WITHDRAWN

Faith Martin was born in Oxford. This is her seventh novel in the Hillary Greene series, which includes *A Narrow Escape, On the Straight and Narrow, Narrow Is the Way, Through a Narrow Door* and *With a Narrow Blade.*

BESIDE A NARROW STREAM

When Wayne Sutton's body is found in a beautiful summer meadow, his head bashed in and a red paper heart left on his body, DI Hillary Greene isn't surprised to learn that the handsome young artist had a reputation as a heartless Casanova. Moreover, it appears that there were numerous middle-aged, married and wealthy women buying his canvases with reason enough for wanting him dead. But, delving deeper into this case of cold-blooded murder, she finds that all is not what it seems. Worse still, her new DS, Gemma Knowles, although pleasant and efficient, has a secret agenda . . .

Books by Faith Martin
Published by The House of Ulverscroft:

A NARROW ESCAPE
ON THE STRAIGHT AND NARROW
NARROW IS THE WAY
THROUGH A NARROW DOOR
WITH A NARROW BLADE

FAITH MARTIN

BESIDE A NARROW STREAM

Complete and Unabridged

ULVERSCROFT
Leicester

First published in Great Britain in 2008 by
Robert Hale Limited
London

First Large Print Edition
published 2008
by arrangement with
Robert Hale Limited
London

British Library CIP Data

Martin, FaithB
   eside a narrow stream.—Large print ed.—
   Ulverscroft large print series: crime
   1. Greene, Hillary (Fictitious character)—Fiction
   2. Policewomen—England—Fiction
   3. Artists—Crimes against—Fiction
   4. Detective and mystery stories
   5. Large type books
   I. Title
   823.9′2 [F]

   ISBN 978–1–84782–481–3

Published by
F. A. Thorpe (Publishing)
Anstey, Leicestershire

Set by Words & Graphics Ltd.
Anstey, Leicestershire
Printed and bound in Great Britain by
T. J. International Ltd., Padstow, Cornwall

This book is printed on acid-free paper

1

May Day that year dawned bright and hot, just the kind of weather to encourage the idiots who liked to throw themselves off Magdalen Bridge as part of the traditional May Day celebrations. In Oxford, uniformed police watched them and shook their heads, whilst the media cheered them on. An enterprising cameraman for the local news show was even taking bets on how many broken bones there'd be by the end of the morning.

Elsewhere, the rest of Oxfordshire woke with a little more decorum and none of the slightly suicidal tendencies that the dozy students were displaying in the city. Among the many people starting up their cars and heading into work for the mundane routine of earning a living, was Detective Inspector Hillary Greene. At least the warm weather was being kind to Puff the Tragic Wagon, her ancient Volkswagen Golf, which started first time. Pulling out of the turning from the tiny hamlet of Thrupp, and heading up the main road on her three-minute commute towards Kidlington, where Thames Valley Police had their headquarters, she listened to the local news, turning it off with a grumpy mutter when it turned to the doings at Magdalen Bridge.

Although she had been a student at Oxford herself — albeit at a non-affiliated college — she'd never felt the least urge to throw herself off a bridge. At least, not until she'd joined the police force. But today she had other things on her mind. Today was the day when her new DS started work, at long last. Her last detective sergeant, Janine Tyler, now Mrs Janine Mallow, had left just before Christmas, and she'd been struggling to cope with only that waste of space Frank Ross, and the new, and still largely untried, Detective Constable Keith Barrington, ever since. A third pair of helping hands was just what she needed.

And DS Gemma Fordham sounded good on paper, at least. Maybe too good? Hillary, over the years, had come to be known as a 'safe pair of hands' when it came to training staff and, as a result, she'd become used to getting not exactly the dregs, but the unusual, the slightly worrying, or the downright politically correct officers that nobody else felt comfortable with. Yet Gemma Fordham seemed to be cast from a very different mould. Young, female, an amateur but

2

successful martial arts expert, she'd joined the force straight from Reading University, and had quickly risen to the rank of DS. It begged the question — why had she been seconded to Hillary's team?

Telling herself she was probably just getting paranoid in her mean old age, Hillary pulled into the HQ parking lot and nabbed the last space underneath the shade of a large horse chestnut tree and clambered out. Already she could feel the heat of the day making her clothes stick to her, and hoped she'd remembered to slip a roll-on deodorant into her bag.

She sighed and headed for the large glass doors that fronted the headquarters of Thames Valley Police Force. Well, she'd soon find out whether or not the estimable DS Fordham lived up to expectations.

★ ★ ★

Whilst others dragged themselves into work, for two young boys who lived in the pretty, ironstone village of Deddington, life had become an unexpected holiday. With their primary school closed for that wonderful creation 'teacher training day' the whole of that Tuesday, 1 May, spread out like a glorious gift.

Until, that is, Jaime Gould's mother unexpectedly turned into a dragon, and turned off her son's computer, on which he and his best friend in all the world, Tris Winters, were playing the latest shoot-em-up game, and thrust aside the curtains determinedly.

'It's a beautiful day out there, just look at it,' Marjorie Gould demanded, pointing dramatically at next door's gabled roof. 'When I was your age, and the weather was this good, I couldn't wait to get outside.'

Jaime, a small boy of ten, with a mop of brown hair and large orange freckles that were quickly becoming the bane of his life, stared out at the neat, new-build detached house of Mr Jardine gloomily. This didn't sound good. Not good at all. He caught his friend's puzzled look and shrugged his skinny shoulders in apology.

'Why don't you play tennis, or go to the park?' Marjorie demanded. 'You spend too much time on that thing,' she nodded at the now defunct computer with a grimace of contempt. 'I want you to get some fresh air and exercise.'

This was even worse than he'd thought.

'But Tris doesn't have a tennis racquet,' Jaime pointed out hopefully, still dreaming of reaching level three, where, rumour had it, the 'creature from the black lagoon' put in an appearance.

'Then do something else,' Marjorie Gould said in exasperation. In truth, she had a coffee morning looming, and needed to get her coconut macaroons in the oven (a recipe straight from the Sunday supplements) and wasn't prepared to put up with her son's presence underfoot. 'Why don't you take some jam jars and bread to the stream and see if you can catch some minnows?' she suggested, remembering, vaguely, doing something like that when she was their age.

Tris Winters, a tall, tallow-haired lad with big brown eyes, blinked up at her from behind his heavy-framed glasses. 'What's a minnow?' he asked, genuinely puzzled.

Marjorie Gould stared at him helplessly. 'If you don't know what a minnow is, then it's high time you learned, young man.'

'It's a fish,' Jaime said miserably, having heard about this activity from one of his other friends at school. 'You tie some string around the top of a jam jar, then put some bread inside, press it down really hard so it squashes into a corner and doesn't come out, then toss it in the river. When you see these little fish swim inside you pull the jam jar out quick and put them into a bucket.'

Tris listened to this with his usual, serious

expression, then said simply, 'Why?'

To this, neither Jaime nor his mother had an adequate reply. But it didn't stop them being ushered out of the house that morning at ten o'clock with two jam jars and a slice of Wonderloaf.

★   ★   ★

Hillary Greene knocked on the door of Detective Superintendent Philip 'Mellow' Mallow's office, and went in before waiting for a reply. As he was one of her oldest friends, she rarely bothered to stand on ceremony, and as she closed the door behind her, she turned to find a very tall woman rising to her feet.

'Mel,' Hillary said, using the shortened version of the superintendent's nickname, by which he was widely known. Tall, impeccably dressed, smooth-voiced and urbane, it wasn't hard to see how he'd earned it, but it was largely a front. As many a villain had come to learn, just a little too late.

'Hillary, come in. This is DS Fordham. We've just been having a chat. Gemma, your new boss, DI Hillary Greene.'

So *this* is Hillary Greene, Gemma Fordham thought, a tight feeling suddenly constricting her chest. Funny how life had a way of playing games with you. She held out a hand, smiling blandly, her thoughts whirling. All those nights I lay awake, wondering what this woman looked like. How she talked. How she dressed. What sort of power she must have been able to access at the drop of a hat. It made Gemma embarrassed, now, to think of herself as so young and so gormless. And so hideously jealous.

Hillary walked quickly across the room to take the proffered hand. Gemma Fordham had to be five feet eleven at least, but she was so lean that she looked even taller. She had short-cropped, spiky hair so blonde it looked almost white. Her angular face was pale, and her large grey eyes dominated it. Her grip was as firm as you'd expect of a brown belt in judo, and who knew what-the-hell-else.

'DS Fordham.'

'Gemma guv,' Gemma Fordham said at once.

The voice surprised Hillary totally, for it was a smoker's growl, low and rasping. Men must find it as sexy as hell. But surely someone who threw people around on mats had to be a keep-fit fanatic as well? Probably didn't eat red meat, and only bought organic veg. What was with the forty-a-day gravelly voice?

7

'Gemma was telling me all about Reading,' Mel said, sitting again and watching the two women curiously. They were, in appearance at least, very different, but there was something tough and no-nonsense about Gemma that he'd instantly liked, and that had reminded him of Hillary herself. Surely the two women would get on like a house on fire? He still felt somewhat guilty for taking Janine Tyler off her team by marrying her, and he was anxious that his old friend should like and approve of his choice for her new DS.

Gemma Fordham smiled down at her new boss with level grey eyes, noting the curvy hour-glass figure, still good for a woman who had to be in her mid-forties, and the thick quality of her bell-shaped shoulder-length cap of dark brown hair with natural-looking chestnut highlights. Dark chocolate brown eyes, shrewd but willing-to-be-friendly, met her gaze head on. Yes. She was attractive in a certain way, Gemma thought, taken aback by the sudden spurt of angst that lanced through her.

She doesn't like me, Hillary heard the thought pop into her head, and turned abruptly back to Mel before the knowledge could reach her eyes. Sometimes, for no particular reason, two people just couldn't hit it off, and she hoped against hope that this wasn't just such an occasion.

Perhaps she was over-analysing things.

Mel, sensing a certain coolness in the air, turned up the charm a few watts. 'Gemma asked to be transferred to your team, Hillary,' he carried on. 'She's a great admirer of yours.'

Hillary smiled briefly and took a seat. Beside her, on a separate chair, Gemma Fordham also sat. She was wearing brown slacks and a matching jacket, with a light silk cream top underneath. She wore no make up and no jewellery save for a practical-looking watch with a brown leather strap. Her feet were in top-of-the-range sneakers. All the better to kick you with?

Hillary dragged her eyes from the sneakers and back to the face. Fordham was watching her with an avid curiosity that she turned off immediately, and replaced with bland inter-est. 'Your arrest and conviction rate is really impressive, ma'am,' she said. 'When my old DCI knew I was determined to shift station houses, he put in a good word for me with Superintendent Mallow. I'm really looking forward to working with you.'

Well that was true, Gemma thought with a wry, internal smile. And may you never know just how much, or why, she added silently.

Hillary nodded. 'I'm sure we'll get on fine,'

she said. And only Mel, who knew her so well, could tell that she was lying.

★   ★   ★

'Sorry about this. I think Mum's got PMT,' Jaime Gould said to his friend as they wheeled their bikes on to the pavement and prepared to mount.

'What's that?' Tris asked, throwing his long leg over the cross bar without even standing on tip-toe. He'd begged his dad for a new bike for the last two Christmases running, so far without success.

'I don't know,' Jaime was forced to concede. 'It's something I heard Dad say on the phone to his friend once, when Mum wouldn't let them have a barbecue on the new lawn.'

Tris thought about this solemnly, then nodded. 'Well, I expect my Mum won't have it. You want to go to my place and play instead?'

Jaime grinned, then reluctantly shook his head. 'Nah, better not. If my mum talks to your mum and finds out we're there, I'm for it. I 'spose we better go and catch some minnows,' he conceded gloomily. 'Hey,' his face suddenly brightened again. 'What say we catch some, take the bucket back to your place, and *then* play on your computer? That way, if we get busted, we can show them the proof!' He held aloft a small, as yet empty and minnow-less bucket that he'd looped over his handlebars. In it rested the two jam jars and bread. 'It shouldn't take us long to catch a few.'

'Sounds good to me,' Tris said obligingly, and the two boys pushed away from the kerb. Living on the outskirts of the village, they didn't have far to go. Simply across the main road (using the traffic lights for safety) and thence down the small B-road leading off to the villages of Michael St John and Barford St John. Leading off this road was an even smaller lane, little more than a farmer's track, where a row of small, one-time farm workers' cottages stood, now all re-tiled, stone-faced, and double-glazed, the property of proud commuters. This track ended at a traditional five-barred country gate, giving access to a water meadow.

The two boys fastidiously used their chains and padlocks to secure the bikes to the gate, as they'd had dinned into their heads by their parents. It didn't occur to either of them that a farmer might actually want to open the gate, and wouldn't be best pleased to have to lug the two bikes with it.

A narrow sheep track crossed the meadow

to a small stream that, about a mile further downstream, ran into a larger tributary of the River Cherwell itself. The two boys, dutifully lugging their fishing equipment, walked across the meadow, oblivious to the buttercups and cowslips, the orange-tipped butterflies and fresh air and sunshine, so beloved of Mrs Gould, and talked instead of far more important things.

'Do you think Mr Harris really is gay?' Tris asked, making Jaime giggle. The deputy-headmaster of the primary school in Banbury they attended was new that term, and the current rumour doing the rounds was too intriguing to pass up. The younger ones, of course, didn't even know what it meant. It was a source of pride to the likes of Tris and Jaime that they understood everything.

'Nah, I don't think so,' Jaime said. 'I saw him with a woman in his car once.'

'That don't mean nothing,' Tris said, ungrammatically. '*I* think he is.'

They were heading for the bend in the stream, where a hawthorn bush was growing close to the edge. A yellowhammer was nesting there, and called out his 'little-bit-of-bread-and-no-cheese' ditty, which neither boy recognized or would have been interested in, if they had.

'Why? You seen something?' Jaime asked,

lowering his voice to a whisper, although the only one who might have overheard was a Jersey cow, munching grass nearby.

'No, not really,' Tris admitted reluctantly, then said 'Ow, yuck! I've stood in it!' He lifted one, now slimy, green sneaker in disgust whilst his friend doubled up laughing beside him. The smelly brown muck, courtesy of one of the Jersey cow's sisters, clung tenaciously.

'Go and wash it off you dope,' Jaime finally managed to advise, over his shrill giggles, and Tris, hopping like a lame giraffe, quickly headed for the stream.

The bank of the stream was eroded where the cows regularly went down to drink, and with just a bit of deft leg-work, the boy was able to dip the sole of his sneaker into the shallow water. On the bank, his friend, now bored with the entertainment, was pushing squishy bread down into a jam jar.

Tris Winters put his foot back on dry land, turned back to face his friend, and then froze. 'Oh heck, there's someone already here!' he hissed to his friend, who looked back, alarmed.

'Where?'

'Over there, look. He's sunbathing,' Tris hissed back. His friend quickly joined him, and looked to where he was pointing. Sure enough, about ten yards further upstream, a man lay on his back on the grass, his face turned away from them.

'Hey mister, we're just catching some minnows, all right?' Jaime shouted, then frowned as Tris grabbed his arm. 'Wassup?'

'You shouldn't have shouted,' Tris whispered back frantically. 'What if he's — you know — a perv or something. A kiddie killer?'

Jaime Gould paled, making his freckles stand out even more on his face. The lads both knew about kiddie killers. Every now and then, some child's picture appeared in the papers and on telly, and everybody's Mum and Dad got all jittery, and nobody was allowed to play outside for a while, or go to town on their own on the bus.

'We could run for it,' Jaime hissed.

Tris nodded, but scowling, said, 'I don't think he heard you anyway.'

'Or he's pretending he didn't,' Jaime said nervously. 'You know, to fool us.'

'Hey, Mister!' Tris shouted, and this time his friend scowled.

'You just told me off for doing the same thing!'

For a while, both boys stood by the bank, watching the sleeping, sunbathing man, wondering if they should run or not.

'Perhaps he's drunk,' Jaime said at last, and giggled. 'Last summer, Uncle Tom got drunk and spent the *whole* night on the sun lounger in the back garden.'

'Let's go see,' Tris said intrepidly.

'You go. Not me,' Jaime immediately replied.

'Wuss,' Tris taunted contemptuously. 'I'll go a bit closer, you stay here. If he grabs me, run for the nearest cottage and scream blue murder.'

Jaime swallowed hard. And when his friend moved off, took a few reluctant steps after him.

★   ★   ★

Gemma Fordham followed Hillary Greene across the crowded, open plan office. 'We're over here, by the side windows,' Hillary said over her shoulder.

Gemma nodded, aware of the eyes following their progress across the room. Small clusters of desks stood in no particular order, manned by uniformed and plain clothes alike. A lot of them were working the computers, or on the phone, but nearly all were watching her. She knew it was only to be expected, since she was the new girl in town. She wondered what the scuttlebutt was about her, but knew there could be nothing tasty. There'd been no scandals in *her* past, after all, which is more than could be said for her new boss.

Probably that old chestnut about her being a lesbian was doing the rounds, Gemma conceded. It was almost inevitable, given her martial arts, tall lean figure, gravelly voice, and the fact that she only ever wore slacks and jackets. But it would soon fizzle out when it became common knowledge that she was shacked up with a man.

'Frank, Gemma Fordham,' Hillary's voice brought her back to the matter in hand, and she felt herself tense up as she turned to look at Frank Ross.

Her only real worry was that Ross might recognize her. Not that they'd ever met, she was pretty sure. But he might have caught a glimpse of her, maybe, when Ronnie was picking her up or dropping her off. It was even possible that Ronnie had shown him a photo of her. But she'd have been much younger then, with longer hair, and more baby fat. Chances are, he wouldn't recognize her face. But he might know her name.

Could she bluff her way out of it if he did?

'Judo girl, huh?' Frank Ross said, not bothering to get up. He was a short man, with greying hair and blue eyes, chubby, with a surprisingly cute Winnie-the-Pooh type face.

Appearances, she knew, were utterly deceptive as far as Frank Ross went. Ronnie had often talked about him, and described him in various ways — a vicious little git, back-stabbing bastard, good old-fashioned copper, or the kind you'd want in your corner during a football riot, depending on Ronnie's mood at the time. Whatever — the fact was, Frank Ross had been Ronnie Greene's acknowledged sidekick for many years, and she found herself curious to meet him, after all this time.

'Judo, kendo, karate and kung-fu girl, actually,' she corrected, and saw Ross snarl a grin.

'Don't cut no ice with me, luv,' he drawled. 'And where'd you get that voice? Cigs-'r-us?'

'Childhood accident,' Gemma said, relaxing. He didn't have a clue who she was. 'Damaged the voice box.'

So that explained it, Hillary mused. She hadn't really believed that the whippet-like Gemma Fordham and nicotine could ever be best buddies. The woman moved with the economical grace of a true athlete, making Hillary feel like a contented cow in comparison. Is that why she was feeling so anti? Did Gemma Fordham make her feel, subconsciously at least, somehow inferior? If so, she needed to get over it, pretty damned sharpish, Hillary told herself firmly. She needed to find some sort of common ground with this woman if they were going to work comfortably together. And the sooner she did it, the better.

'Barrington not in?' Hillary asked, surprised. It was gone ten. It wasn't like him to be so late.

'Nope,' Frank said, with a sly grin. He was so used to being the last one in, it was nice to see someone else in the shit for a change.

Hillary saw Gemma pick up on the spite and give Ross a long, measuring look.

No two ways about it, Hillary mused, Fordham was sharp. And ambitious. Perhaps she saw a stint on Hillary's team as nothing more than a useful leg-up on the career ladder? It was widely known that the Chief Super, Marcus Donleavy, rated her highly. She'd probably work here a year, maybe a little more, then sit her boards and get transferred somewhere with a bigger profile. Which was fine with Hillary. As far as she was concerned, the force didn't have enough good, strong, ambitious women officers in CID. As long as she did her job, did what she was told, and gave her no hassles, everything would work out fine.

Gemma caught Hillary looking at her, and

thought, without any surprise, 'She doesn't like me'.

'Right, well, this is your desk,' Hillary said brightly. 'Get settled in, set up your computer, and then check in with DI Danvers, our immediate boss.'

Ross snorted. 'The Adonis of Thames Valley.'

'Frank,' Hillary said wearily.

⋆　⋆　⋆

'He ain't breathing,' Tris Winters whispered, his eyes round and wide with awe. He was stood about six feet away from the supine man, leaning forward gingerly and prepared to spring back and leg it, should the man so much as twitch a nostril.

'Go on! How can you tell?' Jaime Gould asked, feeling a little braver now, and sidled up to join his friend.

'You just stare at his chest, twit,' Tris said scornfully. 'It ain't going up and down is it?'

Jaime Gould blinked. 'Crikey. It isn't, is it? Do you think he's dead?'

'Duh!' Tris hit his bony head with the palm of his hand. 'You think?' But in truth, and in spite of his brave show of sophistication, Tristram Winters was feeling just a little bit sick. 'Perhaps he *is* just sleeping it off. Drunks do that. Sometimes people *don't* breathe very deep if they're really fast asleep.' He didn't know if that was true or not, but he wanted it to be.

'Hey mister!' he called again, loudly.

The man lying on the grass didn't stir.

'What's that on his tummy?' Jaime asked.

'I dunno. I was wondering that too,' Tris agreed. The stranger was wearing faded denims and a pale mint-green shirt, but on his chest was what looked like a big red paper heart. It was held down by a flat, pale stone.

'I think we should go,' Jaime Gould said, his voice a little tremulous now.

'Yeah, he might need an ambulance,' Tris agreed, backing away. The two boys walked a little away, then turned back to look again.

'Has he moved?' Tris asked.

'Don't think so,' Jaime gulped.

'One of us should stay with the body,' Tris said, because he'd once heard someone say that on an episode of 'Morse'.

'Well, I ain't,' Jaime averred quickly.

'You'll have to go and get somebody then,' Tris said reluctantly. 'Someone in the cottages is bound to be home and have a phone.'

'I ain't asking someone on my own,' Jaime squeaked. 'What if one of *them*'s a perv or a kiddie killer?'

'Well, take your bike and go home then,' Tris said, exasperated. 'No, wait, there's a phone box at the end of the road. Use that.'

'I ain't got no change,' Jaime wailed. 'If only Mum would let me have a mobile, we could have used that.'

'You don't need money to dial 999 you twit,' Tris said. 'Don't you know nothing? Just dial, and tell them we need the police.'

'OK,' Jaime said, and walked a few steps away, whilst Tris stayed where he was.

'Go on,' Tris hissed encouragement, seeing that his friend had stopped and was looking uncertainly back at him.

Suddenly, Jaime Gould turned and ran.

He ran across the meadow, disturbing all the butterflies and trampling the buttercups, and vaulted the gate in a scrambling heap. His hands shook a little as he unlocked his bike, and he wobbled a bit as he first raced off. When he got to the phone box, he felt both unaccountably shy, and in equal measures, undeniably proud, as he dialled the famous number.

A bored woman's voice asked him which service he required.

'Police,' Jaime Gould said importantly. Just wait till they heard about this at school!

When he told the operator on the other end that he and his friend had found a dead

21

body in a field, he hoped they believed him. Sometimes, he knew, adults didn't believe you when you were telling the truth, but *did* believe you when you were telling lies. If they were the kind of lies they wanted to believe.

But the man who'd now been put on at the other end of the line seemed a reasonable sort. He asked him his name, and his age and where he was, and when he told him that his friend, Tristram William Winters was still in the field watching over the body just in case, the man told him, rather sharply, not to go back, but to stay by the telephone and wait for a police car.

This, Jaime did.

He didn't have to wait long.

2

DCI Paul Danvers put down the telephone and walked quickly to the door to his cubicle. Glancing across the large open plan office, his eyes quickly narrowed on his DI, Hillary Greene. As always when contemplating her, his first knee-jerk reaction was physical, and his eyes automatically took in the soft caramel-coloured jacket and skirt she was wearing, today complemented by a pure silk cream blouse. The sunlight streaming through the large glass windows gave her bell-shaped dark brown hair a reddish, almost gothic halo, and as he walked across the room towards her, he felt the expression on his face become bland.

A few months ago she'd agreed to go out to dinner with him, but since then, nothing. Worse yet, she was still seeing that pillock from vice, Mike Regis. And until *that* fizzled out, and he was sure it would, at some point, he was playing a waiting game.

'Hillary,' he greeted her the moment he was in range, his eyes only then going across to the desks surrounding her. It surprised him that Frank Ross was in, whilst Detective

Constable Barrington was absent. It was usually the other way round. But it was the tall blonde-haired woman rising at the sound of his voice that his eyes lingered on the longest.

The new girl. Mel's choice, but he hadn't found anything in his interview with DS Gemma Fordham that worried him. She smiled at him now briefly.

'Sir.'

'Sergeant.' He turned once more to Hillary, and saw her cast a speculative glance at the younger woman. He hid a wince, knowing exactly what she was thinking. But she was going to be disappointed. There was nothing about Gemma Fordham that appealed to him. She wasn't going to shake him loose that easily. 'We have a suspicious death in Deddington,' he said crisply, his voice all business. 'Fancy it?'

'Of course,' Hillary said at once.

'Somebody dead in Deddington. Stop the presses,' Frank Ross chortled, which, for him, passed as wit. Everybody else ignored him.

'Got the call from a schoolboy,' Danvers carried on. 'He and his chum were playing in one of the meadows on the outskirts, and came across a man lying in the grass. According to dispatch, the boy was adamant that he wasn't breathing. Still, it might turn out to be just a drunk after all, or maybe a heart attack victim, or death by other natural causes. Assess the situation and take it from there.'

Hillary nodded. 'Right sir.' She glanced across at Gemma. 'DS Fordham, with me. Frank, you'd better take your own car,' she added reluctantly. She'd rather leave him behind, but he'd only whinge.

'No Barrington yet?' Danvers asked, staring at the constable's empty desk.

'I gave him permission to come late,' Hillary said at once, making Ross snort in disbelief. Gemma Fordham shot her new boss a thoughtful look, but said nothing. Keith Barrington, although relatively new, had proved himself to be a hard worker, bright, and willing not only to take orders but to learn. And Hillary was not about to drop him in the shit without hearing his explanation first.

'Fine,' Danvers said, not believing her, but not prepared to make an issue of it yet. Barrington had been at the nick for six months now, and as far as he knew, this was the first time he'd been late. No doubt Hillary would handle it.

'Report in first chance you get,' he added, already turning around and heading back to his desk.

'Our glorious leader,' Frank Ross whispered in an aside to Gemma, as he grabbed his jacket. 'Your predecessor, Mel Mallow's missus, would have it that he has a thing for our Hillary.' He slipped into his jacket, which had a fried egg stain on the lapel. 'Can't see it myself,' he added snippily. 'She's a bit long in the tooth for him, don't you think?'

'Really?' Gemma asked, her curiosity instantly aroused, and glanced back to the retreating DCI. Danvers, fair, good-looking and dressed in what looked like a hand-tailored suit, had instantly caught her eye, for she liked good-looking men, but she usually preferred them with a serious flaw — something their boss obviously lacked. No doubt a shrink would have made something of that, but she wasn't into self-analysis. So whilst Danvers hadn't rung any of her bells, it was interesting to know that he had the hots for Hillary Greene. Once upon a time, long, long ago, she would have been obsessed with anything to do with Hillary Greene's love life, and it irked her that she still felt such spurious curiosity, even now. Although in her mid-forties, Hillary Greene could certainly still attract them, it seemed, and the knowledge made a sharp little pain lance through her.

'Ready?' Hillary asked crisply, making

Gemma turn her head sharply and focus on business.

'Yes guv,' she said smartly. All she had to do was pick up her bag, which she did, and follow Hillary towards the exit.

Hillary, taking the lead down the wide, concrete staircase, could feel the younger woman's eyes on her back, and made a conscious effort to ignore the itch between her shoulderblades. She gave the desk sergeant a sketchy salute as he acknowledged her, and called over briskly, 'When my DC gets in, point him to Deddington would you Jack?'

'You bet.'

Once outside, however, the first thing Gemma saw was a tall, red-haired man jogging towards them across the car park, and from behind, heard Frank Ross's jeering greeting.

'Thought you'd come in then?'

So this was the errant Detective Constable Keith Barrington. Gemma hoped he would give her no problems. A sharp-eyed and curious DC might just put a spoke in her wheels, and that wasn't something she was prepared to tolerate.

Hillary glanced pointedly at her watch, but only said mildly, 'Keith, ride with Frank. I'll talk to you later.'

The pale-faced man flushed slightly, and said unhappily, 'Guv.'

Gemma walked silently beside her new boss until they drew level with an old Volkswagen Golf, her boss going around to the driver's side. Gemma stared at the car for a flat few seconds and smiled inwardly. Hillary Greene certainly didn't believe in flash motors, which boded well. If she couldn't afford a new car it must mean that her late husband's ill-gotten gains were still stashed somewhere, untouched and safely hidden.

Good.

'It doesn't look much, but it won't bite, Sergeant,' Hillary Greene's dry voice snapped her back to attention and she cursed herself inwardly. She'd have to stop letting her mind wander like this. Greene was too good, too clever, not to pick up on it. And start wondering about it.

'I used to have one just like it, guv,' she lied, smiling brightly and opening the passenger door before sliding in. 'Brought back memories, that's all.'

Hillary took her own seat behind the wheel and said nothing. But as she pulled out on to the main Oxford-Banbury road, and headed north, she wondered why her DS felt the need to lie to her.

★ ★ ★

'I think it must be the other side of the village, nearer Adderbury,' Hillary murmured, nearly twenty minutes later. They'd approached the village of Deddington from the south side, but there were no signs of patrol cars. Driving at the 30 mph limit on the main road, she glanced curiously at either side of the main street. Ironstone buildings, the colour of rust, lined the wide avenue, many playing host to rambling roses and other climbers. Outside a hotel, large colourful hanging baskets added to the rainbow hues, making the village look like a tourist board official's dream come true. Hillary seemed to remember there was some vague rumour of a castle too, and a splendid church with a four-tower turreted spire. Or was she thinking of Bloxham?

'Up ahead, guv, turn right at the lights,' Gemma Fordham said, having contacted the switchboard for further directions.

Hillary nodded, and indicated. Once on the narrow road, the village proper was quickly left behind them, and sure enough, up ahead, parked on the side of the road, was a 'jam sandwich'. The driver, looking in the mirror and seeing a car pull up behind him, got out. He straightened up, just a bit, as he recognized the woman getting out of the car.

'DI Greene,' Hillary said, introducing herself to the uniform, who instantly added her name to the running roster. Apparently, they weren't the first to arrive by a long chalk. It must be looking a bit more interesting than a mere drunk then, Hillary mused, feeling her heartbeat quicken.

'Ma'am,' the uniform nodded. A large, comfortable-looking man, he was sweating a little now that the sun had burned away the last of the morning mist. 'Over the five-barred gate at the end of the track, and straight across the meadow towards the stream. The ME's already here.'

Hillary, who hadn't spotted Steven Partridge's nifty little sports car, looked surprised. 'That was quick off the mark.' It was usually left to the Senior Investigating Officer, in this case herself, to call out the cavalry.

'DC Tylforth, first on the scene, called him in, ma'am,' the constable said, his voice so deadpan it made Hillary's lips twitch. Reading between the lines, no doubt DC Tylforth was a young eager beaver who'd probably jumped the gun before. No doubt his ears were already burning.

'I see,' Hillary said non-committally. 'I don't see the doc's car.'

'Out of commission ma'am. He got a ride

30

in a jam san — In a patrol vehicle.'

Hillary nodded, and walked off towards a row of pretty cottages, shaded by a towering, and majestically flowering, horse chestnut tree as Gemma and the others signed in behind her. It was nearly eleven now, and in the green hawthorn hedges that lined the narrow farm track, she could hear chaffinches, blackbirds, hedge sparrows, a yellowhammer and a corn bunting, all vying for territory. A large lime-green-yellow brimstone butterfly flew past, heading for a patch of cow parsley growing nearby. Already she could feel the top of her head beginning to tingle, and knew the hot sunshine was probably going to give her a raging headache before the day was through. She should have brought a cap. She reached the gate quickly, but since she was wearing her usual comfortable flatties, didn't bother to open it, but merely clambered over it. It amused her to find Gemma Fordham doing the same, with perhaps a little more ease and grace. Frank, being Frank, had to open it, cursing and grunting as it stuck in the dried mud ruts either side, forcing Keith Barrington to give him a hand lifting it up and over.

Walking across the meadow, Hillary could see a small knot of men several hundred yards away, crouched down and looking busy. One was already taking photographs, but there was no other sign of the white-suited boffins that comprised a scene-of-crime officers' unit. Presumably DC Tylforth hadn't called them out yet, Hillary thought with a wry smile.

'Shit,' she heard Frank Ross mutter viciously, and with feeling, behind her.

'That's exactly what it is, Frank,' she heard Gemma Fordham say cheerfully, and grinned. As a country girl, born and bred, Hillary had been picking her way carefully through the cow-pats without even thinking about it.

Keith Barrington, having lived in London all his life, wasn't so adept, but at least he had the sense not to complain about it.

Hillary's pace quickened as she approached the possible crime scene. Incongruously, it had to be one of the most beautiful she'd ever attended. A narrow, fairly shallow stream, obviously a tributary of a much larger river, had cut a meandering path through the lush green water meadow, and a pair of grey wagtails, nesting on the far bank, were flitting back and forth in agitation, long lemon tails wagging frantically. Picturesque-looking Jersey cows, standing some way off, watched curiously. Buttercups and daisies, some low-growing purple orchids and other wild-flowers like speedwell and scarlet pimpernel gave the meadow a wild-garden appearance. With the bright sunlight shining down on it all, it looked like the last place in the world you'd expect to come across death or human tragedy.

But as she approached, Steven Partridge was kneeling down over the supine body of a young man, and frowning in such a way that made her hackles rise.

Hillary, always mindful of the practicalities, immediately glanced down at the hardened, cow-trampled grass and decided she might as well approach the body too. No doubt the two boys who'd found the body, the initial call-out constables, and now the ME had all left traces at the scene. But with the heatwave they were currently experiencing, there'd have been no chance of footprints anyway so it probably didn't much matter.

Steven Partridge sensed her arrival and glanced up. He was dressed in pale powder-blue slacks, and a light-weight cream-knitted jersey. His dyed black hair was shining and quiffed, making him look a lot younger than his fifty-something years. He smiled the instant he saw her.

'Hillary, glad it's you,' he said, by way of greeting, and Hillary felt her heart give a little leap, then settle down. So it wasn't a heart attack then. Or any other natural causes.

'What have we got?'

'Death by drowning, I think,' Steven said. 'But don't quote me until the autopsy's done. But see this dried foam around the mouth?' he turned the corpse's head very slightly, and Hillary, after a quick check for cow-pats, knelt beside the body, the better to see. She easily spotted the dried-bubble marks around the full lips and nodded.

'Classic sign of drowning,' the medic said flatly. 'Once we get him to the lab we can compare the water in his lungs to the water from the stream,' he nodded towards the narrow channel of water not far away, 'but I'd be surprised if it wasn't a perfect match. I haven't come across any signs so far that the body's been moved.'

Hillary nodded. The corpse in front of her looked to be in his early twenties. He had a long, lean body, and she guessed that, standing, he must have been tall — six foot at least. His dark-brown, almost-black hair, looked mussed and dirty, but his face was still classically handsome, with high cheekbones and firm jaw. He was dressed in casual designer jeans and what looked like a raw-silk shirt. Very classy. He must have really looked like something, before death had glazed his blue eyes and left his mouth slack and almost foolish-looking.

'Misadventure?' she asked, but didn't really think so. Already it had the feel of something much more nasty.

'Doubt it,' Partridge said at once, confirming it, and once more turned the head carefully, this time to the left. 'See here, on the temple?'

Hillary saw. 'He's been bashed over the head,' she said flatly. 'Enough to knock him out?'

Partridge nodded. 'Or at the very least, seriously stun him. But not kill him, I think. I still think we're looking at death by drowning.'

Hillary swallowed hard, and rose to her feet, her knees aching a bit with cramp. It was possible the victim might have fallen and hit his head. But if so, how did he end up drowning in the stream? And did he manage to crawl away from the water and slump on to dry land before expiring? It hardly seemed likely. She stamped her feet to get rid of the persistent cramp and looked around. 'So, someone met him here, hit him on the head, dragged him to the stream and held him down till he drowned?'

She glanced towards the stream and sighed heavily. Where the mud might have been kept moist by the water, and thus provide them with a set of the killer's footprints, there was only a plethora of half-moon cuts, courtesy of cow-hoofs.

'Frank, call out SOCO,' she said absently, and saw one of the two officers nearby whisper something to his colleague. Probably DC Tylforth, saying 'I told you so'.

'Things aren't all doom and gloom, we've managed to preserve some good stuff,' Partridge said, nodding towards a middle-aged woman, who'd been taking photographs. 'My assistant, Claudia Wright.'

Surprised, Hillary moved across to shake hands. 'Ma'am,' Claudia Wright said, glancing away shyly. She was dressed in a pair of black trousers and a plain white shirt. She was thin, with hardly any breasts, and had short, brown hair, which was probably why, from a distance, Hillary had mistaken her for a man. She seemed almost painfully shy for this job, and Hillary wondered what had led to her working for someone as flamboyant as Steven Partridge.

'We bagged and tagged this,' Partridge said, nodding towards a plastic evidence bag beside the body. Hillary frowned, walking across to it and peering down. Inside she could clearly see a large, flat, pale stone that had a tinge of rust-coloured stain on one side, and what looked like a few strands of human hair attached to it.

'Shouldn't you have left that for SOCO?' Hillary asked sharply and Partridge held up a hand in a 'peace' gesture.

'Claudia's fully qualified and licensed,' the medico said soothingly. 'She was with me in the lab when I got the call out. I asked her to come. She's used to field work.'

Hillary nodded, appeased. 'Murder weapon?' she nodded down at the evidence bag and Steven smiled.

'I shouldn't wonder. But until we get a DNA link to our vic, we can't say for sure. What I can tell you is that the stone was also used to anchor something down on the vic's chest. Claudia?' he looked up, and the older woman nodded and, from her briefcase this time, produced another evidence bag. This time flat. Inside, was a single piece of paper. Red, and cut out in the shape of a heart.

Hillary blinked and stared down at it, a cold, icy feeling gripping the back of her neck.

This was nasty.

Very nasty.

Usually, people were murdered in a fit of rage; a father attacking the man who'd raped his daughter or run down his wife in a car. Drunks fighting after a night in the pub. Man-and-wife spats with a kitchen knife over who burnt the roast.

Less often, murders were committed with a

bit more malice aforethought, and careful contemplation.

But never before had she investigated a murder where the killer had deliberately left a sign behind. Something taunting and triumphant. Or a signature.

Serial killers liked to leave signatures behind.

'Oh shit,' she said softly.

Instantly, she felt Gemma Fordham beside her, using her few extra inches of height to look over her shoulder. Gemma, too, drew in a breath sharply, instantly leaping to the same conclusions.

'Bloody hell, guv, I don't like the look of that,' she said softly.

'What? What's up,' Frank Ross demanded, crowding closer, never liking to be out in the cold when something tasty was happening. 'A red paper heart? Big sodding deal,' he snorted, turning away.

Keith Barrington, the only one not to crowd around her, frowned thoughtfully.

Steven Partridge got to his feet and peeled off the rubber gloves he was wearing. He shot her a sympathetic look. 'Well, once SOCO have done their thing, you can move the body. I've done all I need to here.'

'Time of death?' Hillary asked, before he could get away.

Steven pursed his lips and glanced around. 'The temperature last night was pretty mild. Rigour's only just passed. Rectal temperature was about as I'd expect if he'd died sometime between, say, seven o'clock and midnight last night. Mind you, that might be off either way if the body spent any time in the water, which is several degrees colder than the ambient air temperature. But I don't think he did. The skin's not puckered enough — no washer-woman's hands on his face or exposed skin. I think the killer pulled his body on to dry land once the deed was done and simply left him there.'

He turned to look down at the good-looking young corpse at his feet. He shook his head. Somebody was going to have a very bad day today. He was somebody's son, maybe husband, or even father. A handsome lad like him was bound to leave a distraught lover of some sort behind.

'Thanks, doc.'

'If the stone on his chest didn't go in the water, and I don't think it did, we might get some skin traces from it,' Partridge continued. 'Which'll give you some DNA to work with, if you come up with a suspect. A rough surface like stone is almost certain to have rubbed off some epithelia.'

'Any ID on the vic?' Hillary asked, but

Partridge shook his head. 'I only did a very brief check of his pockets. Nothing obvious — no driver's licence or even wallet. Last evening was lovely — a fine sunset. He probably just came out for a walk, didn't think to bring anything with him. Also no car keys or front door keys. There was a piece of paper in his shirt front pocket, but it got wet when he was pushed head first into the drink. I didn't dare extract it before it can be dried out properly. You'll have to wait to see what it says.'

Hillary sighed. 'Right. So the first thing we need to do is find out who he is.' She turned to her team. 'Well, you know the drill. House to house, start with the cottages nearest, find out if anybody saw anything last night. Claudia,' she turned to the medico's assistant, who bobbed her head in acknowledgement, but didn't make eye contact. 'Can you take a couple of instamatic shots of the head please? None of the gore, perhaps side-featured. Something my officers can use to show people and help us get an ID?'

The forensic expert nodded, and reached into her shoulder bag for a different camera.

'Everyone take a photo of our vic. He's almost certainly local. Constable,' she called across to one of the uniforms, who obediently trotted over. 'I take it there's been no car parked nearby overnight?'

'No, ma'am. First thing we checked.'

She nodded. 'Right, so he almost certainly walked here from Deddington. It's a big village, and no doubt full of newcomers, but somebody'll know him. A lad that good-looking won't have gone unnoticed.'

'Yes, ma'am.'

'I'll have a quick word with the two lads who found him. They still here?'

'No, ma'am, we took 'em back to their homes.'

'Bit upset were they?'

The constable, a short, lean man in his early thirties, smiled briefly. 'More excited, I'd say, ma'am.'

Hillary smiled and nodded. 'Well, better that than trauma, I suppose. You've got their addresses?' She waited until he'd copied them from out from his notebook and took the sheet of paper he proffered. 'OK, well get to it then, everyone.'

Gemma, Frank and Barrington peeled off to start house-to-house. 'You'd better wait here for SOCO and the coroner's van,' she said to the uniform. 'The body can go as soon as it gets here.' She glanced across at Steven Partridge. 'If you need a lift back, the van's your best bet.'

The doctor grimaced. 'I'll be glad when the MG's back on the road.'

* ★ ★

It was Gemma Fordham who hit the jackpot first. The tenth house she tried belonged to an old lady who twittered and fluttered, but avidly looked at the picture of the dead body, and identified him at once.

'That's that Wayne Sutton that is,' she said judiciously, nodding her permed blue head sagely. 'Lives in one of them cottages other side of lights, near church. Bit of a lad, they do say.'

Gemma nodded and smiled. 'Is that right? In what way?' she asked chattily, settling down on the sofa, all ears. Thus gratified, the old lady promptly spilled her guts.

★ ★ ★

Hillary was talking to Marjorie Gould when her mobile rang. She answered it, surprised to hear her new DS's voice. She hadn't remembered giving her the number yet. Still, for someone as super-efficient as Fordham, acquiring it probably hadn't represented much of a challenge.

Biting back the urge to snarl, Hillary smiled an apology at Marjorie Gould, and turned slightly on her chair, dropping her voice an octave. 'Yes, Sergeant?'

'Guv, the victim's name is Wayne Sutton. He lives near the church,' she gave the address, and carried on smoothly, 'but his parents live on the other side of the village, near one of the farms.' She rattled this off as well.

Hillary jotted it down in her book. 'OK, got that. Well done and carry on,' she said briefly, and hung up. She supposed she could have given her extra instructions but why bother? Gemma Fordham obviously didn't need them. The woman would probably have the case solved by teatime and they could all go home.

She turned back to Jaime's mother and smiled again. 'Sorry about that. You were saying that you had a coffee morning planned . . . ?'

She listened as Marjorie Gould explained her reasons for turfing out her son that morning, whilst the boy himself sat listening, wide-eyed and enjoying himself. When it came to his turn, he related everything that had happened that morning with childish relish, and Hillary thought, probably also with extreme accuracy. He was, she'd noticed, an intelligent lad and, like most children, had a gift for observation.

When she left the house a few minutes later, she didn't feel the need to interview Tris

Winters, sure that his version would tally exactly with his friend's.

Instead, she stood on the pavement, underneath a pink-flowering ribes bush, alive with buzzing insects, and dialled Keith Barrington's number. It was answered quickly, and in the background she could hear a man's voice asking him if he wanted a cup of tea.

'Huh, no thanks, Mr Phillpot. Hello, DC Barrington.'

'Keith. The victim's name is Wayne Sutton. I want you to start a time line on him as soon as you can, tracing his movements from yesterday morning onwards. Get over to his cottage and start interviewing neighbours.' She quickly rattled off the address for him.

'Guv.'

She hung up and took a long, deep breath. Well, there was no putting it off. She needed to get over to the Suttons. Since their son was renting his own accommodation, they probably didn't even know he'd been missing all night. Let alone that anything was seriously wrong.

Breaking the worst possible news to anxious relatives who knew that something was up was bad, but at least they'd had the chance to prepare themselves psychologically

44

for tragedy. Bearing bad news that came like a bolt from the blue was much worse.

Grimly Hillary got into her car and drove to the other end of the village, feeling like the messenger of doom.

3

Hillary parked in front of a small, two-up, two-down cottage opposite a large and smelly farmyard, and wondered if Mr Sutton senior actually worked on the farm, or was simply renting what was, or had once obviously been, a cowman's or farmhand's tied cottage. The white-painted front gate opened on to a no-nonsense concrete path that led straight to a front door, painted a deep cream with a brass knocker.

Hillary walked slowly up the path and rapped the brass ring, noticing the granny's bonnets and peonies growing in profusion in the tiny front garden. Blue forget-me-nots frothed over the concrete path, and in one corner a flowering japonica ran rampant. The door was opened by a middle-aged, well-padded woman with long blonde hair fast going grey. 'Yes, luv, can I 'elp you?'

'Mrs Sutton?' Hillary asked, showing her ID card. 'DI Greene, Thames Valley police.'

'Aye, I'm Claire Sutton. What's up? My Davey can't have done anything wrong. He's home with the summer flu,' she said, half-smiling, but a darkness in her eyes told

Hillary that the woman already knew this call was not about her husband.

'May I come in please, Mrs Sutton,' Hillary asked gently, hoping the woman PC family liaison officer she'd radioed in for would be here soon. 'I'm afraid I have some bad news.'

Claire Sutton swallowed hard but nodded and stepped to one side. She was wearing dark blue leggings and an extra-large T-shirt with a cartoon Tasmanian Devil picture on it. 'Go on straight through to the living-room. Davey's laid out on the sofa, but there's arm chairs. I'll put the kettle on, shall I?'

And before Hillary could stop her, the woman had darted off into a tiny kitchen leaving Hillary to make her way reluctantly to the only other room on this floor. A spiral wooden staircase, set against the living-room wall allowed access to the rooms upstairs. Since the cottage was tiny, she was not surprised that their son had moved out at the first chance he got. Or had the Suttons been living elsewhere when their son had still been in the nest?

'Hello.' The hoarse voice came from the sofa, where a lean, flush-faced man was lying. He had a large, multi-coloured crocheted blanket over him, and beside him, on a small wooden table, was a tall glass of what looked like lemon barley water.

47

'Mr Sutton? DI Greene,' Hillary once more showed her ID, and sank down into the armchair Davey Sutton indicated. He sat up slowly, careful to keep the blanket around him, and from the quick glimpse she got of his hairy legs, Hillary guessed he was wearing little more than a vest and Y-fronts underneath. He coughed painfully and reached for his glass, just as his wife came through with a tray of tea.

'Ah, something hot. Just what the old throat needs,' Davey Sutton smiled, his voice little more than a croak. Claire Sutton sat down abruptly. She looked very pale.

Hillary glanced around the room, which was pretty standard. The furniture suite took up nearly all the space, and a large-screen television in one corner dominated the cream-painted room. Somewhat to her surprise, the walls contained two original oil paintings. Traditional landscapes, painted in baffling, eye-catching colours. Perfectly blue meadows, pale yellow skies, purple and orange trees. Each carefully painted to resemble a Constable-esque landscape, but the colours jarred like a psychedelic nightmare. It was a clever concept, but to Hillary's, admittedly untrained eye, it didn't quite seem to work. The paintings made her feel jittery, and annoyed.

She pulled her gaze away from them and met Claire Sutton's fearful eye. 'They're our Wayne's. He's an artist,' she added. 'A proper one. Earns his living at it and everything. They were some of his earlier works — done when he was still at art college. He wanted us to have them. Do you like them?'

Hillary smiled. 'They're very striking,' she said, truthfully. 'Mrs Sutton, Mr Sutton, as I said, I have some bad news.'

At this, Davey Sutton suddenly erupted into a coughing fit. He had thinning dark brown hair and large brown eyes, now red-rimmed from the summer cold that was shaking his lean form. He banged a fist on to his chest, hacked and hawked, and reached for his tea. He took a sip, then glanced at his wife, then at Hillary, then cleared his throat again.

'What kind of bad news then?' he eventually asked.

Hillary took a long, slow breath and decided to ease into it gently. 'Have you heard from your son Wayne recently? I understand he rents a place on the other side of the village?'

'No, not since last Thursday. He came over for some supper,' Claire Sutton said. 'What's happened to him then? He crashed that fancy car of his? Always said it was too fast for him.

Sports cars!' she snorted. 'What's he want with one of them, I ask you. Is it bad? The crash, like?' Her voice wobbled on the last few syllables, and wordlessly her husband reached across to take her hand in his and squeeze it hard.

'He hasn't crashed his car, Mrs Sutton,' Hillary said gently, then added softly, 'This morning, a young man's body was found in a meadow by two young boys. An elderly woman has positively identified him as being Wayne, but of course, that was only from a photograph, and isn't yet official.'

Claire Sutton blinked. 'So it might not be him?'

Hillary shrugged, very gently. 'We need someone to go to the mortuary and make a more formal identification,' she hedged, not exactly answering her question, whilst at the same time, giving the impression that it probably wasn't a good idea to hold out too much hope. On the way over here, Keith Barrington had called in to say nobody was answering at Wayne Sutton's cottage, and the next door neighbour was positive he hadn't been in all the previous night.

'Davey can't do it, he's ill,' Claire Sutton at once.

'Do you have any more children, Mrs Sutton? Perhaps Wayne's brother or sister could do it?' she suggested carefully.

'Can't. He's our only one,' Claire Sutton said forlornly, and began to cry.

⋆ ⋆ ⋆

The WPC came a few minutes later, and competently took charge. Within the hour, Claire Sutton and her mother, Wayne's grandmother, who had driven over from her home in nearby Aynho, were on their way to Oxford to view the body.

With a small sigh of relief, Hillary stepped outside into the high noon heat and leaned against the fence. A blackbird, busy tugging worms from the lawn, cocked her a quick look, and flew off, cackling. From across the farmyard opposite, a woman watched her from an open doorway.

Hillary straightened her shoulders and walked over.

The farmer's wife, a woman maybe a few years younger than Claire Sutton, watched her approach with pale blue eyes that gave away little. Hillary showed her ID card, and once again introduced herself.

'Jenny Somerleigh,' the woman nodded, making no move to invite her in. But the shade under her porch was nice and cool, and Hillary had had enough of sitting anyway.

51

'Do you know the Suttons well?' Hillary asked, by way of opening gambit.

'Few years. We rented them the cottage back in 2002. Nothing wrong, I hope?'

'There's been something of a family tragedy,' Hillary hedged. Whilst she was in little doubt about the identity of the corpse, she had to be discreet for a while longer yet. 'Any problems? They ever late with the rent, loud parties, anything of that sort?'

'Nah. Mark didn't like it when that son of theirs parked a tatty old caravan out the back, but then, you couldn't see it from the front, and there ain't no near neighbours either side to complain. But we was glad when he left, nevertheless, and they sold it on.'

'I see,' Hillary nodded. 'The son any trouble? I hear he used to be an art student. They can be a bit of a handful.' She smiled encouragingly.

Jenny Somerleigh nodded seriously. 'Drugs you mean. And booze? No, nothing like that. Plenty of naked ladies though,' she added, grinning widely, and showing a row of very badly kept teeth.

'Really? I thought he was into landscapes,' Hillary said, but supposed any young lad, given a legitimate excuse to stare at naked women all day long, was hardly going to turn up his nose.

'Oh, I dunno about that. But I didn't mean that he painted them,' Jenny said, and grinned again. 'Wayne's too good-looking for his own good. And knows how to use the old charm. He liked more mature women — or so he always said. Know what I mean?'

'Oh,' Hillary nodded wisely. 'Funny, his mother tells me he's got a regular girlfriend. A woman a few years younger than himself.'

'That pretty thing with long hair? Young, drives a battered mini?' Jenny tapped the side of her nose. 'Too poor for our Wayne, I'm thinking. But then, she's young and pretty and he probably needed some relief from the rest of his blue-rinse army, as my Barry calls 'em.'

Hillary smiled. 'Sounds like Wayne wasn't exactly monogamous.' And into her mind flashed the image of a cut-out red paper heart. A valentine? A cruel joke? Or a calling card that represented the very real anguish and rage of a female killer?

The farmer's wife laughed again. 'You can say that again.' She seemed about to say something more, but just then the sound of a baby's angry cry rang out behind her from the house, and she glanced over her shoulder quickly. 'Look, sorry, gotta go,' and before Hillary could say another word, took a step back and promptly shut the door in her face.

53

Hillary's lips twisted wryly, and she wondered what else Jenny Somerleigh might have said and decided to come back for a return visit later. First, she'd try some more of the neighbours.

There were one or two cottages scattered far and wide on either side of the muck-strewn lane, but nobody was in at any of them, confirming her supposition that nearly all were rented out to workers who commuted either to Banbury, Oxford, or even further afield. Maybe Barry Somerleigh worked the farm alone?

She was just returning to her car when her mobile phone rang. It was the family liaison officer. Claire Sutton had confirmed the ID. Hillary thanked the WPC and rang off, opening her car door and then standing back as a wave of heat blasted out. She unwound the two front door windows and stood back outside the car, letting Puff the Tragic Wagon air a bit. Then, making a rare snap decision, she radioed HQ and got Gemma Fordham's mobile telephone number, quickly entered it into her phone's memory and hit speed-dial.

It was answered promptly.

'DS Fordham.' The deep, gravelly voice sounded alert and upbeat.

'Gemma, it's me,' Hillary said, expecting to be recognized, and not disappointed.

'Guv,' Gemma Fordham said smartly.

'I want you to leave off house-to-house and get back to HQ. Have a word with the PR Officer — I want you to do a radio broadcast on both BBC Radio Oxford and Fox FM, to catch tonight's commuter traffic, appealing for anyone to come forward who met or saw Wayne Sutton yesterday.'

It was throwing the new girl in at the deep end, but Hillary had no doubt she was up to it. Besides, she hated doing radio interviews herself.

'Right, guv,' Gemma said, totally unfazed, as if she did radio slots every day of the week. 'ID's confirmed then?'

'Yes. I don't usually go public so soon,' Hillary said, then wondered why she felt the need to explain herself to her new, super-efficient DS, and carried on, a bit more sharply, 'but the crime scene's too far out of the way to make any witnesses to the actual event likely, and I need to get any interesting worms to come out of the woodwork as soon as possible. And from something one of the Suttons' neighbours told me, I think there are plenty of worms of the female variety about who could tell us a thing or two.' And, she thought silently, given that red paper heart, it would be interesting to see which women volunteered to come forward, and which had to be winkled out.

'Right guv,' Gemma Fordham said, and waited for Hillary to hang up first. When she did, she put her phone away thoughtfully, and allowed herself a small smile. The boss either trusted her with the radio appeal, or else wanted to give her enough rope to hang herself. Either way, she was obviously making an impression.

Then she felt the smile fall from her face and gave herself a mental kick. Making an impression was not exactly what she was there for. If she was going to get that pot of gold at the end of the rainbow she needed to be unobtrusive. To fly below the radar, to watch, listen and learn, then nip in and out again and be off before anyone could wonder why.

Damn it, she was going to have to keep her need to impress and outshine Hillary Greene firmly in check.

Oblivious to the glories of the late spring day around her, Gemma Fordham walked quickly back to the crime scene, and got a lift back to HQ with a patrol car, already planning the radio appeal in her head. Quiet, calm, concise. Nothing flashy but enough to get the job done.

That was going to be her motto from now on.

★ ★ ★

Monica Freeman, the victim's girlfriend, lived in a small block of red-brick flats overlooking a large car park in the nearby market town of Banbury. According to Claire Sutton, she worked as a trainee veterinary nurse at a practice in town, so Hillary wasn't particularly surprised to find no one in at the flat. It didn't take her long to walk back to her car or track down the surgery.

The Fairways Clinic was situated not far from the famous Banbury Cross, in a small, fairly new-looking industrial estate. Hillary parked in a surprisingly spacious car park and made her way to the clinic doors, feeling the sun beat down on her back and make a trickle of sweat run down her shoulderblades. Inside, a large black-and-white cat was yowling from the depths of a carrier-cage, and an excitable Jack Russell pup, wearing what looked like a lampshade around his neck, barked at the cat like a thing demented.

Hillary walked over to the reception desk and, low-voiced, asked if she might have a quiet word with Monica Freeman. She showed her ID card yet again, and the receptionist, a little wide-eyed, left the desk and moved quickly into the back, where something was whining pitifully.

57

Hillary hoped it wasn't a vet.

A few minutes later, the receptionist came back. 'Please, follow me. You'll have to use an examining room, I'm afraid. We're a bit short of office space.'

Hillary smiled to show that was fine, and followed the woman through a narrow maze of corridors, obviously made of thin hardwood. The tap-tap of the woman's high heeled shoes on the linoleum flooring sounded weirdly amplified. Again something whined pitifully, and Hillary was glad she didn't keep pets. The wild mallards and moorhens who regularly congregated around her boat of a morning to beg for breakfast didn't count.

'Through here,' the receptionist said, pushing open a door to reveal a small cubicle containing a very high table, shelving full of plastic containers of various liquids and drugs, and a tall, ash blonde young woman, who was wearing a white coat and a puzzled, vaguely worried frown.

'Thank you,' Hillary said firmly to the woman still holding open the door, who then flushed and quickly withdrew. 'Monica Freeman?'

'Yes. Vera said you were with the police?' Wide grey eyes watched her nervously and Hillary once again withdrew her ID card.

'Yes. I've just got a few routine questions. Can you tell me what you were doing yesterday, from around four o'clock onwards?'

Monica Freeman blinked her big, fine grey eyes and looked about to object. Then she seemed to change her mind. 'Well, at four I was still here. I worked until six, then I went to Mum and Dad's. I usually have dinner there once or twice a week. It keeps us in touch, and well, the wages here aren't much so I appreciate the free meal. We had meatloaf,' she added, with just a touch of ironic belligerence. 'I stayed with them until about nine or so, then came back here, to the flat.'

'You live alone?'

'Yes.'

'Did anyone see you return to your flat? Neighbours, the caretaker?'

'No.'

'And your parents live . . . where?'

'Deddington. Look, do you mind if I ask what this is all about?' She wore her long hair held back in a pony tail, and when she moved it swung around the back of her head like a live thing. She didn't have many curves, but her face was intriguing, with high cheekbones and a very sharp chin and delicate lines to her jaw. Hillary could well understand why a good-looking young man would be attracted to her. They must have made a fine-looking, even eye-catching couple.

Hillary nodded to herself as she took apart the witness's words. The first part of the evening sounded like a solid enough alibi, and before she left here she'd make sure that Monica Freeman had indeed worked until she'd said — but parents often lied for their children, and after nine she had no alibi at all. So she was firmly in the frame.

'It's about Wayne Sutton. He's your boyfriend, I understand?' she said, a touch more gently now.

Monica Freeman opened her mouth, then slowly closed it again. Her eyes, already large, seemed to grow bigger. 'What's happened to him?' she asked, her voice quiet, almost whispering. 'Did he crash his car?'

Hillary wondered what sort of driver their victim had been if both the women in his life instantly assumed he'd had a car accident. According to the data she'd so far accumulated, Wayne Sutton had only been 25-years-old at the time of his death, so perhaps the assumption was understandable. As a beat officer, Hillary had quickly learned, and only too well, that young men and fast cars should be kept far apart.

'No, he hasn't been involved in a traffic accident, but I'm afraid I have some very bad news, nonetheless,' she said softly.

Slowly Monica Freeman leaned back against the high table, her hands shaking as they clasped the edges of it.

'The body of a young man was found in a meadow just outside Deddington this morning. His mother has identified him as being Wayne Sutton. I'm sorry.'

Monica Freeman nodded. 'Oh,' she said blankly.

★   ★   ★

About a half an hour later, Hillary drove a short distance up the road, where Monica's parents, Victor and Pauline, owned and operated a small garden centre. She found them both in a handkerchief-sized outside area that was crammed with every climbing plant imaginable — something of their speciality, Pauline Freeman quickly informed her.

She was tall and lean, like her daughter, but her hair was a riotous mass of brown curls. Monica's ash-blonde looks and triangular face came courtesy of her father's genes, Hillary noticed, when Pauline called him over to join them.

Yet again, Hillary brought out the ID. 'I've just come from speaking to your daughter,'

Hillary began, and saw by the quick look of surprise they gave each other that this was news to them. Hillary was just a little surprised herself. She'd expected Monica to call them and tell them the news straight away.

Why hadn't she?

'Our Mon's not in any trouble I hope,' Pauline Freeman said, half-laughing, half-worried.

'Oh no, nothing like that,' Hillary lied. Being a suspect in a murder inquiry could probably be classified as 'trouble' in any-body's book, but she knew that that wasn't what the girl's mother meant. 'It's about Wayne Sutton.'

'Huh, I knew it,' Victor Freeman said, putting down a huge tub of flowering 'Montana' clematis, and glancing quickly into the shop to make sure that there were no customers waiting. 'Always thought he was going to end up coming to your lot's attention at some point.'

'Oh now, Vic, don't be daft,' Pauline said, casting a worried look Hillary's way. 'He don't mean nothing by it. He just thinks Wayne's not good enough for his daughter, that's all. I expect all doting daddies feel the same way.'

Victor Freeman frowned at his wife and

shook his head. 'That boy's trouble waiting to happen. I always said so. So what's he done? Killed someone in that car of his? Knocked some kiddie over? Or has somebody's husband put him in hospital?'

Hillary smiled grimly. 'Neither, Mr Freeman. He's been murdered.'

Pauline Freeman sat down abruptly into the empty wheel-barrow that was pressing against the back of her legs. Victor Freeman gaped at Hillary. 'Murdered? So one of them murdered him. Bloody hell, I didn't think it would ever come to something as bad as that.'

Hillary held his gaze firmly. 'One of who, Mr Freeman?'

Victor shook his head, blinking. 'What? Sorry, what?'

'You said 'one of them murdered him'. One of who, Mr Freeman?' she reiterated patiently.

From the wheelbarrow, Pauline Freeman groaned. 'Oh Vic, you shouldn't have said that. You don't know, not for sure. It's probably just gossip. Jealous old biddies. You know how villages are. We come from Birmingham originally, you see,' she glanced across to Hillary. 'Came down here when our Mon was just a baby. Thought country living, and village life would be safer. Better for her. But some of those cats in Deddington are vicious, I can tell you.'

Suddenly becoming aware that she was sitting in a wheel-barrow, long legs dangling incongruously over the side, she struggled to get up. Her husband thrust out a hand to help her, but his mind was obviously still on other things.

'I'm still waiting to hear who you're talking about, Mr Freeman,' Hillary said, not about to let it go.

'Huh? Oh. Well, I dunno,' he began to look worried for the first time and under his wife's admonishing gaze actually blushed.

'Like I said, Vic never liked Wayne,' Pauline Freeman said quickly.

'And you, Mrs Freeman?'

The other woman shrugged. 'Well, he had a bit of a way with him. He was obviously happier with ladies than with men, I can tell you that. But then, he was a good-looking young chap, and an artist to boot. Most men tended not to like him.' She shot her husband another frowning look, and then shook her head. 'I'll have to go to our Mon. She'll be right upset. Vic, you'll have to stay, keep the shop open. I don't know when I'll be back.'

Hillary decided it was in her best interests to let her go, and a few minutes later, when silence had once more settled over the clematis and wisteria plants, the rambling roses and honeysuckles, Hillary glanced pointedly at Victor Freeman.

The lean, gangling man sighed heavily. 'He was a bloody gigolo, wasn't he?' he said helplessly. And when Hillary said nothing, added more forcefully, 'I mean, literally. He lived off women. Conned them silly. That car of his was a 'present' from some besotted divorcee who should have known better. And that cottage he was so-called 'renting'. Hah!' he snorted inelegantly. 'I doubt the owner of that ever saw a penny. Not that he wouldn't have paid her in a different kind of way.'

Hillary, by now not altogether surprised by this revelation, simply nodded. 'His mother said he was a professional artist,' she pointed out quietly.

Victor Freeman laughed. 'Oh yeah? And just who do you think it is that *buys* those bloody awful paintings of his? Women, that's who. All of a certain age, all either divorced or widowed or unhappily married. You won't find a gallery owner or a true art lover buying them, I'll tell you that for nothing. Have you seen them? He gave one to our Mon for her birthday, and it's hanging in our front room. I tell you, looking at it gives me eyestrain. She's better off without him.'

Hillary nodded. 'Your daughter tells me she came to your house last night?'

'That's right. For dinner. She arrived at

about quarter to seven.'

'And she left, when?'

'About quarter past nine. Look, you can't think our Mon had anything to do with this? She's just a strip of a girl! Besides, she hasn't got a violent bone in her body. She loves animals, even as a little kid. She hates to see anything suffer.'

Hillary nodded. 'And after she left, Mr Freeman? What did you do?'

'Me? I went out to the greenhouse out back. We've got a large series of glass houses there — we've not got much space here as you can see, so we tend to grow a lot of our stock at home.'

'Did your wife help you?'

'No. There was something on telly she wanted to watch. I came in about ten-thirty and we went to bed.'

Hillary nodded thoughtfully. So not only did Monica Freeman not have an alibi. Her father had no alibi either.

Interesting.

4

By the end of the day, they'd covered a lot of ground, but learned very little about the victim's movements on the day of his death. The owners of the cottages nearest the meadow had returned home from work, to be greeted by officers on their doorsteps, notebooks at the ready, but nobody remembered seeing Wayne Sutton yesterday evening.

One bright PC had ascertained that there was a short-cut from the village to the meadows that by-passed the lane altogether. Once the last house of the village was left behind, the footpath kept mostly to the sides of hedges before opening out into the meadow where the victim was found, so it was possible that Wayne Sutton had never even walked down the farm track past the cottages on the day of his death. Hillary wearily told the uniforms to find out, next day, who the regular dog walkers were, since they were bound to use the path, and question them instead.

After a half an hour back at HQ talking to Danvers, outlining the case so far and receiving further instructions, she was more than ready to call it a day. As she pulled out of the HQ car park, she heard a faint church bell toll eight o'clock. Her stomach was rumbling, and when she passed a fish and chip shop, she almost whimpered at the delicious smell. Telling herself that she really *did* want the cold tinned salmon and cobbled-together salad that awaited her back on the boat more than a greasy fry-up, by the time she finally pulled into the car park of The Boat pub, where she habitually parked, she was almost convinced.

She locked the car and headed for the towpath, glancing at the other boats as she walked towards her own, noting which of the 'regulars' had moved on, and which visiting, mostly tourist craft, had moored in their spot.

She had to smile at *Oodunnit*, a boat that had painted inside each of the two 'O's a worried-looking eye, and wondered if the owner was a mystery writer. As she neared the *Mollern* her own narrowboat, she sighed to see that *Willowsands* was still absent. Nancy Walker, who owned her, had been Hillary's nearest neighbour since she'd had to move on to the *Mollern* after the break-up of her marriage to Ronnie Greene. Last winter, however, Nancy had chugged her way up to Stratford-upon-Avon, and Hillary still missed her raucous, humorous, blithe presence. A swinging divorcee, who loved younger men — and many of them — she had decided to trawl for fresh pickings from the many actors and wannabes who flocked to Shakespeare Country. Hillary hoped she'd come back soon.

As she approached her predominantly grey-and-white boat with black-and-gold trim (the colours of the heron, after whom her boat had been named) she saw that she had a visitor. Stretched out on a patch of sun-dried grass beside the boat, was the figure of a man. He lay with his forearm across his eyes, his shirt undone almost to his navel as he sunbathed in the setting sun.

'Put it away before you get arrested,' Hillary advised cheerfully. 'It's still too white and pasty-looking to be out on public display anyway.'

DI Mike Regis, from Vice, slowly lowered his arm and opened one eye. 'I'll have you know that,' and he patted his flat belly proudly, 'is now the colour of clotted cream. Tomorrow it'll be the colour of ripe wheat, and by the end of the week I'll be so bronzed I'd make a Hollywood leading man jealous.'

Hillary laughed. 'Sure you won't just look like a lobster?'

Mike Regis rose lithely to his feet. Although her own age, he moved with the subtle fitness of a much younger man. True, his dark hair was thinning, but he had spectacular green eyes, and a killer smile. He reached forward and kissed her gently on the lips.

'Been waiting long?' she asked, worried that they'd arranged to meet, and she'd forgotten.

'Nope. I got off late, didn't fancy home, or the pub, and took the off chance you'd be here. You weren't, but it was such a lovely evening, I thought what the hell?'

They'd been seeing each other for over six months now, but it was rare for him to come to the boat. Hillary had a sneaking suspicion he wasn't overly fond of it. And, to be fair, she could remember that, at first, she hadn't exactly been enamoured of the narrowboat either. But the *Mollern* had been much better than staying at her marital home, which had resembled a battlefield, and over the years, she'd come to love the boat. So much so, that she'd finally took the plunge and bought it off her uncle, who'd originally owned it. And after the death of her husband before their divorce could be finalized, she'd made the decision to sell the house and keep the boat.

Now she stepped on to it and felt the slight movement beneath her with a sense of coming home. 'Mind your head,' she called automatically over her shoulder, as she negotiated the few steep steps down into the narrow corridor that ran the length of her home. She walked on through to the front, where a single armchair, a narrow bookshelf, a small portable telly, and a gas fire, comprised her 'parlour'. She pulled out and opened a folding chair, and slung her bag under it. Then she took one step to one side so he could get past her, and walked back a few steps to the open-plan galley.

'It's salmon salad. OK?'

Regis nodded, sitting down gingerly in the chair, and feeling like a rabbit in a hutch. Outside the window, set higher above him than he was used to, he saw a pair of legs walk past, closely followed by a black button of a nose, belonging to a curious dog. It sniffed the window, cocked its leg, and moved on.

'I bought some bread and wine,' he added, realizing he'd left it outside on the side of the grass. 'I forgot to bring it in.'

'Don't worry, I'll get it,' Hillary said quickly.

The bread turned out to be still warm, crusty and brown, the wine a rich Chablis. Just as well, since the tinned salmon was minuscule and the lettuce a little wilted. The bag of fresh tomatoes she thought she had in the fridge turned out to be only three in number, and just wrinkling. A small tin of new potatoes, warmed up, and a wedge of cheese — strong enough to walk out the fridge on its own and pop the cork of the wine without benefit of an opener — would just have to do. She spread it all out on to two mismatched plates, grabbed some cutlery and took it through.

'I'll have mine on my lap,' she said. 'But there's a small side-table you can use for yours — that's it, flush to the wall. It pulls out,' she watched him fiddle with the latch that kept it pinned to the wall, then wince as it hit the top of his knee with a bang. He scrunched down in the chair a little, and she eased his plate on to the small square of wood. 'No salt, I'm afraid, I haven't been shopping this week.' She tended to buy only small, strictly needful items of grocery, since she didn't have the storage space on the boat that most home-owners were used to.

'This is fine,' Regis lied gamely, and prodded a piece of rather soggy fish experimentally. Hillary went back for the wine and poured out two large glasses.

'So how's Vice?'

'Busy,' Regis grunted. 'With the summer comes the grockles, and you know what comes with them.'

Hillary grinned. 'Grockles' was Regis's favourite word for tourists, and she did, indeed, know what came with them. More prostitutes, more drug dealers, more illegal gambling. All the things that were Vice's bread and butter.

'And you?' He looked up over his plate, his eyes softening on her as she sprawled tiredly in her chair. Her hair was mussed and clung to her cheeks, making him want to push it gently away. Her big, doe-like brown eyes that had always made his heart beat just a bit faster, looked strained and yet eager.

'Got a new murder case today,' she said simply, and he nodded knowingly.

'Ah.' That explained it. 'You're getting quite a rep for them.'

Hillary shrugged. It was her Chief Super, Marcus Donleavy, she suspected, who'd been responsible for her being in charge of so many murder inquiries. And Mel Mallow, of course, her oldest friend, who, as Danvers's immediate superior, was in charge of who was assigned to what.

'So, what's it all about?' Regis asked, staring suspiciously at a tomato. He prodded it and it rolled obligingly across the plate.

'Young guy, bit of a Casanova. Found dead in a meadow with a red paper heart weighted on his chest.'

'Blimey.'

'That's what I thought. A bit over the top. Already his girlfriend and her father might be in the frame, and I've got the feeling that before long, we're only going to add to their number.' Briefly she outlined her day. 'So I expect we'll be up to our eyeball in female suspects once we know the extent of his list of clients.'

Regis smiled. 'Bit of a change from your last case then. As I recall, you were struggling to find even one person with a motive.'

Hillary sighed and sipped her wine. She bit half-heartedly into a lettuce leaf, thinking of cod and chips. The bread though was nice, especially lathered with naughty butter. A rare indulgence, but she'd bought a half-pound on impulse and was now glad that she had.

Outside, the evening light slowly died and the stars came out. She cleared and washed the dinner things, putting them away neatly before opening all the windows to let in a cool, evening breeze.

'Are you staying?' she asked softly.

'Do you want me to?' he asked, almost diffidently.

She frowned. 'Of course. Why? Don't you *want* to stay?'

'Don't talk daft, woman,' he growled, and let her lead him to the bedroom, a tiny cabin with a single bed that could pull out to make an almost three-quarter bed. He watched her undress with lazy-lidded eyes, and when she was finished, took a step back into the corridor to do the same. To attempt to strip in the tiny space would have had him scraping his elbows and bumping his knees and toes — and who knew what other protruding bits — into the walls or furniture.

Hillary giggled as he got naked into bed beside her, then gave a muffled yelp of laughter as she turned to face him and he nearly fell out the other side. 'Come here,' she said helpfully, pulling him on top of her.

* * *

It was nearly four in the morning when Regis finally admitted defeat and slipped out of the bed. No matter how much he tried, he simply couldn't sleep with so little room. It wasn't so much the crowded bed — when you had such lovely curves as Hillary's pressed against you, who cared? But he could lift his hand and touch the ceiling, or move his arm parallel, anywhere in a 360-degree radius, and touch walls. He felt as if the air was thickening, pressing him down, making it hard to breath. He dressed quietly, with the full moon shining through the round port-hole in the bedroom and illuminating her sleeping face.

He sighed softly, wishing she'd move in with him. He was renting a fairly spacious flat out Botley way, but if that didn't suit her, he was more than willing to move. But so far, all his gentle, tiny hints, had fallen on to stony ground. Dressed, he bent and kissed her forehead, and let himself off the boat.

The moment she felt his weight rock the boat slightly as he leapt on to the towpath, Hillary opened her eyes and sighed. She'd thought he would never go. He was so restless, it had been impossible to sleep. But she could hardly shove him from her bed, could she?

She sighed, waited five minutes, until she was sure he'd be gone, then turned on the light. She knew it would be no good trying to get off just yet. Instead, she went into the galley and made herself a cup of coffee, and then, reaching for her mail, extracted a literary magazine she subscribed to, and took it back to bed.

The magazine was one she used to read as an undergraduate at Oxford, and it was filled with local gossip as well as articles. As she opened it out to the middle-spread, always her favourite part, she instantly noticed the headline: **'Jane Austen find in obscure Oxfordshire village?'**

She gave a small grunt of disbelieving pleasure, and began to read, slightly disappointed to find that the article wasn't about a long-lost Austen manuscript, or even the outline or notes for one, but of a 'possible' portrait of the famous author instead. Apparently, there was only one authentic portrait of the novelist in existence, painted rather indifferently by her sister Cassandra, and currently hung at the National Portrait Gallery. However rumours were flying that another painting of her might have been discovered not far from the city of Oxford. Experts and sceptics gave conflicting statements, and the reporter promised more revelations to come.

She put the magazine down, wondering just what she was going to do about Mike Regis. She sighed, finished her drink, and turned off the light.

Without a restless partner taking up all the room, she was quickly asleep.

★   ★   ★

Keith Barrington woke up the next morning with a vague feeling of dread. It took him several moments to realize why.

The autopsy.

Before he'd left the office the previous day,

Hillary had asked him to attend. It was only the second one he'd ever had to do, and although he'd had to dash to the loo to be sick at his first go-round, at least he hadn't fainted.

He knew that it was protocol in a murder case that someone from the investigating team be present, but he wished she'd asked the new girl to do it. He swung his legs out of bed and rubbed his face tiredly.

He wasn't quite sure what to make of Gemma Fordham. Born and raised in London, he'd spent all his working life in the city, until an unfortunate incident with his sergeant had forced him to relocate. He'd been lucky to keep his job, he knew, and saw his move to Thames Valley as his last chance to turn things around.

And he'd been lucky in his new boss. Hillary Greene was fair, straight-forward, intelligent, and one hell of an investigative copper. He'd learned more from her in the last six months than he'd have learned in six years at his old nick. And Gemma Fordham was said to be something of a high flier too. She certainly came across as one tough woman, with her gravelly voice, kung-fu persona and no-nonsense wardrobe. Already he sensed that half the men at the nick either fancied her rotten or were dead scared of her. And probably both. He felt neither, but then he had a certain immunity.

He felt a sleepy body stir on the other side of the bed, and then a warm hand slipped up his back, resting between his shoulderblades. 'Come on, Kee, it's still way too early. Come back to bed.'

Keith smiled. 'Some of us don't have rich daddies to keep us in luxury. Some of us have to work for a living.'

'How bloody boring! Come on, come back to bed. If you *have* to live in this shit-hole, the bed's the only place habitable.'

Ignoring the invitation, Keith got to his feet. 'You've already made me late once, and don't think my boss didn't notice. Besides, I have an appointment with a dead body. Gotta go see that it's sliced and diced properly.'

'Ugh, don't. Who'd do your awful job? I don't know why I put up with you. And as for leaving London — I still think you're out of your tiny mind. If you come back, you know I can always line you up with something. A job with a bit of class.'

Keith laughed at the thought of himself in a stockbroker's office, and shaking his head, reached for his clothes. Doc Partridge would be starting the autopsy at 8.30 on the dot. And he meant to be there.

He thought it would probably be a good idea to skip breakfast though.

Gemma Fordham wasn't surprised to find the office still largely deserted. It wasn't yet seven, and whilst the night shift was preparing to leave, most of them buggering off early, the day shift had yet to arrive. Which was just what she wanted. Some peace and quiet and privacy.

She settled herself down at her desk, pouring a cup of camomile tea from her thermos before reaching into her capacious bag for the first of the files she'd checked out of records.

It was Hillary Greene's first murder case.

If anybody saw her reading it, they would only assume that she was boning up on her new boss. A worthwhile, maybe even necessary, precaution on her part, some would say.

But, in truth, she had little interest in how clever the woman had been, or thorough, or even lucky. In fact, the murder of David Pitman didn't interest her at all. She only wanted to discover what could be gleaned about the investigation into corruption that had been going on at the same time. Gemma already knew that some officers from York had been brought down to investigate the corrupt Ronnie Greene's missus, and had gone back with their tail between their legs. Ronnie, as had already been proved by then, had been running a very lucrative and illegal animal parts smuggling operation for years before he was caught. The fact that he'd died in a car accident had been the only thing to save him from prosecution. The money had never been found.

But what Gemma desperately wanted to know was what they might have found out about his saintly spouse. Needless to say, those records were sealed. All she'd been able to find out was what had circulated on the grapevine. Namely, that no case had been made against her, and that nobody had ever seriously considered that she was in on it.

But since Hillary was investigating her first murder case at the same time as all this was going on, there was no knowing what might be discovered from some astute reading between the lines.

Quickly, she opened up the file and began to read.

⋆   ⋆   ⋆

Steven Partridge looked across the naked body of Wayne Sutton and assessed the young, red-haired constable opposite. A little green around the gills, but holding up. Best of

81

all, no tell-tale swaying back and forth. He might even not have to rush out to the loo.

Good for him.

'Well, you can tell your boss that cause of death has been confirmed. Water in the lungs and the diatoms say that he was drowned at the scene. And my original guess at time of death hasn't changed significantly, either.'

Barrington nodded, but wasn't bothering to take notes. Everything the medico was saying was being recorded, and before he left, he'd get a copy and transcribe it on to the computer back at HQ. Hillary would expect a full summary of it by the end of the day.

'Also, see the bruising here, and here.' The small, wiry doctor rolled the larger and heavy corpse of Wayne Sutton from side to side with a strength and ease that spoke of long practice. Keith forced himself to look. 'These small, round-ish bruises on the small of his back. They're consistent with someone holding him down with their knees.'

Keith swallowed hard. 'Poor bastard,' he muttered.

'Yes,' Steven Partridge said softly. 'But I think the bash to his temples had probably rendered him all but senseless. A man flailing about on a riverbank, fighting for his life, not to mention his breath, would almost certainly rip out mud and grass with his hands as he tried to get free. But there was nothing like that under his fingernails. I think he drowned without any significant struggle.'

'So a woman would have had the strength to do it?' Barrington asked, mindful of that red paper heart found on the body. And from what he'd learned yesterday from house to house, Wayne Sutton had something of reputation as a ladies' man. If they weren't looking for a female killer, he'd be very surprised.

'Oh yes,' Partridge confirmed. 'A woman could certainly have done it. And now, something that'll please your boss. It's over here, at trace.'

Keith, glad to leave the gaping cadaver, followed the doctor to one of the side tables, where the victim's clothes had been meticulously searched. The doctor lifted one, apparently empty, tiny plastic envelope.

'This hair, found on the victim's shirt, does not match his own. As you can see, the victim's hair is black. This hair is a dark-brown. In fact, I wouldn't be surprised if it wasn't dyed. I'll know if I'm right once the lab has a go at it.'

Barrington nodded. 'DNA?'

'Oh yes, it's got a root. Not torn out, I would have said, just naturally shed. The stone weighing down the paper heart is with the lab now. If the DNA from the skin particles on that match up with the DNA from this little beauty,' he rattled the plastic envelope jauntily, 'then all your boss has got to do is find a suspect to match. And you do know how juries like DNA at crime scenes that match the one on trial. Gives 'em no end of confidence to bring in a guilty verdict. Oh, and tell Hillary that the piece of paper in his pocket is drying out nicely. I'll be able to let her know its contents soon.'

Keith nodded, eager to leave and glad to bring such good news to his boss.

★   ★   ★

Hillary pushed open the door to the office and saw Gemma Fordham glance up, move forward in her chair and unobtrusively thrust the folder she was reading back into her voluminous bag. She was leafing through her note book when Hillary reached her.

'Morning, guv. Another scorcher.'

Hillary stared out at the bright morning sunshine. According to the radio it was going to hit over 90 degrees before the day ended. But she doubted that that would worry her new sergeant much. She couldn't see the lean Gemma Fordham so much as breaking out in a sweat, despite the fact that she was wearing dark slacks and a jacket.

'Gemma, can you do the biog for me?' Hillary said, shrugging off her own light-weight jacket, and reaching for her coffee mug. 'I forgot to assign it yesterday.' At the beginning of a murder investigation, information about the victim came from lots of various sources. As well as the bread-and-butter stuff that could be gained from access to a computer, friends could relate telling incidents that gave insight into character. Witness statements, scrap books, photos, diaries, and anything else needed to be collated together to produce a detailed picture of their victim.

'Sure, guv, I've already started on it,' Gemma lied. 'Once Keith is in, and Frank, I can add their stuff to mine. Give me an hour.'

Hillary smiled and walked over to the side, where a perpetual coffee pot was on the go. It was nice to have an efficient sergeant who didn't need to be supervised all the time. Someone competent and able, who didn't give her any grief or back chat.

Janine Tyler, her last DS, had upped and married Mel Mallow, had taken orders with reluctant grace, and was so ambitious she needed to be checked constantly.

Gemma Fordham's cool, self-assured nature could only be an asset.

And as soon as her back was turned, Hillary was damned well going to find out what was in that file she'd been reading and had oh-so-casually put back in her bag.

* * *

Frank Ross turned up a few minutes after Keith Barrington, smelling faintly of stale beer and cigarettes. Whereas Barrington had been to an autopsy, Frank had no excuse for rolling in two hours before lunchtime. But Hillary merely gave him a sour look, and gathered her team together for a confab.

'Right, Keith, you can kick off.'

They listened to the pertinent titbits provided by the pathologist, all of them relieved by the potential of the DNA evidence.

'Sounds like it's a straightforward case of *cherchez la femme* to me,' Frank said, strangling the French, and picking his teeth with a paper clip. 'From what they were telling me at his local boozer, our Wayne was a randy git, who specialized in middle-aged crumpet. The doc said the brown hair was dyed, so we're probably looking at a fifty- or sixty-something old gal who didn't like to share the young meat around.'

'Very elegantly put, Frank,' Hillary said

dryly. But he had a point. 'Any thoughts about the red paper heart anybody?'

'Just goes to prove my point,' Frank said, before the others could open their mouths. 'Typical over-the-top gesture. I dare say the poor old dear who bumped him off was having trouble with her hormone replacement therapy or something. A red paper heart is just the sort of soppy, goofy thing that would appeal to a randy tart with no sense. Probably thinks she's committed some grand crime of passion. Silly cow.'

Hillary let him run down, then glanced at Gemma. 'I don't like that heart. I didn't like when I first saw it, and I don't like it now.'

Gemma Fordham nodded. Her short spiky blonde head bobbed forward as she selected a slim folder from the stack in her On-Going tray. 'I did some research on serial killers who leave a 'signature', guv. Thought it might prove useful.'

She handed it over, and Hillary glanced at it briefly. 'I'll be sure to read it later. But I've been wondering since, whether the heart wasn't so much a calling card, as a bit of misdirection. I mean, here we have Wayne Sutton, a bit of a Casanova, and more likely than not, a straight out-and-out gigolo. And when he dies, someone leaves a red paper heart on his chest.'

Gemma's grey eyes narrowed slightly. 'Too much icing on the cake, you think?' she asked sharply. 'Yes, possibly. If someone wanted to lead us up the garden path, that's the obvious direction to take us.'

'What, you think it's got nothing to do with his private life?' Keith asked, catching on.

Frank Ross grunted. Typical. Shoot down his suggestion without even bothering to give it a proper airing. He didn't know why he kept on doing this job.

'It's only a thought,' Hillary said sharply. 'So don't let's get too hung up on it. Chances are, Frank's spot on. If it waddles like a duck, swims like a duck, and is always quacking, it probably *is* a duck. Wayne Sutton may well have been killed by one of the women in his life . . . '

'Or one of their hubbies who didn't like being made a fool of,' Frank Ross butted in.

' . . . So let's concentrate on them first,' Hillary carried on. 'I want a list of all the women who might have had an interest in him . . . '

''Course, it needn't be an actual husband,' Frank Ross said. 'Could be an ex-husband, who doesn't like the fact that his big fat alimony cheques are being spent on a poncy lothario.'

' . . . And find out how many of them have solid alibis,' Hillary went on. 'I take it time of death is confirmed as the evening of the 30th of April?'

'Yes, guv,' Keith said quickly.

'OK. Gemma, any response to the radio appeal yet?'

'Filtering through, guv. You want to be kept appraised?'

'Please.'

'One other thing, guv,' Gemma said. 'Before you pulled me off house-to-house, I was talking to a woman who goes to night-school in Banbury, and she was telling me that she thought she saw an art club advertised that had Wayne Sutton as either president or founder or something. Want me to check it out?'

'Yes. It sounds like a good place for our vic to find more potential customers to me. Get a list and start interviewing them. Keith, you help her out. I want a short précis on them all when you've finished. I might want to re-interview.'

Keith, who was beginning to learn her methods, was already nodding. His guv had a way with witnesses, and was no desk jockey. She liked to get out and about and do things hands on. Gemma Fordham, however, looked slightly surprised, but quickly got to work, phoning the college in Banbury and asking if she might come over and photocopy some-thing from their notice board. Given the go-ahead, she grabbed her car keys and quickly left.

Taking her bulky, file-filled bag with her.

Hillary ground her teeth.

Frank strolled off, talking about more interviews — no doubt at Wayne Sutton's local pub — and Keith began to transcribe the autopsy notes.

Hillary sighed, and reached for a pile of witness statements, but barely ten minutes later, she was buzzed from downstairs by the desk sergeant.

Someone had come into the station after hearing the radio appeal that had been repeated on that morning's breakfast news. And she wanted to talk to the officer in charge.

5

Gemma Fordham stood at the top of a flight of concrete steps and looked around at the technical college spread out before her. The sight, sound, and smell of it, was taking her right back to her own student days, and she sighed, just a shade regretfully.

At nineteen she'd just got her first belt at karate; studying criminology, she was half-shacked up with a chemistry student and worked a bar at nights to make ends meet. But she hadn't yet met Ronnie Greene. Looking back at her life then, she wondered what she'd have done if she could have time-warped herself ten years to this spot, and this moment. Would she recognize herself?

Probably not.

She scrutinized the signs pointing out various departments, and decided that her best bet was probably the Administration Office. At this time of day, the students were all in classes, and the institutional corridors were eerily empty. At Admin, a secretary listened to her request, obviously dying to ask questions, but restraining herself.

'Sounds like you want the common room,' she said, when Gemma had explained what she was looking for. 'If the woman was at night school here, that's where she'd probably have seen the general notice board. Take the stairs back down to the front, turn left, and you'll see a big green door. Go through, take the first right, then it's the second door on the left. Or maybe the third. Anyway it'll have a sign on the door. There's a small office just opposite — the Principal's secretary's place. She'll have a photocopier and if you ask, she'll run some copies off for you.'

Gemma thanked her, and followed her instructions with ease. The witness had indeed remembered it correctly. The 'Ale and Arty club' promised a combination of pub crawls where real ale was the primary motivating force, plus ad-hoc 'art lessons' by, amongst others, Wayne Sutton. Founder members were listed, as well as some endorsements by happy recruits.

With the notice copied and in her bag, Gemma returned to her car and slipped inside. She glanced at her heavy tote bag beside her, and frowned. Was she just being paranoid in believing that Hillary Greene would have gone through the bag had she left it behind? Were her own less than lily-white motives for joining the team colouring her own judgement? She didn't think so. There were no flies on her new boss, and Hillary *had* noticed her slipping the folders out of sight when she'd come into the room. No, she was going to carry on being just as careful. Before she went back to the open-plan office she shared with the rest of her colleagues, she'd take the incriminating reading material back to records.

With this in mind, she opened up the file to where she'd left off and began to scan it quickly.

★   ★   ★

Hillary pushed open the door to Interview Room 2, and smiled as a woman rose slowly to her feet. A watchful WPC stood in one corner, saying nothing, as Hillary approached the single table, which was bolted to the floor, hand held out in greeting.

'Hello, I'm DI Greene.'

The visitor was short, about five feet one, with curly brown hair and large hazel eyes. Her handshake was passive and slightly damp. She was wearing a voluminous, rainbow-hued kaftan of pure Indian silk, over lightweight white slacks. The outfit probably cost more than Hillary made in a month. Or two months. She was wearing long dangling

93

turquoise and silver earrings, and her make-up was light but clever. A diamond and platinum lady's watch adorned one small wrist, that was already tanned a deep brown.

'I asked to speak to the man in charge,' the woman said, her voice accentless but high-pitched. 'But I suppose he's busy?'

As the woman sat down again, Hillary smiled wryly. 'I dare say he is,' she said, disinclined to put her right. She was obviously one of those women who played off her dainty, feminine charms, a woman who much preferred the company of men. It had probably never occurred to her that a member of her own sex might be heading up a murder inquiry, and Hillary was in no mood to enlighten her.

'Mrs Berdowne, isn't it?' Hillary said, glancing at the scrap of paper the desk sergeant had given her.

'Stella Berdowne, yes. Of Berdowne Ceramics.'

Hillary nodded. She'd never heard of it. Probably the woman made pots in her expensive studio conversion and sold them to long-suffering friends.

'You have something to tell us about Wayne Sutton?' she asked, coming straight to the point.

'I heard on the radio this morning that he was dead. Is that true?'

'Yes.'

'And the radio said that you were treating his death as suspicious?' the voice rose even higher in pitch. Stella Berdowne had long, peach-painted fingernails that fiddled with the clasp of her bag, then moved up to stroke one earring, then went back to the table top, where she absently scratched a loose sliver of wood.

Hillary watched all the twitching, trying to decide whether the woman was on something, nervous, or terrified. Or all three.

'Yes, it is officially a murder inquiry, Mrs Berdowne. I take it you knew Wayne Sutton?'

'Yes.'

'Socially?'

'Oh no. Well, sort of. That is, I took private art classes with him. I'm a potter by inclination, but I wanted to improve my general painting skills. A friend of mine told me about him. I admired one of her paintings at a coffee morning, oh, about four months ago now, and she told me it was a Sutton original. When she told me he also took on a few select students, I asked for his number, and . . . ' the peach-painted nails spread wide before moving to the toggle on her kaftan and pulling on it, ' . . . he came to my studio to see my work, and liked it, and agreed to give me some classes. He was a wonderful artist, a generous man with his time and talent.'

Hillary nodded. She'd just bet he was. 'And you became friends?'

'Well, of course,' Stella Berdowne laughed falsely, and her nails went up to her hair, patting the curls, fluffing, smoothing. 'He was a friendly young man. Interested, and so supportive of my work. Throwing pots isn't all that easy, and the market for original works isn't all that great.'

'You make a living at it, Mrs Berdowne?'

'Oh, well, not really. My husband is a market research analyst for a major pharmaceutical company.'

Hillary nodded, her face perfectly straight. 'We're looking for anyone who saw Mr Sutton on the thirtieth of April, the day before May Day. Did you see him that day?'

Stella was already shaking her head before she'd finished speaking. 'The last time I saw Wayne was for my regular Friday afternoon lesson.'

'He came to your studio, you said?'

'That's right.'

'Do you happen to know how many other students he had, Mrs Berdowne? Or their names? Did he visit all of them at their own homes, or did some of them go to his place?'

As she expected, the question made the other woman very uncomfortable, and the

96

restless fingernails went into overdrive.

'Oh, well, I'm not sure. I mean, I didn't like to pry. I know he saw several other students, that's all. Some, to be honest, didn't sound very exceptional. One woman in particular he was rather annoyed with.'

'Oh?' Hillary asked sharply. 'Why was that?'

'I'm not quite sure. Wayne didn't talk about his other students very much — it wouldn't have been nice, would it? But I got the impression that this woman wasn't very talented. From what he let drop, I got the feeling she was jealous, you know the type. A bit of a drinker, maybe, clinging. I mean, a man like Wayne, he was very good-looking, and charming, and had a warm heart. He didn't have it in him to turn anyone away.'

'But you don't know her name?'

'I'm sorry, I don't.'

'Or where she lived?'

'No, sorry.'

'And can you tell me where you were on the evening of the thirtieth, Mrs Berdowne? And please, don't take offence, it's a question we're asking absolutely everybody,' Hillary assured her, seeing her start to protest.

Stella Berdowne ran a peach-painted nail across her lower lip and then shrugged graphically. 'I was throwing a little dinner party for Duncan. My husband. He had some

Danish party over — his company's got contacts over there. Or were they Swedes? Anyway, I did a nice little salmon and dill mousse for starters, duck of course, then tiny little wild-strawberry tartlets with home-made elder flower ice-cream afterwards. I spent a year taking cookery lessons when I got married. I think it's so important to be able to help your husband in his career, don't you?'

Hillary thought briefly of her corrupt, womanizing, late and totally unlamented husband, and smiled widely. 'Of course, Mrs Berdowne.'

★   ★   ★

Back upstairs, Hillary wondered how much Mrs Berdowne paid their victim for her 'lessons' and supposed that however much it was, her husband had been well able to afford it.

Then she made a note to assign Frank to check out the Berdowne woman's alibi, sighed, and returned to her stack of witness statements.

★   ★   ★

Keith Barrington jotted down the last of the list of names that Gemma had just rattled off over the phone, and said, 'Got it. How do you

98

want to split them up?'

Still sitting in her car outside the technical college, Gemma Fordham scanned a report signed by DCI Philip Mallow. 'I'll take the 1st page,' she said distractedly into the mouthpiece of her mobile. 'You take all those on the 2nd.'

Barrington assented amiably and hung up. He checked the list, then radioed into dispatch for a current address on a Mr Marcus Lyman.

*   *   *

Hillary Greene tossed aside the last statement from the house-to-house inquiries, glanced at her watch, and decided it was time to get out of the office. She grabbed her bag and checked her papers, deciding to interview the owner of their victim's cottage, a Mrs Margaret Eaverson.

Driving back to Deddington, she turned the radio station to a golden oldie channel, smiling as The Move began to sing all about a 'Night of Fear'. Outside, the sun baked the tarmac, causing a shimmer of heat-haze to dance before the car. On the pavements, pedestrians dressed in shorts and skimpy tops looked cheerful and oblivious. She wondered what Claire and Davey Sutton were doing right now, and doubted that the bright sunshine would be making any difference to their world.

As always with a murder case, she could feel the heavy weight of responsibility sitting on her shoulders, and when she parked outside a large, detached house in the older part of Deddington village, she scanned it carefully. According to Monica Freeman's father, the woman who rented Wayne Sutton his cottage was another donator to the Wayne Sutton fan club and benevolent society.

Which made her definitely suspect.

The gardens were large and well-kept, with late-blooming cherry trees, flowering, pruned bushes, and manicured lawn. A tiny fountain tinkled merrily away by a large and shady porch, making Hillary feel instantly cooler. She rang the bell and the door was answered almost at once, as if the occupant had been expecting her, and had been lurking closely nearby.

'Yes?' the woman who held open the door was short and dumpy, with a red sweating face and white hair that clung to her forehead and cheeks.

'Mrs Eaverson?' Hillary asked, uncertainly.

'She'll be out by the pool, luv. Come on in,' the cleaning lady stepped back and closed the door behind her. 'Straight on down the tiled corridor, luv, and on into the conservatory. The pool's tacked on, off to the right. Gotta get on with these banisters.' So saying, she retrieved a tin of furniture polish and her orange cleaning rag and set to on the wooden staircase.

Hillary followed the directions easily, pausing only to admire a grandmother clock ticking away melodiously in a small recess. The conservatory was full of overpoweringly fragrant mock orange blossom, and the instant, sticky heat made Hillary gasp. She was glad to step through to a slightly less warm, half-glass, half wooden construction that housed a large, aquamarine pool.

The water itself was undisturbed, and Hillary quickly spotted a woman lying on a sun lounger at the far end. Beside her was a long glass filled with ice, a pale lemon liquid and fruit, with one of those jaunty little paper umbrellas to cap it off. She was reading a paperback novel, but glanced across curiously at Hillary as she moved around the pool to join her.

'Hello, did that gormless charwoman of mine let you in? I keep telling her to escort visitors herself, but I might as well talk to the wall. If you're selling something I'm not interested. You're not a burglar are you?'

Hillary grinned and held out her ID card.

'No, I'm with the other lot, Mrs Eaverson.'

'Madge, please. Everyone calls me Madge. Oh my, the coppers no less.'

She made no move to get up. She was one of those women with short honey-coloured hair, heavily tanned faces and laughter-lines around the eyes, who could be any age between thirty and sixty. She was wearing an apricot-coloured swim suit with a matching beach jacket, and still had the figure — just about — to carry it off. A pair of sunglasses loitered on the table next to the drink, which smelt faintly of rum, pineapple and coconut.

It's all right for some, Hillary thought, with just a pang of envy.

'You're here to talk about Wayne, of course,' Madge Eaverson said, her light and bantering tone suddenly gone. 'It was a bloody tragedy what happened to him. He always managed to cheer me up. My old man is a bit of a grumpy bugger, but Wayne was always good for a laugh. And he was talented too. I asked him to paint that mural for me,' she added, pointing to the wall opposite. Because it was on the same side as the door through which she'd entered, Hillary had had her back to it during her brief walk to the lounger, and now she turned and looked back.

And blinked.

The wall was covered with flowers, but flowers that were actually comprised of individual cars. The petals consisted of Cortinas and Rovers, racy old Morgans and sleek elongated E-type Jaguars. Leaves were petrol station pumps, stems were hose pipes. Stamens were exhaust pipes and the blue sky had painted over it, very lightly, what looked like a map from a road atlas.

'Clever, isn't it?' Madge Eaverson said admiringly. 'It's an ecological statement as well as a stunning, visual work of art. Cars and petrol, our obsession with travelling in comfort, is actually poisoning the air. Plants breath in carbon monoxide, and give out oxygen as a waste product? Did you know that? I didn't, until Wayne told me.'

Hillary, who *had* known that, blinked again. The whole effect managed to be somehow both hideous and eye-catching at the same time. She didn't like it, but she could tell that some art critics might rave over it, whilst others vilified it.

'I understand you're the owner of 18 Westside Court, Mrs Eaverson?' she said, turning her back firmly on the mural.

'What? Oh, Weeping Willow Cottage. Yes. I used to live there, before I got married. Then I had it done up and rented it out. But it got a bit down-at-heel after fifteen years of tenants, and when the last lot left, I was going to sell it. Then I met Wayne, who was living in a caravan outside his parents' house, for Pete's sake, and so I let him have it instead.'

Hillary, forced to stand simply because there was only the one lounger, scribbled somewhat awkwardly into her notebook. 'You say you 'let him have it'. Do you mean he paid no rent?'

Madge laughed. 'Oh, peppercorn only. Wayne, like most real artists, was always short of cash.'

Hillary somehow rather doubted that. She'd read Keith Barrington's report, and when he'd visited Wayne's home, he'd found expensive stereo equipment, the latest wide-screened digital television, and a wardrobe full of designer gear. Even the bathroom cabinet was full of the most expensive toiletries.

'How long had he been living there, Mrs . . . Madge?'

'Oh, who knows. Time has a way of getting away from you, have you ever noticed that? Must be, what, two years by now. Maybe even more.'

'And can you tell me what you were doing two nights ago? Say between six and midnight?'

Madge Eaverson rose one, artfully plucked eyebrow and smiled. 'Am I really a suspect?'

'We're asking anyone who knew the victim the same, standard questions, Mrs Eaverson.'

'Madge, dear, please. I insist. It makes me nervous to have a copper keep calling me Mrs Eaverson. Especially since I don't have an alibi. I was alone here all evening, I'm afraid.'

'So your husband wasn't home?'

'Good grief no,' Madge snorted. 'He practically lives at the office. Don't know why, when he doesn't exactly get paid overtime. Still, he's a manager, as he keeps on telling me, and has to set an example for the junior execs who want to rise to the same giddy heights.' She shrugged as if to say, 'what-can-you-do?'

'And your husband works where?'

'Collings. Out by Cropredy. Largest agricultural supply company in five counties.' She rolled her eyes, 'As I've been told, every day for the last fifteen years of marriage to the man. What I don't know about tractors and combine harvesters isn't worth knowing. Can I get you a drink?' She reached for her own glass and gave it a shake, making the little paper umbrella dance.

'No, thank you. Did you have any callers that night, or speak on the phone with anyone?'

'Don't think so. Look, seriously, why on earth would I want to kill Wayne?' Madge

Eaverson said, sucking on the straw in her drink and leaning back on her lounger. 'He was a sweetie pie.'

★ ★ ★

Keith Barrington, after six months in Oxfordshire, was beginning to know his way around the county, and being told that Marcus Lyman lived in a small village called Souldern worried him not at all.

Now, parking under a magnificent red-flowering hawthorn, he paused to smell the air and could even identify the predominant scent as belonging to wallflowers, growing, not surprisingly, beside a nearby wall.

He'd first come to the countryside from the bright lights of the city in the depths of winter and, at first, the grey overcast days, and the monochrome scenery had depressed him. But with the spring had come a rejuvenation, and now he wasn't so unnerved by mile upon mile of green fields, or the surprises that Mother Nature threw at you, all of which were so much more apparent out here than in the capital. And when a hovering kestrel in the field nearby suddenly plummeted to earth, he didn't even wince as he imagined some small rodent being dispatched.

Marcus Lyman lived in a compact, neat and modern little house, with a spick-and-span, unimaginative garden. Keith instantly put him down as a more 'Ale' than 'Arty' member of the club. So when Mr Lyman answered the summons to his door a few moments later, Keith wasn't surprised by the rather broken-veined red nose or large beer belly.

'Mr Lyman? DC Barrington. I'd like to talk to you about the Ale and Arty Club? You may have heard in the local press that one of its members, Mr Wayne Sutton, has been murdered?'

'Oh ah, right you are. Yes. Come on in.' Marcus Lyman was a grey-haired man, pear-shaped, and moved in a rolling walk. He led Keith to a small, neat front room, that was musty and obviously little used. He instantly opened a window, then sat down in an armchair, indicating to Keith to do the same.

'Wayne Sutton. He's the good-looking one, always going on about honesty in art whilst ogling the ladies, yes?'

Keith Barrington nodded. 'Probably, sir.' He showed him a photograph of the victim, and when the witness nodded in recognition, carried on smoothly, 'So, what can you tell me about him?'

'Not a lot, really. I didn't like him much, truth to tell. But then, I wasn't in his gang.'

'His gang?'

'Yes,' Lyman said, then frowned. 'How to explain it? The club's a bit of a mish-mash really. I do calligraphy,' he paused, to see if Keith knew what that was, and when the red-haired youngster nodded his head, carried on brightly, 'and there are others in the group who throw pots, some who do creative knitting, one chap who does metal sculptures for garden centres, that sort of thing. More arts and crafts, you might say. Then there's the paint crowd. They see themselves as the real 'artists' as it were. Anyway, we all have a love of good booze to create a sort of bond between us, and we all take it in turns to 'find' a good pub, and every two weeks we all troop to this pub for a booze up and talk art.'

Keith nodded, to show he understood the set up.

'But, like I said, somehow the painters have formed a sort of splinter group, within a group. As if painting canvases is the only one true art, and the rest of us are just artisans. And that Sutton was the worst of the lot. Bit of an artistic snob if you ask me. Not that he ever bothered to bend my ear much. I was the wrong sex. Wayne was only interested in something if it wore a skirt.'

Keith nodded. That certainly sounded like their victim all right. 'And can you tell me the names of any of the 'skirts' he was particularly interested in, sir?'

★   ★   ★

Hillary smiled at Tommy Eaverson's secretary, and waited whilst she slipped through a door to the boss's inner sanctum to give him the bad news. She doubted that the woman had ever had to tell the MD of Collings International that a police officer wanted to talk to him before. Unless, of course, it was about security arrangements, or pranged cars or lost wallets.

'You can go right through,' the secretary, a twenty-something with dyed red hair and an eye-catching diamond ring on her engagement finger, said brightly. Hillary murmured a thanks and slipped past her, into a fairly modest-sized office with a large window overlooking a carefully landscaped cluster of yellow-bricked buildings.

'Mr Eaverson?'

'Yes. Please, sit down. What can I do for you, Detective Inspector?'

'I'm heading the Wayne Sutton murder inquiry, Mr Eaverson,' Hillary said, sitting

109

down, but never taking her eyes from his face. He was a thickset man, wearing a well-cut grey suit. His hair was silver, rather than white, and his somewhat small grey eyes were almost the exact colour of his suit. She saw him wince slightly at the mention of Sutton's name, then he shrugged.

'Then you should be talking to my wife. He's her friend, rather than mine.'

'I've just come from your home, Mr Eaverson,' Hillary replied, not missing the antagonism implicit in his choice of words. 'I need to confirm where you were on the night of the thirtieth. That's not last evening, but the evening before.'

'Oh?' Eaverson said flatly.

'It's purely routine sir. Your wife tells me she was home, alone. Is that true?'

'I expect so. I was here,' Tommy Eaverson said, a shade reluctantly. 'There's always a lot of work to be done, this time of year. Winter can be a bit slow. Then, just when it's needed the most, farmers discover that their machinery has broken down, or they need new seed drills or whatever, and suddenly there's a massive rush.'

'Did your secretary work late too?'

'Of course not. She keeps regular office hours.'

'So you were here alone?'

'More or less. Young Greenstock was here

for a time. I think he left about seven, seven-thirty. Look, I can assure you I didn't kill the man, Inspector.'

'Your wife tells me he paid only a peppercorn rent on Weeping Willow Cottage.'

Tommy Eaverson flushed. 'Nothing to do with me. That's Madge's property. Always was. Now, if there's nothing else, as I said, I really am busy.'

Hillary nodded, but on the way out, got the full name and address of 'young' Greenstock.

She got the distinct impression that Tommy Eaverson hadn't liked Wayne Sutton. That he hadn't liked him at all.

★   ★   ★

Gemma Fordham visited the first two art club members on her list, a Mike Armstrong and a Nancy Bates, and found them both absent from home. She could chase them up at their places of work, but instead she decided to drive to the small market town of Bicester.

There she made her way to the large, newly-built nick on the outskirts of town, where she had an old acquaintance, put out to grass in the evidence locker.

Sergeant Pete 'Fit me up' Glover was the same age as Ronnie Greene would have been, had he lived, and looked both surprised, but pleased, to see her. It was Ronnie, of course, who was responsible for her knowing Glover at all. They'd met during those long ago nights spent going from the pub to the betting track, and then on to a curry house, when Ronnie had briefly worked out of the old Bicester nick, the one up near the sports centre.

She explained that she was newly arrived to Kidlington, but carefully didn't mention that her new boss was Hillary Greene, no less. The old days were well and truly given an airing, with Pete vociferously defending his old, dead friend.

'You ask me, those charges against him were trumped up,' he continued belligerently. 'I'd bet anything that it was Frank Ross, that skanky git, who was behind it all. Ronnie was a good bloke, would give you the shirt off his back. Well, you know, luv,' he mumbled, not quite meeting her eyes.

Gemma smiled gently. Oh yes. She knew.

'Don't suppose he ever got back here much?' she asked sadly, and wasn't surprised when Pete shook his head. A big, rambling shaggy-haired man, he looked as if he should have been tossed out on to the scrap heap a long time ago.

'No, never saw him after he got transferred.

First I heard he was dead was when I clocked in for my shift. Seen his son, though.'

'Gary?'

'Right. He came here a couple of years back now. He's working out of Witney nick. Or he was. His dad had left a bit of gear behind. Not a lot. Just a cardboard box full of stuff, left over from his locker. He'd asked me to keep it for him, like, until he came to pick it up. Well, when I heard he'd gone, I thought his son should have it.'

Gemma felt a flicker of excitement bolt through her. At last. A solid lead! It would have been just like Ronnie to keep something important hidden in plain sight. And why would any internal investigation team be interested in his six-month stint in Bicester all those years ago? Besides, Ronnie had always said Pete was trustworthy, simply because he had no imagination. It simply wouldn't have occurred to him to go through his old mate Ronnie's left-over locker leavings.

'So you gave it to Gary,' Gemma said thoughtfully. 'That's nice. How is he, these days?'

After a few more minutes reminiscing, Gemma left.

As she walked back to her car, her steps were just that bit lighter. At some point in the very near future, she was going to have to 'run into' young Gary Greene.

6

Keith Barrington glanced across the largely empty pub and spotted Gemma Fordham immediately. He wasn't sure whether to feel pleased by her phone call to join him for a drink and a catch-up or not. On the one hand, she was his new sarge, and he needed to get to know her, and keep on her good side. On the other hand, he was somewhat wary of her reputation as a ball-buster. So far, he'd found her cool and wary, but perhaps he should put that down to first-week blues. When he'd first come to Thames Valley, he hadn't exactly been all sweetness and light either. But he had the feeling that Hillary Greene was also wary of her, and that made him feel deeply uneasy. Over the last six months working with the DI, he'd come to respect and trust her judgement.

He moved past two men, who were sitting at widely spaced intervals at the bar, nodding towards the landlord to indicate that he'd be ordering a drink soon. It was nearly three, and the pub looked to him to be one of those that kept to the old-style opening hours.

Gemma pushed a plate away that had the

remains of an uninspired ploughman's and made room for him at the table. 'I thought it made sense to meet up and compare notes before we did any more interviews,' Gemma said, by way of greeting. 'What you having?'

'Mineral water, thanks, Sarge, but I'll get it.'

Gemma rose firmly and walked to the bar, ordering two Evians, and paying. When she got back to the table, Keith Barrington was rereading his notes.

Gemma knew a little of his background and history, but was only mildly curious. There seemed little point in getting to know her team-mates well, when she didn't intend to stay long.

Still, it paid to be friendly. And you never know what titbits you could pick up. 'I hear you're settling down at Kidlington well. There was some that thought you'd be out on your ear by now,' she said, letting a small smile soften the statement.

Keith glanced at her sharply, met the large grey eyes without looking away, then slowly nodded. 'Yeah. If the guv had made it hard for me, I dare say I'd be out of the force by now. But she's all right.'

Gemma nodded. 'Yeah, she seems pretty straight to me too. She's got a good record. Well, apart from that old trouble with her husband.'

'That was all about him. Not her,' Keith said flatly.

Sensing his withdrawal, she instantly backed off. 'OK, about the art club. I've only interviewed two so far, but the vibe I'm getting is fairly standard. Wayne Sutton, and a bloke called Colin Blake, seem to be the 'stars'. You getting that?'

Keith Barrington took a sip of his water. 'Oh yeah. There also seem to be two schools of thought regarding them. Our vic is more experimental, and prized originality above talent. Colin Blake seems to be a more traditional, but finer artist. A craftsman, like.'

Gemma laughed, a husky, sexy laugh that made both the men at the bar — and the barman — turn and look at her. 'Very intellectually put. The last woman I interviewed had a more down to earth approach about it. How did she put it.' She checked back a few pages in her notebook and grinned. 'Oh yeah. *If I wanted to hang a painting on my walls, I'd buy a Blake. If I wanted to impress a philistine, I'd buy a Sutton.*'

Keith nodded. 'Yeah, that sums it up pretty well. Seems that this Colin Blake fellah could paint the kind of things that you could show your mum, and not have her screw up her nose. But our vic liked to shock.'

'I get the feeling Wayne Sutton wasn't as good, though. I mean technically. I was chatting to this man out Bloxham way, a retired lecturer. He seemed to rate Blake far higher than Sutton,' Gemma said thoughtfully. Although she didn't think the relative artistic merits — or otherwise — of the murder victim were going to mean much to the investigation. Unless an irate art critic bashed him over the head and drowned him because he couldn't stand the way he handled his gouache.

'Think that made our vic jealous?' Keith asked curiously.

'Bound to,' Gemma said firmly. 'A guy like Wayne Sutton needed to be praised and petted. He'd have wanted top spot in the limelight. But I just can't see anyone committing murder over jealousy about who painted a better landscape.'

Keith shrugged. 'I dunno, Sarge. Artists can get fairly het up, I reckon. Rage and jealousy can fester.' He took a sip of his own drink. 'Might be a good idea, from now on, to find out just how much resentment between the two actually existed.'

Gemma shrugged. 'Couldn't hurt. Although I think our boss is looking more at the female angle. And he could certainly put it about a bit, our Wayne. I got the feeling he was boffing the old gal I talked to, even though she wouldn't have hung one of his paintings on her walls.'

Keith grinned. 'So, how have your first few days at the new job worked out? Enjoying it?'

'Sure. Getting a murder case right away was a bit of luck.'

Keith grunted. 'Tell me about it. I did too. So, you found a good place to shack up? I'm still in a cramped bedsit in Summertown. Bit of a dump, but accommodation in Oxford is a nightmare. You're from Reading, originally, right?'

Gemma took a sip of water. 'Right, yeah, but my fellah's from Oxford, so when things started to get serious, I just stopped commuting and moved in with him. Saved me a lot of hassle. Plus, he's got this really nice place on the Woodstock Road.'

Keith Barrington whistled silently. The north Oxford suburb surrounding the Woodstock and Banbury Roads consisted mostly of large, detached semi-mansions, and was very des res.

'He's a don,' Gemma said, as if reading his mind. 'St Bede's. He's the master of music there. Holds one of those fancy international chairs. Always off to Vienna or Salzburg.'

And totally blind. But Gemma didn't mention that.

'Are you musically minded?' Keith asked

118

curiously, and Gemma laughed.

'Two tin ears. Well,' she drained her drink, 'back to the grindstone. I was going to wait to catch Colin Blake at home this evening, but after this, I think I might take a shufti to his place of business. Scope him out.' She got up, riffling through her notes for his business address, then raised one slender, plucked brow. 'Well, well, the Michaelangelo of the Ale and Arty Club is a butcher no less. What would Freud have made of that?'

Keith Barrington dreaded to think.

★   ★   ★

The pub where they'd chosen to meet was in Adderbury, about mid-way between their locations when she'd called, so Gemma drove the short distance north, towards the old market town of Banbury, whilst Keith, about to interview a mother-and-daughter team in the village of Wootton, took off in the opposite direction.

Gemma's car was a 7-year-old Fiesta, which she kept immaculately clean and polished, but when a grey-haired man in a classic E-type Jaguar pulled up beside her at the traffic lights, she cast a long, covetous look at it. She'd always dreamed of driving a sports car — something that would have made James Bond drool. She'd been leaning towards something more modern and kick-ass, but the long, sleek lines of the classic 1960s icon surely did look good.

Her attention drifted to the driver, who, sensing eyes on him, glanced her way. No doubt he was used to his car turning heads. But when his eyes met the large grey eyes of the striking-looking, spiky-haired blonde woman, they widened slightly in appreciation.

Gemma gave him the long, slow, sexy smile. The smile that was so meaningless to Guy. Had she been so attracted to Guy Brindley, the blind maestro, solely because she couldn't use her killer smile on him? Had he represented more of a challenge solely because he couldn't admire her long, lean, grace? Her bony, intriguing face? But then, it had been her own damaged, gravelly voice that had first caught his attention, so perhaps her seduction of him hadn't been much different from her seduction of other men.

He was still attracted to the physical. Only the specifics had changed.

The driver of the E-type was still staring at her when the lights changed to green, and it was Gemma, her foot already poised over the clutch, her hand ready on the gearstick, who raced away first. Uninspired Fiesta or not.

She smiled in triumph, but as she headed

into the suburbs of Banbury, she felt a hard, hot, familiar glow spread into her stomach.

One day, she was going to have that sports car. That villa in the sun somewhere. That designer wardrobe, the jewels, the expensive perfumes that had been specifically made up for her by her own 'little chemist' in Paris.

And they wouldn't be provided for her by a lover, either.

Well. Not technically.

⋆   ⋆   ⋆

Keith Barrington turned off the main Oxford-Banbury road a mile or so south of a little spot on the map called Hopcroft's Holt, and found himself driving down a narrow country lane. On all sides of him, pungent May blossom was in bloom, and the roadsides frothed with cow parsley. In all his explorations of the countryside surrounding Headquarters, he'd never made it to this particular village before.

A narrow bridge over a twisting river led him to a small but pretty enough place, and as he pulled up on a grass verge, he heard ducks fighting.

He found Number 23, Laburnum Terrace, after a bit of searching. A modern-build, with neighbours crowding in all around, it still managed to look pretty and cottage-like, and he wasn't surprised to see the garden host to not one but two, spectacularly flowering laburnum trees. He eyed the dangling, grape-like clusters of yellow flowers with a vague sense of unease. Weren't they supposed to be poisonous or something?

He walked up a garden path bordered by all sorts of flowering things, stopping now and then to let ponderous bumble bees have the right of way. By the time he reached the tiny upside-down V of a porch, smothered in flowering clematis montana, the door was already opening. Obviously, his arrival hadn't gone unnoticed.

Marion and Judy Druther, according to the last Ale and Arty club member he'd talked to, were specialists in stained-glass. Now, Keith found himself showing his ID card to Marion Druther, a pleasant-faced forty-something with a large mass of curly dark hair and slightly small, button-like dark eyes. Her fingers were stained a funny yellow, he noticed, as she reached to draw his card nearer her face. Whether that was due to the nicotine stains of a heavy smoker, or something to do with the mysterious process of creating stained-glass, he wasn't sure.

'Sorry, haven't got my proper glasses on,' Marion Druther said, and from behind her, she heard a younger voice laugh.

'You haven't got *any* glasses on, Mum! They're still hanging around your neck.'

They were too, on a black silken cord. Keith tried not to look at them as Marion Druther made a tutting sound and slipped them on to her nose. 'Oh yes. Of course, you're that nice policeman who called earlier. Well, come on in.' She stood to one side and let him pass. Keith thanked her and stepped into a small hall. From there she led him straight through into a small lounge. Dried flowers in a vast arrangement stood in front of an empty grate. Large lampshades, all made of stained-glass, stood atop tall stands at strategic points around the room. In the window, several small, stained-glass mosaics had been hung, catching the light and reflecting a rainbow of colours on to the plain white walls.

A tall young woman, also with masses of dark curly hair and small dark eyes, was just folding her length into a comfortable-looking chair.

'Oh, yes, please sit down,' Marion said. 'This is my daughter, Jude. Her real name's Judy, but she refuses to answer to it. Don't know why. It isn't even as if she likes the Beatles,' Mrs Druther said, without pausing for breath, making her daughter scowl at her fondly.

'Don't worry, Sergeant, she's not mad. Just scatter-brained. Now, what is it we can do for you? Mum, stop hovering.'

Marion Druther sat down, smiling vaguely.

'It's Constable Barrington, ma'am,' Keith corrected her with a smile. 'And I'm part of the investigation into the murder of Wayne Sutton. I take it you've heard about that?'

Mother and daughter swapped looks. 'Yes. Millie phoned us last night. Millie Fair-weather. She used to be a member of the club, but she dropped out last year. Couldn't afford the price of real ale anymore, or so she said,' Marion began, then subsided as her daughter cut in.

'I'm sure the constable doesn't want to know about Millie's problems, Mum,' she said, just a touch of warning in her voice. 'Millie always has her ear to the ground, so she's our source of all information really,' Jude Druther carried on. 'We tend not to watch too much telly, and we never get the papers. Far too depressing. And when we're in the workshop we only have the radio on Classic FM, so without her we'd be totally out of the loop. But yes, we know about Wayne. It was a shock, wasn't it, Mum?'

'I'll say. You don't expect anyone you know

124

to be murdered do you? I mean, you know it happens, but you don't think it'll ever be someone you actually *know*.'

Keith, who'd come across this reaction often in the past, nodded his head sympathetically. 'So, what can you tell me about him? You must have known him well?'

'Well, yes and no, really,' Jude said, when her mother cast her a rather helpless look. 'The club meets every fortnight, at some pub or other, and we have a drink and swap success stories. Some of us have small businesses, others just sell the odd commission here and there. Wayne . . . well, Wayne was almost the only professional artist amongst us. Even Colin has a day job.'

'This would be Colin Blake?' Keith clarified.

'That's right.'

'I've been hearing good things about him,' Keith said craftily. 'A lot of people seem to rate his work.'

'Oh yes, he's good,' Marion said at once, and pointed to a small watercolour. In it, a dilapidated, crumbling red-brick river bridge spanned a small stream at the height of summer. The water was low and translucent, the river weed almost lime green in colour and flowering with tiny white flowers. A large stand of bulrushes, in the foreground, added

125

a velvety contrast. Tiny drifts of gossamer seeds floated in the air. It was charming — well painted and almost brought the sound of gently flowing water into the room.

'That's one of Col's. It took me and Jude all year to save up for it, but we had to have it. Didn't we, Jude?'

'I love it,' the younger woman confirmed with a grin.

'Do you have any of Wayne Sutton's paintings?' Keith asked, and again the two women exchanged meaningful glances.

'Well, no,' Marion said, somewhat uncomfortably. 'We're not really into his style, are we, Jude?'

'What Mum means,' Jude said, eyeing Keith carefully, 'is that we're not members of his fan club. Wayne sold almost exclusively to . . . er . . . older, middle-aged women. Fairly well-heeled women.'

Keith smiled and nodded. 'Yes. We know about that. And were there any such women in the club?'

'Well, only Denise Collier,' Jude said, somewhat defiantly, ignoring her mother's gasp. 'Well, it's true. She only joined the group to meet Wayne. Once he'd signed her up for some of his 'private art lessons',' here Jude Druther held up her hands and crooked her fingers to make speech marks in the air, 'she soon dropped out, didn't she?'

Jude seemed to be speaking more to her mother than to Keith. But he didn't mind. He was learning a lot. If Marion Druther hadn't fancied being one of Wayne's 'clients' he was a Dutchman's uncle. And the fact that the daughter didn't approve couldn't have been made more clear if she'd been wearing a T-shirt sporting a logo that said as much.

Marion toyed with one curl of her hair, refusing to meet the policeman's eye.

'Going to pubs and drinking real ale was all a bit too plebeian for our Denise, Constable,' Jude said, as if determined, now that she'd started, to be as catty as possible. 'She was supposed to be interested in pen-and-ink sketches, but she never showed us any of her examples, did she?' Again this seemed to be addressed to Marion, who shrugged.

'Those of us who did work small enough to be shown at the pub crawls brought it along to be 'critiqued'. Wayne liked to do quite a bit of that,' Jude said sardonically, and from the way she flushed, Keith got the distinct impression that, at some point, their murder victim had said something less than compli-mentary about a piece of Jude's work.

'I don't suppose you have Mrs Collier's address?'

'No. But she lives in Lynn Sutton

127

somewhere,' Marion said. 'Please, Constable, don't think our club was all about backbiting and nastiness. It isn't. Most of us have a good time.'

'Did Wayne?'

'Well, he was, how shall I put it — a bit more serious about everything than the rest of us,' Marion sighed. 'Take Jude and me, for instance. We get by selling our stuff at craft fairs, and some of the antique shops in Woodstock and Bourton-on-the-Water, places like that, take our lampshades and stuff, strictly to sell to tourists. Hand-made, local glass; Americans especially go for stuff like that. And it pays the mortgage on this place, and keeps us in shoes. But Wayne . . . well, he was a *serious* artist. I didn't much like his stuff, it's true, but it *was* talked about.'

'Yeah, this little student rag did a write up about him once,' Jude said, smiling. 'You'd think it was one of the major art review mags from London the way he went on about it, instead of some little back-room, two-man outfit from Wadham College.'

'But he had a piece shown at the museum of modern art,' Marion said. 'Once.'

'It was a public exhibition, Mum,' Jude said, exasperated. 'You know, members of the public got to show off their stuff to a panel of so-called judges, and the museum displayed a selected few for a summer show.'

'It was bought though,' Marion said.

'Yeah, and you know who by?'

Marion flushed.

'Denise Collier,' Jude crowed.

Keith glanced at Marion curiously. He got the impression that mother and daughter were close, but had Wayne Sutton put some kind of serious wedge between them?

'And Colin Blake? Did he sell many paintings?'

'Oh yes,' Marion said, obviously relieved to change the subject.

'And to real punters too,' Jude put in, not so willing to it let go. 'There are one or two galleries locally that regularly take his work and sell it,' Jude mused. 'I've seen some of his stuff in the Woodstock galleries. And the one in Summertown, in Oxford. Wayne was always furious about that. You should have heard him go on about it. He claimed Colin only managed it, because of his 'friends in aristocratic places'. That's how Wayne put it. Real sarky he was. Remember mum?'

Marion sighed heavily. 'Yes. I think Wayne was a bit jealous, poor boy.'

Keith frowned. 'What did he mean by 'aristocratic friends'?' he asked. 'I thought Mr Blake was a butcher by trade.'

'And so he is,' Jude said. 'And what's

wrong with that? Wayne used to make fun of him, as if there was something wrong in selling sausages. At least Colin works for a living, which is more than Wayne was ever prepared to do.' Jude's voice rose indignantly.

Marion coughed gently. 'I think Colin was friends with someone out Duns Tew way. Or was it Heyford Sudbury? You know, one of those pretty villages almost in the Cotswolds. They're all becoming rather touristy nowadays.'

'That's right,' Jude said, snapping her fingers. 'I think Colin first met him when he bought one of his paintings. I can't remember his name, can you, Mum?'

'No. But he's something of an anachronism. That's how Wayne put it, anyway. You know the kind — almost landed gentry, but of course, they've all lost their land now. I believe his family used to be important once, but now they've sort of, dwindled down, somehow. They live in these big, rambling houses but can't afford to pay the fuel bill.'

'I think I get what you mean,' Keith said.

'Anyway, Wayne said Colin only got half his commissions because this upper-class pal of his put his name about amongst his set,' Jude carried on. 'I think this friend of Col's had an ancestor who used to live in Bath a few hundred years ago, and gave parties for the rich and famous. You know, Wellington slept in his spare room before going off to Waterloo, that sort of thing. It made Wayne wild.'

Jude suddenly giggled, and Marion winced.

'I remember him once, at that pub in Wolvercote, when he heard Colin had just sold an oil to some gentleman farmer type. 'Just because he's got a pal who's great-great-great-great-great-grand-daddy showed Beau Brummel how to tie a cravat or something.' He said it was pathetic. He went on and on about how he sold his own stuff on the merit of the paintings themselves. Which was a laugh of course. His women only bought his canvases because . . . '

'Jude! Please, that's enough. I'm sure the constable can't be interested in any of this.'

But Keith was very interested in all of this. What's more, he thought his boss, Hillary Greene, would be too. Before he left, he asked, as casually as he could, 'And where were you two ladies, say between six o'clock and midnight, on the last day of April?'

Marion Druther blinked. 'Here, I think. We tend not to go out much.'

'You live together?'

'Can't afford to rent a place of my own,' Jude said with a sigh. 'And yeah, we were here. We stayed in and watched that programme on the telly you were so keen on,' she added to her mother, who nodded.

Keith wrote it all down and left. It wasn't much of an alibi, and both, in his opinion, would back the other up without a second thought. Of course, it was possible that they could have killed Wayne together. Two women would have a better chance of overwhelming a man, than just one.

But Keith couldn't see it somehow.

⋆   ⋆   ⋆

Hillary Greene tapped on the door to Detective Superintendent Philip 'Mellow' Mallow's door and went in without bothering to wait for a summons.

She and Mel had been friends since her first days at Kidlington, and when she took the seat in front of his desk, she sighed heavily. 'You don't still have any of that decent Colombian blend left do you?'

Mel grinned and walked to the coffee pot kept constantly perking on a nearby shelf. Tall, lean, classically good-looking, he was wearing a dark blue suit and red tie.

'How's Janine?' she asked automatically, accepting the mug he offered her. Janine Tyler had been her DS before embarking on an affair with Mel that had nearly proved disastrous for them both. It had resulted in Mel being overlooked for a promotion, and his career seemed doomed to fizzle out. And then, out of the blue, the pair had decided to marry, which meant that Janine had been transferred out of HQ to Witney.

'She's resitting her Boards next month,' Mel said. It had come as a shock to his confident, ambitious wife, when she'd failed her Inspector Boards at first try.

'She'll get there,' Hillary said soothingly. 'But you didn't call me in to chat about the wife.'

Mel smiled. 'No. The murder case, how's it shaping up?'

Briefly, Hillary filled him in. Mel frowned when she was relating the finding of the red paper heart on the victim's body, and when she'd finished, it was the first thing he went back to.

'You did a check, to see if any other killings fit the MO?'

Hillary smiled grimly. 'My new DS did. Relax, there were no matches. I really don't think we're dealing with a serial killer. Well, not yet. But if another young Lothario turns up dead with a paper heart attached to his body, you won't forget to let me know, will you?'

'Don't!' Mel shuddered, then narrowed his

eyes thoughtfully. 'Did I detect a bit of angst back there? When mentioning your new DS?'

Hillary smiled blandly. 'No.'

Mel regarded her thoughtfully. 'Gemma Fordham gave an excellent interview. She's experienced, smart, and can obviously work without supervision. After the year you've had, what with a new DC, and with Frank like a constant albatross around your neck, I thought you'd welcome someone competent and quick on your team.'

'And so I do,' Hillary carried right on smiling blandly.

Mel watched her for a moment more, then smiled slowly. 'Miaow?' he said thoughtfully.

'You carry on like that,' Hillary said amiably, 'and I'll scratch your eyes out, Mel.'

★   ★   ★

Gemma Fordham walked into a room full of dead flesh and looked around with a vague sense of distaste. The butcher's shop was located in tiny side street off an already narrow lane, which was typical for a market town that went back to medieval days. There were places in Banbury where you could still walk down ancient cobbled streets and come across a fifteenth-century coaching inn.

Inside Blake and Waincott, however, all was

modern strip lighting, refrigerated units, and EC regulation meat products. She hastily turned her eyes away from bright red piles of minced beef, and turned her head towards the back, where a young man with red cheeks and a white wrap-around hat, appeared.

'Yes, madam?'

'I'm looking for Colin Blake please.'

The youngster looked surprised, then hurt, as if he suspected that she didn't trust him to be able to fillet a joint. 'Hey, Col!' he yelled, turning his head to face towards the opening, the better to be heard. From out the back came the steady thunk, thunk, thunk, of a cleaver on wood. The noise stopped abruptly, and a moment later, another man stepped into the serving area. 'Hello?'

Colin Blake was about the same height as herself, with well-kept, dark-brown hair that Gemma instantly suspected was dyed. He had dark, chocolate-brown eyes, a large, Roman nose and extremely well-shaped lips. He was sexy, even in a white apron spotted with blood.

Another reason why Wayne Sutton would instantly dislike him. Not only did Colin Blake rival him in the painting stakes, he could probably turn a few ladies' heads himself.

Gemma showed her card. 'It's about Wayne

Sutton, Mr Blake. Is there somewhere we could talk?'

'Oh, sure. Let's step outside. There's a nice place just across the way.'

He walked from behind the counter, taking off his apron and leaving it just inside the door. Outside, the closeness of the other buildings blocked out the worst of the dazzling sun, and he led her to a small area, centred around a large tub of flowering pansies, with a baker's on one side, and a charity shop on the other. He sat down with a sigh, and spread his long legs out in front of him.

'I heard about it on the radio,' Colin Blake said at once. 'At first I thought they must have been talking about another Wayne Sutton. Then they mentioned he lived at Deddington, and I realized they weren't.'

'I understand you were both members of the Ale and Arty Club, sir,' Gemma said smoothly. 'We've been interviewing all members, asking for background really. Anything you can tell us about the victim?'

Colin Blake jerked on his seat. 'You know, it's really odd to hear him referred to like that. As a victim, I mean. Wayne always struck me as one of nature's survivors. He had a hard edge to him. You know, ambition, drive. He was young, of course, but I always felt he had an old head on his shoulders. I simply can't imagine someone getting the better of him.'

Gemma blinked in surprise. Now that was something she hadn't considered before, but she should have. Oh yes, she definitely should have. Because Wayne Sutton was a taker. A man who played on people, especially women; who read them and used them. That kind usually were wary.

It was very astute of the butcher to pick up on that. And she knew, right then and there, that Hillary Greene would probably want to reinterview Blake herself, once she read the report on him. It made Gemma more determined than ever to do a good job of it herself, first time around.

'So, Mr Blake,' she said brightly, eyeing the butcher closely. 'What can you tell me about Wayne Sutton?'

7

Thursday dawned bright and clear, giving no sign that the spring heatwave was going anywhere in a hurry. Hillary got into the office early, and quickly read through the updates.

She gave Gemma Fordham's interview notes with Colin Blake a second reading, and made a note to herself that a follow-up interview might be called for. With both Barrington and Fordham coming up with evidence of a rivalry between the two men, it needed looking into. But that red paper heart, found on the victim's body, kept intruding into her thoughts, and just before nine o'clock she lifted the receiver of her phone and dialled Steven Partridge's number.

An assistant answered, telling her that he was currently doing the autopsy on a nine-year-old girl found mysteriously dead in her bed, and didn't want to be disturbed. Hillary left a message, gently but firmly emphasizing that she needed to know, as soon as possible, the contents of the soggy note found on their murder victim, Wayne Sutton. She carefully recited the case number, and hung up, just as Barrington walked in through the door.

Hillary got up and grabbed her bag, and met him halfway across the floor. 'Come on. We're going to interview Denise Collier,' she said crisply, not surprised when Barrington looked pleased.

It was one of the leads he'd picked up himself, and he was glad his DI was letting him follow up on it.

As they drove to Lynn Sutton, a small village near Banbury where Denise Collier was currently living, she had him go over the interview with Marion and Jude Druther again. By the time they were making the final turn-off towards the small village, he'd finished.

'You got the impression then, that this Collier woman was possessive?' Hillary asked, after a small silence.

'Yes, guv. She was obviously one of his women, but from what the Druthers were saying, it sounded as if she fancied herself as being well and truly a cut above the rest. It's why I ran a preliminary check on her before I left the office last night. No known priors. Married in '91, to an airline executive, divorced ten years later. No kids. Typical middle-class background. Mother, a small-town solicitor; father, a headmaster of a small

139

private prep school.'

Hillary nodded. Just the sort of woman who'd end up in a genteel village like Lynn Sutton, in fact. They were approaching the village now, a small village of perhaps a hundred or so houses and cottages, clustered around a large church with a Norman tower. A village school, now closed down and turned into a private residence, rubbed shoulders with what had once been a large vicarage, probably now converted into large, desirable flats. There was the obligatory village pub, called intriguingly The Angry Cat, but there were no signs of any sixties-construct council house cul-de-sacs. For some reason, the council town-planners must have overlooked Lynn Sutton. Cottages, some thatched, some not, ran the length of a dog-leg main road called, not so surprisingly, Freehold Street. A village square, rather than a green, had planted firmly in its centre a gloriously green oak tree. Probably planted for Queen Victoria's jubilee or coronation.

'Collier lives at 31, Freehold Street. Green Acres. See it?' Hillary asked.

'Not yet, guv.'

She parked her ancient car under the shade of the oak tree and got out, glad to stretch her limbs. From above her came the raucous calls of jackdaws. 'You walk up, I'll walk down,'

Hillary instructed, wishing she'd thought to bring her sunglasses. Already the glare was making her eyes ache, and before long, she'd have a headache.

A small stream, almost running dry now, ran down one side of the street, and clusters of the palest-of-pink cuckoo flowers grew alongside it. Hillary hadn't gone far, however, when she heard a sharp whistle. Looking over her shoulder, she saw Keith beckoning her over.

Green Acres wasn't set in many green acres, but the garden it did have was impressive, in a modernistic, low-maintenance kind of way. Low-lying evergreen shrubs, designed to provide the patch with winter interest, gave way to large, impressive tubs, each holding a single banana plant, fern, or other dominating specimen. Most of the garden was landscaped in shale, patio bricks and gravel, off-setting a tinkling water feature, with not an inch of grass that needed to be mown.

The house itself was large, and had probably once been two, or maybe even three tiny cottages now converted to one roomy residence; large picture windows and a pair of French doors to one side had been added. Hillary rang the bell and waited.

The door was eventually opened by a short woman, no more than five feet one or two, with a cap of rather startlingly red hair. Snapping green eyes went straight from Hillary, fixed on Barrington assessingly, then moved back to Hillary. From Keith's background check, Hillary knew that Denise Collier was 51-years-old, but this woman could easily have passed for thirty. She was wearing a pair of white slacks, with four-inch, high-heeled sandals, and a silver lamé top. Platinum and diamond earrings sparkled at her lobes, and a large diamond ring glittered on the third finger on her right hand.

'Yes?'

Hillary held up her ID card, and Denise Collier's face closed down. It had, somehow, the effect of highlighting her make-up, which was heavy but cleverly applied. Her green/silver eyeshadow seemed to glitter that bit more, and her plum-coloured lipstick turned garish. The blusher on her rounded cheeks looked faintly ridiculous.

'This is about Wayne,' she said abruptly, almost accusingly, her voice breaking on the first syllable of his name. 'Come in, then,' she added, with obvious reluctance. She stood aside to let them pass, and led them, not to a lounge or living area, but to the kitchen.

It was a well-appointed kitchen, and had obviously been arranged by a designer's hand. An old Aga, lovingly restored, stood cold and aloof in pride of place. Copper-bottomed saucepans, that looked as if they'd never been used, hung down from a low, black-painted beam. An oak 'island' stood in the middle of a terracotta-tiled floor, and it was to this, and the tall chrome and black-leather stools placed around it, that Denise Collier headed. She drew up a stool and with a little hop that reminded Hillary of a robin, seated herself.

Hillary followed suit, and, after a moment's hesitation, so did Keith Barrington. Denise Collier rested her slim white hands in front of her on the counter. Hillary noticed her nails had been painted plum, to match her lipstick. She could see that this woman probably spent two to three hours, at least, on grooming herself before starting the day.

'I loved him, you see,' Denise said at once, looking out of the window to where a small patio gave way to a seating area incorporated into a small garden wall. 'I was the only one who did.'

Hillary settled down to watch the performance. That Denise Collier was acting, she was sure, but that didn't necessarily mean she was being untruthful. Some women, Hillary knew, needed to play their own starring roles in a melodrama, and the death of a lover was simply too good an opportunity to pass up.

And Hillary didn't mind being the audience. You could learn some interesting things from watching a performance.

'Oh, I know all about his other women,' Denise went on, still without looking at her, and waving one hand limply in the air, as if swatting at a vaguely annoying fly. 'They meant nothing. An artist needs fawning sycophants. And women especially flocked to him. Well,' she gave a short, sighing laugh, 'why wouldn't they? He was an Adonis. But I was his only true lover.'

Hillary let her get on with it, and glanced around. As she expected, a large canvas hung on the main wall, above a small dining table and chairs. It was a painting of the sky. Nothing else was in it. Just blue sky and a variety of white clouds. But the clouds, of course, weren't clouds. They were double decker buses, spanners, dustbins, hubcaps, washing machines, computer keyboards. All white and fluffy.

'He called it *Skydiving*,' Denise said, finally dragging her tragic gaze away from her patio, and finding the eyes of the detective not on her, but on the painting. 'I have others of his. Do you want to see?'

Hillary, now that she'd got her full attention, wasn't about to let it go. 'Perhaps later, Mrs Collier. Let's start with a few basic

144

questions first,' she kept her own voice firmly matter-of-fact. 'Where were you on the night of the thirtieth of April, from say six, until midnight?'

Denise Collier laughed dryly. 'So I'm a suspect, am I? How Wayne would have laughed! He had a wicked sense of humour, Sergeant, really wicked.'

Hillary let her demotion down a rank, slide past. She had no doubts at all that Denise Collier knew exactly her correct title, but didn't intend to get drawn into any little power games. 'I'm sure,' she said blandly, instead. 'Were you out that evening?'

Denise Collier blinked, then turned her gaze back to her patio. 'No. Not that night. I was here.'

'Alone?' Hillary persisted patiently.

Denise sighed heavily. 'Yes, alone. I saw Wayne mostly on the weekends you see. Friday and Saturday. Sometimes we'd go away, book into a quiet hotel somewhere.'

Hillary didn't bother to ask who paid the bills. 'Do you know of any enemies Wayne had, Mrs Collier?'

'Oh, not really. I mean there were people who were jealous of him, of course there were. His silly women, and their even sillier husbands. And other so-called artists, who were eaten up with envy of his talent. But

145

nobody who'd want to *kill* him.' Her voice broke on the last two words, and she hung her head and sobbed.

Barrington started to look around for tissues, but Hillary, after a quick glance, could see that, though the narrow shoulders were shaking up and down, no actual tears marred the make-up on her face. Keith eventually settled for a roll of kitchen towels, which he awkwardly placed on the work top beside her. Denise took a strip off and daintily dabbed her eyes — careful not to smear her mascara.

Hillary pursed her lips thoughtfully. Of all the people in the case so far, Denise Collier was the only one she could see leaving a red paper heart on the corpse of her lover. It would no doubt appeal to her sense of the dramatic. But was she the kind actually to kill?

Well, if Wayne Sutton really had been the 'love of her life' and if she'd found his cavalier womanizing too much, Hillary supposed it was possible. Sutton wouldn't ever regard Denise as a threat, so she might just have taken him by surprise. But was she tall enough to have committed this particular murder? To swing a stone at a tall man's head and reach his temple, even in high heels, would have been an effort. And did she really

146

have the physical upper-body strength necessary then to drag his inert dead weight to the stream, hold his head down until he was drowned, and then drag his corpse back on to the river bank?

It didn't seem likely somehow.

And if she *had* been wearing high heels, even with the sunscorched ground trodden by cattle, wouldn't SOCO have found some trace of tell-tale little round indentations?

'Tell me about his girlfriend, Mrs Collier,' she said flatly, deciding on shock tactics, and saw Denise's whole body go rigid. A moment later, she shot her a scornful look.

'He didn't have a *girlfriend*.' She said the word as if it was something vile.

'Monica Freeman?'

'Never heard of her,' Denise hissed. And there was something just a shade . . . demented, just a bit . . . touched . . . about her voice that gave Hillary pause for thought. She was trembling, very slightly, all over, her pretty made-up face almost snarling.

She's crazed with jealousy, Hillary thought. Utterly possessive. Maybe just a little delusional? No doubt Wayne Sutton used her as a never-ending source of money, but he'd have had to earn his pay with this one. She must have clung like a limpet. Had he finally had enough and told her it was all over?

Maybe. But she had the feeling he liked his easy money too much. Still. If he *had* dumped her, it could have been enough to send Denise over the edge and . . .

The sharp, shrill sound of a mobile phone shattered the moment, and Hillary glanced around sharply. She'd turned her own phone off automatically before ringing the doorbell. It must belong to the suspect. Then she saw Keith Barrington's pale, freckled face blush red with mortification, and she shot him a half-angry, half-disbelieving look.

'Sorry,' he muttered, stepping off the stool and hurrying outside into the hall. Hillary, turning back to Denise Collier, was just in time to see a look of relief cross her face. Evidently, she must have realized that she was in danger of loosing control and giving herself away, and was quickly burying the rawness of her emotions behind a vague smile.

There'd be no getting to her now. She was too alert to danger. Hillary mentally cursed Keith Barrington and his mobile. Time to take the witness through her movements the night of the killing.

In the hall, Keith pressed the answer button, lifted the gadget to his head and heard a familiar voice.

'Kee, listen, I've got to talk to you. Something awful's happened.'

'I can't talk now,' Keith said brutally, glancing anxiously towards the kitchen. 'I'm in the middle of something.'

'But it's urgent. I have to see you. Meet me somewhere during your lunch hour. The plod do let you eat, don't they?'

'OK, fine,' he whispered quickly. 'The Bread Oven at one-thirty. Now I gotta go.' He hung up and returned to the kitchen, where Hillary Greene was writing something up in her notebook.

'And did you receive any telephone calls, or did a neighbour drop by to visit you? Did you go out in the garden at all and see anybody walking past, perhaps taking their dog for an evening stroll?'

'No, no, nothing like that, I've already told you,' Denise Collier said peevishly. 'I just stayed in, listened to some blues, a little jazz. Read a few magazines.'

Hillary sighed, not believing a word of it. But with Denise Collier in this sort of mood, there was no point pressing it. She'd have to come back and try again later. 'Very well, Mrs Collier, that's all for now,' she said flatly, and Keith felt his heart plummet. He knew it was his own fault the interview, that had begun to get so promising, had fizzled out so abruptly.

He was in for the high jump. And deserved it. Never before had he let his personal life interfere with the job.

'If you can think of anything at all that might help, please phone,' Hillary said, handing her a standard card with the HQ phone number and her own extension listed.

Denise Collier took it with a moue of distaste, then showed them to the door. It was closed behind them before they'd even reached the garden gate.

'Next time we go into an interview, Constable, turn off your phone. Yes?' Hillary said sharply.

Keith swallowed hard. 'Sorry, guv. I normally do. I don't know why I forgot this time.'

Hillary glanced at him as they walked back to the car. He looked distinctly miserable. 'I've noticed you seem a bit distracted lately,' she said, not so much a question, as an opportunity for him to talk.

Keith ducked his head and said nothing.

Hillary sighed, and dug into her handbag for the keys. 'You can drive, Constable. But keep your mind on the road, please.'

Keith slid behind the driver's wheel feeling about two inches tall, and knowing he had no one to blame but himself. It was only when he'd started to drive back to Kidlington that he felt suddenly anxious. Before, he'd thrust the contents of the phone call to the back of his mind, wanting only to get his lover off the line. But now he wondered. What was the 'something awful' that had happened? Dammit, he didn't need any more hassles in life. Not now!

He was careful to drive at a sedate fifty miles an hour all the way back to HQ.

★   ★   ★

Back in the open-plan office, Hillary found the desks empty. Frank Ross had apparently been in, and, finding the boss gone, had quickly taken the opportunity to nip back out again, leaving behind only a pile of badly-typed notes on his activities of yesterday, and a hand-written scribble that he was following up on a lead.

Yeah, right. At the nearest betting shop, Hillary supposed. She sighed and crumpled up the note and tossed it into the bin. She scowled at Gemma Fordham's empty desk, got on the phone and dialled her number.

'Fordham,' the voice that answered sounded as if it was suffering from a bad cold. Only someone who actually knew the DS would know it was her normal speaking voice.

'DI Greene. Where are you?'

'Kidlington, guv, talking to another Ale and Arty member. Want me to come in?'

'When you've finished. Then I want you to concentrate on Denise Collier for me. You know who she is, right?'

'I read the murder book last night before I left, guv. She's the lead Barrington dug up, yeah? One of the vic's women?'

'Right. I've just finished talking to her, and I got a definite whiff of instability from her. Do a bit of deep digging. Find out why her marriage failed, talk to the hubby, past lovers, you know the drill. She's the clinging, possessive type. I wouldn't be surprised if there hadn't been some trouble somewhere. We know she's not got form, so it never came to our notice, but even so.'

'Think she did some stalking?' Gemma cut straight to the chase.

'It wouldn't surprise me. Find out who her GP is, see if she has any history of mental trouble as well. The doctor probably won't want to tell you, so lean on him or her, stress the murder inquiry angle, and if you still get no luck, see if you can find out via the back door.' Hillary knew there was always more than one way to skin a cat, especially for a clever and resourceful girl like Gemma Fordham.

'Right, guv,' Gemma said, unfazed, and Hillary hung up.

Slipping her phone back into her pocket,

Gemma smiled at the middle-aged man perched on the edge of his sofa. And Gerald Heydon, 52, semi-retired boat-builder, gazed back at her, all but drooling.

'So you sculpt in wood,' Gemma said. 'That's how you came to hear about Ale and Arty?'

'That's right. Sure I can't interest you in a class of merlot, Sergeant Fordham. It's a vintage year. One glass won't hurt, I'm sure.'

Gemma smiled and let him pour her a glass.

It was, after all, a very good year.

★   ★   ★

Back at HQ, Hillary watched Keith Barrington glance at his watch for the fifth time in the last half hour, and wondered what was biting him. Whatever it was, she hoped he'd get it sorted out soon. He was driving her crackers.

'Why don't you get off to the canteen, Keith,' she said, a shade impatiently. 'Take an early lunch break. I'll hold the fort down here.'

To her surprise, Barrington looked almost stricken. 'No, it's all right, guv. I mean, I'm not hungry yet,' he glanced at the wall clock desperately. It was barely twelve fifteen. 'But if you want to get off and have a bite yourself . . . '

Hillary slowly leaned back in her chair and narrowed her eyes. Keith Barrington flushed.

'Lunch date, Constable?'

'Only a quick one, guv. I need to see someone. A friend. He's in a bit of trouble.'

Hillary blinked. 'Our kind of trouble?' she asked sharply. Keith Barrington was already here on sufferance, and with one big black mark against him. The last thing he needed was to be mixed up with people on the wrong side of the law!

'Oh shit, no, guv,' Keith said, spontaneously, and truthfully. 'Nothing like that.'

Hillary instantly believed him, and relaxed, but when his eyes drifted away from hers oh-so-casually, she also knew that something was definitely eating him.

She deliberately let the silence lengthen.

Keith fiddled with his pen, fighting the urge to confide in her. It wasn't that he didn't think Hillary Greene would be sympathetic. Nor did he fear her being judgmental or, even worse, antagonistic. But he'd always kept some things secret, instinct telling him to do so, and he didn't feel happy breaking the habit of a lifetime now.

'All right, constable,' Hillary said at last. 'I'll be in the canteen if you need me.'

She was just about to rise, when her phone rang. She grabbed the receiver. 'DI Greene.'

'Hillary. I hear from my assistant that you're breathing down our neck?'

Hillary smiled, recognizing the voice instantly. 'Sorry Steven, didn't mean to. I just need to know what that note on Sutton's body was all about. I take it it's dried out by now?'

'It has. I was about to photocopy it and send it over when I got your message. You want me to read it out over the phone?'

'Might as well. Unless it's particularly sensitive?' she said cautiously.

'No, I don't think so. Nor is it pornographic, so we wouldn't be corrupting any delicate little ears that are listening in that shouldn't be.'

Hillary laughed, knowing the lines in and out of HQ were as secure as they could be, in this IT age. 'Fine, go ahead then.'

'OK. The paper is bog standard note paper, can be purchased at any W.H. Smith's in the country. The ink, likewise, the pen used just your average biro.'

Hillary sighed. It didn't sound promising so far.

'I take it you want me to send it on to the handwriting boffins?' Doc Partridge asked, just for form's sake.

'Yes, please,' Hillary agreed. Usually, experts could gather all sorts of information from a handwriting specimen. Whether the author was right- or left-handed, male or female, sometimes even age, and occasionally, from the language used, punctuation, and so on, details as to the writer's education or even birthplace.

'Hmmm. Don't know how much joy they'll get, though,' the doctor warned. 'The immersion in water didn't help any. But at least it's legible. Got a pen?'

Hillary, her own biro hovering over her notebook, nodded. 'Shoot.'

'OK. First line — *Wayne darling* — no comma. Second line — *We have to talk. The worst has happened.* Third and fourth lines — *Meet me at our special place by the stream, I'll try to be there by eight.* Fifth line, *I love you. I trust you.* And it's signed, *Annie.*'

Hillary scribbled furiously.

'Oh, and the name 'Annie' is ringed in a big heart.'

Hillary looked across at Keith. 'Go through the files. See if we have any suspects or witnesses by the name Annie. Include anyone called Anne, Ann, or Anna. Make that Hannah, as well.'

'Right, guv.'

'Sounds like someone was desperate,' Steven Partridge's voice sounded again in her ear, and Hillary turned her attention back to the pathologist.

'Hmm. I wonder what 'the worst' was?' she mused.

'Pregnant?' Steven guessed. 'That's what women usually mean by it.'

'Or the husband's found out,' Hillary said dryly.

Steven Partridge laughed. 'Or that,' he agreed, and after a few more pleasantries, rang off.

Hillary put the phone down thoughtfully and filled Barrington in.

So, their victim had been going to the stream to meet someone. Obviously, they'd met there before if it was their 'special place'. And it made sense as a rendezvous point — it was quiet and out the way, somewhere where they couldn't possibly be overheard, and some serious talking could take place. At eight o'clock at night, it wouldn't yet have started to get dark.

So did they now have the killer's name? Had Annie, whoever she was, lured him there not to talk, but to kill? Or had someone else come instead? If this Annie had a jealous lover or husband, could the message have been somehow intercepted? Or had it even come from Annie at all? No, that wouldn't work. Presumably, Wayne Sutton would have known her handwriting. Unless someone had forged it. Perhaps Annie had been forced to write it, or maybe she'd deliberately set him up?

'No one called Ann, Anne, Annie, or any other derivative has so far come up in our enquiries, guv,' Keith Barrington's excited voice interrupted her musings. 'Denise Collier's second name is Angelique, though.'

'That's stretching it,' Hillary said. 'OK. Well, make sure everyone on the enquiry is on the alert for that name. If they come across anyone at all of that name, even remotely connected to Wayne Sutton, I want to know about it. And remind everyone that Annie might well be a nickname, and not a given Christian name at all.'

'Right, guv.'

Hillary nodded, and rose slowly to her feet. 'Right. I'm going to snatch a quick bite. I'll be in the canteen if I'm wanted.' She grabbed her purse from her bag and headed for the exit.

Keith watched her go and glanced at his watch. She'd be back before one, easy. After that he could nip off. He looked up as he sensed a shadow moving over him, and

158

smiled as Gemma Fordham took her place behind her desk.

Quickly, he filled her in on the message found on the victim's body. Gemma quickly checked her own notes, but was sure that the name hadn't been mentioned in any of her inquiries. She was right.

'Why don't you go downstairs and tell the desk sergeant that if anybody named Annie calls in, he's to make sure the guv comes down straight away?' she suggested, flicking her notebook shut. 'We don't want to miss her, if she does decide to come in, because of some communications balls-up.'

Barrington gave her a quick look, but shrugged and obligingly got up. A phone call would have done it, in his opinion, but perhaps she was just being extra careful. And he knew what it was like to be the new guy. You could get almost paranoid about messing up.

Gemma watched the constable go, and the moment he was through the door, pulled her own chair away from her desk and towards Hillary's. She'd seen Hillary's bag, beside her chair, the moment she'd sat down, and knew she'd never get another chance like this one.

Opening her own bag, she drew out a large, flat tin. After a quick glance around to make sure that no one was watching, she reached down, unzipped Hillary's bag, and fished inside. Hillary's large bunch of keys was easy to find, and she quickly sorted through them, dismissing the car keys, and taking a guess as to the one she wanted. She knew, for instance, that Hillary Greene lived on a canal boat, and that the key to a padlock was probably more likely to get her access to Hillary's home than, say, the more conventional Yale key.

Heart pounding, she opened the tin and quickly pressed the key, front and back, into the wax inside, to make two clear impressions. Then, palms just a little damp, she snapped the tin box shut, returned the keys, and zipped her boss's bag back up, careful to leave it in exactly the same position on the floor as it had been in before.

She knew that Hillary Green would notice if it had been moved.

When she straightened up and looked around, she could tell that nobody had noticed her manoeuvre. Her face a little flushed in triumph and relief, she pushed her chair back to her own desk, and logged on to her computer.

A small smile played around her lips.

8

Hillary opted for the mushroom risotto and the fruit salad, and found a quiet table by one of the windows. Since she was so early, the canteen was largely deserted, but she knew it would get busy soon, and ate quickly.

Outside, nesting blackbirds hunted for insect food for their chicks, flitting about the trees and the bushes among the hard landscaping. Petals from multi-blossoming trees drifted by in the breeze like fragrant pastel snowflakes, and already she could see a mirage-like shimmer of what looked like rippling water, rising off the white concrete pavements and black tarmac.

But her thoughts were far from appreciating the beauty of spring, and firmly settled around the mysterious Annie. Why hadn't they come across her name before? It wasn't as if Wayne Sutton had been particularly discreet about his lifestyle. There was something hole-in-the-corner about the whole set-up that sat uneasily with her image of the free-living, free-spirited, couldn't-care-less artist. After a moment's thought, she reached for her mobile and phoned his parents, Davey Sutton answering, his voice still hoarse from the summer flu.

'Hello? If this is a reporter, I've told you lot before, no comment.'

'Hello, Mr Sutton, it's Hillary Greene,' she said quickly, and heard a sharply indrawn breath.

'News?' he whispered the word, as if afraid someone might overhear. She knew what he was asking, of course, and felt instantly guilty. She knew it was ridiculous to feel that way, but whenever she talked to the loved ones of a murder victim when the perpetrator had yet to be caught, she always felt personally responsible for the lack of a result.

'Of sorts, Mr Sutton, but there's been no arrest as yet. I wanted to know if the name Annie meant anything to you? Perhaps your son had a friend of that name?' She wasn't sure how much his parents knew about their son's gigolo lifestyle, or what they were prepared to acknowledge if they did know, so she asked the question delicately.

Davey Sutton was silent for a moment, then said quietly, 'No, I can't say it means anything to me. Hold on a minute while I ask his mother. She's more likely to know about stuff like that.'

She heard the phone going down, and absently forked the last few pieces of rice and mushrooms into her mouth. She was wiping her lips on a paper napkin when he came back on the line.

'His mother says no. Is it important?'

'It could be, Mr Sutton, yes.'

'You have to understand, our Wayne was a good-looking lad. And he had a way with the ladies. He was young too, and not really settled down. His mother and me, well, we hoped that Monica Freeman might take him in hand. A girl about his own age. But, well, we know Wayne liked to romance women, Detective. His mother seemed to find out about all his ladies, one way or another, and she's sure there wasn't any Annie.'

Damn, Hillary thought. 'All right, Mr Sutton, and thank you. Your family liaison officer has been keeping you updated on the inquiry, I hope?'

'Oh, yeah, she's been lovely.' He coughed hoarsely into the phone, and cleared his throat. 'You will let us know, won't you, when you get our boy's killer?' The hope in his voice made her own throat close up, and Hillary coughed herself.

'Yes, Mr Sutton, I will,' she said softly, and hung up. She sighed and reached for her fruit salad, but her appetite was suddenly gone. She was still pushing tinned pineapple chunks around her dish, when she realized someone

163

had come up to her table. She looked up to see a young, fresh-faced constable she vaguely recognized, hovering a few feet away, waiting to be noticed.

'Yes?'

'Ma'am. PC Thorndike. I was on house-to-house on the Sutton inquiry, ma'am. Thing is, I've only just finished talking to the last of the stop-outs, and thought I should report something direct to you, seeing as you're here, like, ma'am.'

Hillary nodded. The 'stop-outs' were those who always seemed to be out whenever you called at the house to get a statement, and often you couldn't nail them down for three or even four days. Obviously Thorndike had been snatching an early lunch like herself, and instead of going through Gemma or Barrington, had taken the opportunity to approach her direct. Which boded well.

'Something interesting, Constable?' she asked with a smile.

'Might be, ma'am. My stop-out was a seventy-two-year-old lady who'd been visiting her daughter for a few days. She lives opposite the row of cottages that border the farm track, where we initially approached the crime scene, ma'am?'

Hillary nodded, knowing where he meant.

'She told me that on the day of the murder,

164

late afternoon 'about teatime' is how she put it, she noticed a sports car parked up near the farmer's gate. It was still there, she thought, an hour later, but was gone before the evening news finished.'

Hillary frowned. Too early, she thought instantly. For an old woman of her mother's generation, teatime could be anytime between four and five-thirty. And the evening news finished around seven. If their victim was meeting Annie at eight, the car had been and gone by then. Of course, Doc Partridge's official time of death was anywhere between six and midnight. Perhaps she was pinning too much emphasis on the Annie note. And she had no way of knowing for sure that Wayne Sutton had died around eight o'clock.

'Could she describe the car?' Hillary asked, and the young man's face screwed up.

''Fraid not, ma'am. She wasn't much interested in cars. I tried to talk her through it, but all she could say for sure was that it was . . . ' he checked his notes, 'a 'real go-er, one of them old sporty things, low to the ground, that make a lot of noise'. She thought it might be dark-green, or maybe blue or black in colour.'

Hillary nodded. 'All right, thank you, Constable. Be sure to give one of my team your written report when it's ready.'

'Yes, ma'am.'

Hillary pushed her plate away and picked up her purse, walking downstairs thoughtfully. When she got halfway down the stairs, she noticed Keith Barrington coming out of the main office, and wondered what his lunch date was all about. So far, he hadn't come in late again, so that was OK, but she'd be watching him. He'd put in a good, solid, six months, and she didn't want him backsliding now.

As she walked across the office, she noticed Gemma Fordham, sitting with her back to her, typing into her computer. Then the sergeant glanced around, caught Hillary's look, and something in the way her shoulder blades tightened, made the hairs on the back of Hillary's neck rise.

She's been up to something.

The thought so strong, it was almost like a voice in her head.

She walked slowly to her desk and sat down. It was no good to keep on telling herself that she was just being paranoid. And there was little use in putting it down to a personality clash, or even repressed jealousy either. Hillary, over the years, had come to trust her instincts.

She sighed heavily. There was always something.

She reached down for her bag and opened it up, slipping her purse inside. As she did so, she smelt Gemma's perfume. Faint. But not coming from where Gemma was sitting, by her desk. But right under her nose.

From her bag.

Hillary slowly put her bag away, and pulled her chair up to her desk. Her eyes were bland as they met Gemma's. 'A possible lead. One of the constables doing house-to-house found a witness who saw some kind of sports car parked by the access gate to the meadow where our vic was found. She lives in one of those cottages overlooking the farm track. I want you to get some basic pictures of different sports car types and take them over to her, see if you can get at least some sort of a match. We need to trace that car. If necessary, get back on the radio to make an appeal for whoever owned it, and was parked there that day, to come forward.'

'Right, guv.' Gemma turned back to the computer, got on to the net, and before long, Hillary saw several photographs being disgorged from the printer.

Next, Hillary picked up her phone and chased up the path labs. The DNA from the strand of hair found on the vic, and the skin traces found on the stone anchoring the paper heart to Wayne Sutton's chest would be available no earlier than in three days' time. Hillary tried to get it bumped up the queue, but hers was not the only top-priority murder case on the list. She'd just have to wait her turn.

She hung up in an ever-worsening mood, wondering what the public would think if they realized that, contrary to what popular forensic science-based television programmes would have you believe, you couldn't get instant answers at the touch of a computer button.

'Guv, I thought I'd run a check on our list of suspects.' Gemma said. 'Only Tommy Eaverson owns and drives what I'd call a real sports car. A nineteen-seventies GB GT.'

'What colour?'

'Bottle-green.'

Hillary grunted. 'Make sure the witness sees an example when you see her.'

'I'll go now, guv. Got the number of her house?'

'Ask PC Thorndike.'

'Guv.'

Hillary watched the tall, elegant blonde woman grab her stuff and go, and Hillary slowly leaned back in her chair. The woman had been rifling in her bag, she was sure of it. But why? What had she hoped to find? She doubted, somehow, that Gemma Fordham was some sort of kleptomaniac or sneak thief. Just what the hell was she going to do about her new DS? Until she could figure out what she was up to, it was no good going to Mel. Oh, as a pal, he'd probably transfer her, if Hillary really cut up rough about it, but it wouldn't make her popular. Besides, after six months without a DS, she couldn't really afford to have her team reduced to just herself and Barrington again. (Ross didn't count.) And with a murder case in full swing, she needed all the competent help she could get. On the other hand, it felt as if she was sitting on a ticking bomb. What the hell was Gemma Fordham after?

⋆ ⋆ ⋆

Gemma found the little house without any difficulty. Nestled within a small set of 1930s-built, council house semis, it was standing the test of time far better than most of today's modern builds probably would, she suspected.

Miss Phillipa S. Grant lived in the third house, with a clear view of the farm track leading to the meadow where Wayne Sutton's body had been found. As she walked up to the door, the blonde sergeant noticed that the kitchen window did indeed overlook the road.

169

So the old girl could well have noticed a car parked opposite, when she was making and eating her tea. So far, her statement rang true.

When she answered the door, Gemma smiled at a woman nearly as tall as herself, but even thinner, with a long swathe of iron-grey hair held up and back in a somewhat messy bun. Her pale-blue eyes looked washed out, but alert, and when Gemma showed her her ID, she smiled but sighed.

'Best come in then. But I warn you, I told that young lad all I know.'

Gemma murmured soothingly that she was sure that she had, and wasn't surprised when she was led into a small, obviously little-used front room that overlooked a rugged and overgrown garden.

'I just wanted to show you some pictures, Miss Grant.' Gemma sat down on the wooden, hard-backed chair shown to her, and laid out the first photograph on the table set between them. The old lady put on a pair of glasses and looked at the glossy print in almost comical surprise.

'It's a car,' she said, baffled. She might just as well have said 'it's a UFO'. Obviously, she'd been expecting mug-shots, or something along those lines.

170

'Yes, Miss Grant,' Gemma explained patiently. 'You saw a car parked just across the road, on the thirtieth of April. The same night that a young man was killed over there. Does this car look anything like the one you remember seeing?' The top picture was of a 1995 Maserati in dark-blue.

'Oh no. No, like I said, it was a *classic* car. Low down on the ground. Must have been draughty to ride in it, I can tell you.'

'Draughty? You mean it had an open top,' Gemma said, craftily selecting a picture of a convertible. 'Like this?'

Phillipa Grant looked at the picture of a Lotus and sighed testily. 'No, no, dear. It's like I told that young man, it was a really *old* sports car. You know, like something the Great Gatsby would drive.'

Gemma smiled tightly. 'Something from the 1930s then,' she said through gritted teeth. 'A classic. Like an old Morgan?'

Phillipa Grant blinked. Gemma sighed, thanked her, and took her leave.

★ ★ ★

Hillary was feeling restless. With Barrington still sorting out whatever was bugging him, and with Ross AWOL as usual, she didn't even have anyone to bounce ideas around with. Until the DNA results came back, there was little forensic evidence that needed checking out, so that left talking to people.

Not that Hillary had any objections to that. She was quite good at listening. She grabbed the list of the Ale and Arty Club and picked a 'stop-out' at random, seeing that a certain Ms Felicity Wilson had been out both times that Barrington had called on her. She lived not far away, in the village of Yarnton, and worked at the big garden centre there. Figuring that Wilson was more likely to be at work than at home at this time of day, she drove straight to the sprawling centre, and had to hunt around for a parking space. What with the glorious weather, and with spring all around, the place was packed.

She tried the woman at the till first, who called a supervisor, who informed her that 'Flick' was working in the insect house that day. Like most garden centres, Yarnton had diversified, and sold not only begonias, but whole conservatories, daisies and the ceramic pots to go with them, daffs and hamsters, petunias and cat carriers. And, in the insect house, lizards, parrots, cockroaches, snakes and spiders. And rabbits. Who mostly eyed the snakes with worried, twitching noses.

Flick Wilson was a thirty-something, rounded woman, with a pink face courtesy of the heat, and surprised eyes.

'Police? Good grief, what did I do?'

Hillary smiled. 'Nothing, I hope Ms Wilson. I just wanted to ask you a few questions about Wayne Sutton.'

'Wayne? Why, what's he done now?' she laughed. She had thin, mousy-brown hair, which kept sticking to her damp cheeks, making her constantly push it away and tuck it behind her ears. She shot Hillary a slightly nervous look. 'I know he's a bit of a bad boy, but surely he hasn't done anything that *you* would be interested in.' She opened up a glass-fronted cage and threw some dead grasshoppers inside. Hillary tried not to watch as a corn snake slithered out of hiding and glided forward.

'Don't tell me one of his women finally made a complaint!' Flick carried on, her voice becoming more and more tense. 'He must be losing his touch if they have.'

Hillary shrugged. 'You like him, Ms Wilson?'

Felicity Wilson reached down to pick up a small bale of hay, which she took over to the rabbit pens. 'He's all right. Not interested in me, of course. Not got any dosh,' she smiled wistfully. 'But he's OK. I'm into oil painting; abstracts. Most people think that artists who do abstracts, only do so because they can't paint cows or sheep, or country cottages covered in roses. You know. 'Proper' painting. But Wayne understood abstract art. He's one of the few who did. Look, is he really in trouble?'

'You've been away, Ms Wilson?' Hillary asked softly.

'Yes. A few days up north. There was a big exhibition of post-nihilism. I tend to take the odd two or three days here and there, rather than a long two- or three-week holiday in the summer. I get to see a lot of exhibitions that way, and get constant little breaks away from this place, which can be a madhouse, let me tell you. Why do you ask?'

'I'm sorry to have to tell you bad news, Ms Wilson, but Mr Sutton was murdered last Monday evening.'

Felicity Wilson dropped the entire bale of hay into the pen and stared at Hillary for a long, shocked moment. Then she swallowed hard. 'Look, why don't we go to the coffee shop? I could do with a cup of tea. We can talk easier there.'

Hillary agreed, although one look at the packed café changed their minds, and instead they went outside, finding a wooden bench in the shade near a display of wisterias.

'What can you tell me about him?' Hillary asked curiously. 'You seem to be in a unique position to understand him.'

Felicity smiled grimly. 'Not one of his paying customers, you mean? No. Well, what can I say? He liked living well. Good wine, fast cars, designer gear. His mum and dad are strictly working-class, but Wayne was a Champagne Charlie if ever there was one. He let women provide for him, and in return . . . well, you know what he gave them in return. He lived for art, was sort of clever, but spiteful sometimes. I felt sorry for him, but I'm damned if I know why. He lived a lot better than I do.' She suddenly broke off, as she realized that now, of course, he wasn't living at all.

'Did he have any enemies that you know of? I mean beside jealous women or cuckolded husbands?'

Felicity sighed. 'I wouldn't know. We talked mostly about our art. You've seen some of his stuff?' she asked eagerly.

'Yes,' Hillary said blandly. But not blandly enough, it seemed.

'You didn't like it?' Felicity said, her voice hardening, becoming defensive.

'It's not that,' Hillary said, trying to head her off. 'What I saw seemed to me to be quite clever. And technically competent. I just felt, that, for me personally, it never really quite worked.'

Felicity looked at her for a moment, then slowly looked away. Her shoulders slumped. 'No. I always felt that way too, but of course, I never said so. And I think a lot of other people felt the same, to be honest. He was almost, but not quite, really good. It must be horrible to be like that. I'd rather be piss-bloody-poor awful, or an absolute genius. But I rather suspect I'm only merely pretty good too. Wayne was a bit more than merely good, but he wasn't, somehow, top quality.' She sounded ineffably sad. At last, someone truly mourning the dead man?

Hillary nodded. 'Do you think he knew himself?' she asked, genuinely curious.

'No,' Flick said at once, and confidently, but then she hesitated. 'At least, I'm not sure. There was this man at the club, Colin Blake. Now he was good. A 'proper' painter, you understand, but good. And Wayne was jealous of him. Oh, he tried to disguise it, mostly by making fun of Colin's upper-crust friends. I don't think it helped that Wayne really wanted to swan around in that set himself — you know, the real old money, the aristos. Instead, he was stuck with the nouveau riche. And even then, only women who wanted to get into his trousers. It drove him wild that Colin, who was only a butcher, seemed to be able to sell canvases to 'Right Hons', when he couldn't. I told him not to worry about it, that caring about that sort of thing diminished him. That always cheered him up, and we'd have a right spitefest, sticking knives into the traditionalists. But even so . . . '

Hillary nodded. It was all very interesting, but not necessarily helpful. 'What we look for in a murder case, Ms Wilson, are anomalies,' she explained carefully. 'Things in a victim's life that don't quite gel. Specific events that might start a catastrophic chain that results in murder. Can you think of anything in Wayne Sutton's life that gave you cause for concern, or felt out of place, or just, for some reason, gave you a vague sense of 'something being wrong'? Anything like that at all?'

Felicity Wilson thought for a while, then shrugged. 'The only thing that stays in my mind is something he said a few weeks ago. We'd all met up at this pub near, oh hell, where was it. The Rock of Gibraltar. That was it, the name of the pub. Anyway, me and Wayne were the last to leave, and he'd had a little more to drink than I thought he should have had, given that he was driving. I offered to drive him home, but he wouldn't have it. You know how men are. Anyway, I tried to keep him chatting, you know, hoping the cold night air would clear his head a bit, and we got to talking about selling paintings. I'd just had what was for me a big sale — one of the big racing car outfits near Enstone had bought a giant canvas off me to put in their new showroom. Anyway, Wayne made some typical smart-mouth reply about selling one of his canvases to some matron or other, then he laughed and tapped the side of his nose, and said he wouldn't be selling many more of his masterpieces to fat dozy cows who couldn't appreciate them. He was off tomorrow to Heyford Sudbury to make his fortune.'

Hillary felt herself tense. Blackmail? It sounded possible. 'Did he say how he was going to make this fortune?'

Felicity smiled and shrugged. 'No. But how else did Wayne make his money? I just assumed he'd found another woman, but this time, one with really deep pockets.'

One called Annie, maybe, Hillary mused. 'Did he go, do you know? To Heyford Sudbury, I mean?' Hillary asked.

Felicity shrugged. 'Beats me,' she waved away a bee, that had droned drunkenly close to her face, before flying on. 'He never mentioned it again. Mind you, like I said, he *was* a bit tipsy. It could just have been the wine talking.'

Hillary nodded. But doubted it. Doubted it very much. At last, she felt as if she was on to

178

a tangible lead. 'And nothing else springs to mind?'

The other woman shook her head.

'Do you know anyone called Annie? Or Anne, or something like that, someone that Wayne would have known too?' she persisted.

Again, Felicity Wilson shook her head. 'No. Sorry.'

Hillary sighed, thanked her, and left.

★　★　★

Gemma was on a roll. Armed with a whole sheaf of pictures of open-topped cars from the twenties and thirties era, she'd managed to track down the car.

Only to find it led to a dead end.

On the afternoon of the murder, the occupant of the last cottage on the farm track, had had an old friend over for tea, something already mentioned in the notes of the interviewing constable. The dark-blue Morgan, that had been parked outside, belonged to this visitor. A fact that the PC had *failed* to make note of. Gemma would give him a right rollicking when she got back to HQ.

The owner of the car currently resided in Liverpool. She doubted that Hillary would want her to go all the way up there to question him, so she got his phone number instead, and headed back to HQ.

There was only parking to be had towards the back, and as she crossed the car park, making her way to the entrance, she was unaware that she was being watched.

DS George Davies was only five weeks away from retiring. His allotment beckoned, along with long summer days spent sunbathing in an old deck chair and drinking his home-made rhubarb wine. No more hooligans who'd just as soon sink a knife into you as look at you. No more endless paper-pushing, and saying 'yes, sir' to so called superiors who knew nothing about walking a beat or proper community policing.

He was returning to HQ after sorting out a domestic, and something about the tall blonde woman, walking parallel to him about fifty feet away, struck a bell.

He swivelled his head to watch her. Nice. Bit on the skinny side for his taste, and he preferred long hair on a woman, but nice, nonetheless. He found himself admiring the way she moved — like an athlete, all economical grace. It was the walk that he remembered most.

His memory twanged. A nice young bit, walking alongside ... who was it now?

Somebody else. Someone he hadn't liked much.

George walked a bit faster, and got to the door just ahead of her. He went in first and turned to keep the door open. She smiled vaguely as she went past. Sharp, bony face, but somehow attractive. Yes, he'd definitely seen her before, but a long, long time ago. The features had been softer, the hair longer. Young. Yes, he'd thought at the time how young she was for . . . whoever the hell it was she'd been with.

The woman went on up the stairs towards the CID offices, and George sighed. That was the trouble with getting old. The bloody memory began to let you down. But he knew it would come back to him. Things like that tended to niggle away at his subconscious.

He sighed and made his way over to the desk sergeant for a bit of a gossip. Everyone knew that desk sergeants always made the best cups of tea going, and more often than not, had a plateful of biscuits they were willing to share. And it *was* still lunch-time.

Just.

9

Keith Barrington stared at Gavin Moreland, and could actually feel the colour leaving his face. His cheeks felt suddenly cold, but that was nothing compared to the clammy hand that was twisting around inside his stomach.

Gavin, a 22-year-old recent graduate from the London School of Economics, twisted his square-faced visage into a spiteful grin. 'Yeah, I thought that might get a reaction. At last. Ever since I found you in that disgusting fleatpit you call a bedsit, you've been about as responsive as an old tabby cat on Prozac.' His striking hazel eyes, slightly up-tilted at the end, suddenly shimmered with unshed tears. His voice, upper-crust and just slightly on the nasal side, trembled with tension. 'Anybody else would be flattered to be chased. But oh no, not you. It's been nothing but moan, moan, moan, ever since I got here.'

'That's not true,' Keith mumbled, glancing around nervously. The café was a cross between an old-fashioned tea shop and a health food bar, and most of its clientele were young, working, upwardly mobile types, who were taking no notice of the two young men at all. They'd taken a pavement table, but the striped blue and white awning kept the sun off, and if everybody wanted to pretend they were on a street café in Paris, Keith didn't feel like arguing. Besides he had his back to the street and the worst of the petrol fumes.

Gavin, seeing his unease, smiled grimly again. 'Don't worry,' he said bitterly — and quietly. 'I know enough not to embarrass you in public. I won't suddenly reach across and squeeze your hand.'

Keith flushed at the palpable hit. His being in the closet was something they were never going to agree on. Back in the capital it hadn't been so much of an issue, in their social life at least. They'd been together for nearly three years now, and had always been able to find out-of-the-way pubs, clubs and meeting places.

At first, Gavin, the son of a wealthy businessman, had found the red-haired, working-class copper something of an amusement. It had made him laugh, especially when Keith came home in uniform, to tease and taunt. But he'd never expected the entertainment to last for long though. His previous boyfriends had lasted anywhere from a month to, at a real pinch, six. So he'd been frankly astonished when he'd found himself unable to give up his painfully prosaic, working-class, repressed PC Plod. Worse was to follow. Gavin found himself actually in love.

It was embarrassing.

All his friends were 'out' and being with someone so firmly in the closet gave him a headache. He loathed Keith's job, and was always taking pot shots at his so-called 'superior' officers, and sniping whenever he had to arrest a black shoplifter or stop an Asian for speeding. The fact that Keith wasn't in the least a racist only made his vitriol more vicious.

Keith's final falling out with his sergeant, which had led to him almost being dismissed, threatened to be the final straw. Oh, if Keith had been made to leave the force, Gavin would have cracked open the champagne at the speed of light. No, it was the fact that he'd been transferred to Oxfordshire that had sent Gavin stamping out of Keith's life like the prima donna he could sometimes be.

But it hadn't lasted.

For nearly six months, Gavin had sweated it out, pretending he was doing fine. But now here he was, in Oxford, putting up at the Randolf Hotel for the most part, and trying to pretend that Keith was going to take him back. In his more hopeful moods, he imagined Keith coming out of the closet, thus enabling them to become a proper, serious couple at last. All of this, in spite of the fact that he'd hardly been welcomed back with open arms. Gavin was nothing if not an optimist.

But now, this latest catastrophe.

Keith leaned forward on the table, his voice little more than a whisper. 'What exactly did they say when they took him in?'

Gavin took a long, deep, breath. He wasn't as tall as Keith, but had a slender, wiry strength that came from playing near-professional tennis. He'd gone to LSE to please his father, but his dream was to be a tennis pro. 'They said they wanted him for questioning in connection with a shipment of Greek crockery.'

Keith blinked. Gavin's father, Sir Reginald Moreland (the knighthood had been bestowed eight years ago for services to industry, and wasn't hereditary) ran a large import/export company, as well as owning several vineyards in France and Italy. Sir Reginald was prosperous, hard-working, high-living, and Keith had never heard of anything dodgy about him. He wasn't even divorced, and his wife of the past twenty-eight years ran her own chain of beauty salons.

'It sounds as if they're fishing,' Keith said hopefully. 'Perhaps Customs and Excise got a tip-off about one of your father's containers.'

Gavin's face paled. 'Drugs?'

Keith felt that coldness wash over him again. It was the most obvious thing to think of. But of course, as any copper knew, smuggling could cover anything — from the old favourites like booze and tobacco, to human trafficking.

'I don't believe it,' Gavin said tightly, shaking his head. But he knew more than most how his father, raised in tower blocks in Hackney, was ferocious about money. Earning it, spending it, keeping it. And, most of all, never, ever, being poor again.

And drugs were very lucrative business.

Keith looked across at Gavin's unhappy, uncertain face, and fought back the urge to reach across and give him a cuddle. 'Look, they haven't arrested him — that's a good sign. It means they don't have a case yet, or the evidence. He asked for a lawyer right away, yeah?'

Gavin snorted. 'Naturally. You don't think there are any flies on my old man, do you?'

Keith shrugged. 'Look, there's not much I can do. It's not as if I've got the clout to pull a few strings and find out what's going on. Your dad probably has his own cronies who are doing that anyway.'

'Yeah, I know,' Gavin sighed heavily, running his thin, strong, shaking hands through a thatch of thick, dark hair. 'I don't expect you to be able to help. Not in any professional way. It's just that when I got the phone call from Frank, my first thought was to see you. I needed to hear your voice and know everything would be all right. Daft, right?' his voice trembled again. Keith nudged Gavin's knee with his own, under the table, and got a brief smile in response.

Frank Perkins was one of Moreland's vice-presidents. Since Gavin was supposed, nominally at least, to work for Moreland Exports as a young executive, Frank was laughably called his boss. In reality, Gavin was hardly ever in the office. Normally he could be found playing somewhere on the top amateur tennis circuit. Lately, of course, he'd been in Oxford. Keith wondered how much Frank Perkins, or even Sir Reginald himself for that matter, knew about Gavin's private life. And what they thought of Keith.

It made him nervous.

Worse, if Sir Reginald *did* turn out to have criminal tendencies, what would the likes of Hillary Greene, Mel Mallow and Detective Chief Superintendent Marcus Donleavy, all back at HQ, think about a certain DC Barrington being such good friends with a villain's son?

★ ★ ★

Hillary listened as Gemma Fordham told her about the Morgan sports car, and its owner, now resident in Liverpool.

'Better ring him up and check him out. But we're just being thorough,' Hillary mused. 'I take it the cottage owner he was visiting confirmed that they were with each other the whole time?'

'Guv,' Gemma confirmed flatly, and reached for the phone. Hillary, still feeling restless, stared out the window. From what she could overhear of Gemma's side of the conversation with the man in Liverpool, the results were turning out to be pretty much as they'd guessed.

When she'd finished, Hillary grabbed her bag. 'Come on, let's have another word with Tommy Eaverson.' She had no special reason for wanting to see him again, but she liked to interview people more than once, and the office walls were closing in on her.

Gemma grabbed her own gear and followed silently. She noticed Hillary glance across at Barrington's empty desk, and wondered where the ginger nut was today. Frank Ross was still absent, but Gemma was beginning to learn that that was normal. Nobody complained, obviously, because nobody liked working with the poisonous little git.

No wonder Ronnie had found him so useful.

★   ★   ★

Back at the Eaverson place, Hillary was just climbing out of her car when a neighbour, mowing a pocket-handkerchief-sized front lawn, turned off his Hovermower, and watched them approach curiously. When they were nearest to his hedge, he made a small head-bob, indicating he wanted to chat.

Hillary, who loved gossiping neighbours, headed his way immediately. He was a small man, red-faced from the heat and the exertion, with a bald spot on the crown of his head and deep-set, twinkling blue eyes. A moustache sat on his upper lip like a discouraged caterpillar.

'If you're here to talk to Mr Eaverson, I'm afraid he's gone.'

Hillary felt her heartbeat trip. Gone? Her first thought was that he'd done a runner. That somehow she'd slipped up and let him get away. Then, she took a calming breath.

'Gone?' she asked casually. Beside her, she could feel Gemma's silent, watchful presence.

'You know,' the neighbour said, lowering

his voice to a conspiratorial whisper. 'Left her. Packed his bags and went. I heard them having a real barney last night, and this morning, when he got in his car, he had suitcases with him. And you're not telling me he needed three big cases, plus two carry-ons, just to go on a business trip.' He took a much needed breath, and nodded his head solemnly.

'Funny, I thought their marriage was pretty steady,' Hillary said, knowing that would open the floodgates. There was nothing human nature liked so much as to know more than the next man.

'Oh no,' the other man said at once. 'Oh, on the surface, maybe,' he waved a vague hand in the air. 'But you should hear the arguments sometimes! He's been spending more and more time at the office over the last few years, and my wife thought, once, that she saw him having dinner in that posh hotel near Chesterton with this attractive brunette. And as for her! Well, you know about that so called tenant of hers, don't you? The one that got killed? Some sort of artist they tell me. Well, if he ever paid a pound in rent, I'm the tooth fairy.'

Hillary managed to keep a straight face, in spite of the fact that she was suddenly picturing him with gossamer wings, and wearing a white tutu. A look that, rather alarmingly, suited him — in her mind's eye at least. 'Do you know where he might have gone?' she asked, shaking the image from her mind.

'Can't tell you, I'm afraid. But he'll be at work right now though, won't he?' he added craftily.

Hillary smiled brightly. 'Yes he will, won't he?' she agreed softly.

★ ★ ★

They brought Eaverson in. Hillary had already talked to him on his own territory, and now she wanted to shake him up a bit, and see how he liked it on hers. Besides, she wanted to make sure they got his new address, and could lay hands on him again in a hurry, and impressing on him the fact that he was in the middle of a police investigation might not be a bad thing. And if the split with his wife *had* been brought about by her relationship with Wayne Sutton, Hillary wanted to know about it. It went to proving motive, if nothing else. And his alibi was non-existent.

Interview Room Two was identical to all the others — high placed windows, tiled floor, bolted-down table and chairs. A harsh,

bright, overhead light illuminated the proceedings.

Tommy Eaverson, dressed in a dark-blue
suit and mint-green tie, looked both nervous
and angry, upset and belligerent. The
moment he saw her, he began to rant.

'This is ridiculous! Pulling me away from
my work in the middle of the day. And for
what? It'll be all over the place by now! My
secretary could hardly meet my eye!'

Hillary, sitting opposite him, turned to a
fresh page on her notebook, totally unruffled.
'I understand you've left your wife, Mr
Eaverson?'

'So? Is that a crime now?' Tommy Eaverson
tried to laugh, but didn't quite pull it off, and
looked sullen instead. 'That's been coming on
for some time, anyway,' he said flatly. 'And I
don't see what that has to do with anything.'
He folded his arms defensively across his
chest.

'Was it her relationship with Wayne Sutton
that was the catalyst?' Hillary asked calmly.

'Relationship?' Tommy echoed, his voice
rising a decibel. 'Don't make me laugh. They
just had a roll in the hay in return for him not
paying her any rent. You don't call that a
relationship do you? He had women fawning
all over him. Silly cow, thought she was
special.'

'And that made you mad?' Hillary asked quietly. 'Seeing your wife make such a fool of herself? She became a laughing stock, didn't she? But what was much worse, she made you one too, by association.'

'Well, not any more,' Tommy said flatly. 'I'm seeing a solicitor. It's time I got free of her, anyway.'

'And did you want to get Wayne Sutton out of the way too? Is that why you killed him?'

'Eh?' Tommy looked genuinely surprised. 'No. Hey, wait a minute, no!' he sounded genuinely frightened now. 'I wouldn't kill someone. I'm not like that!'

Hillary smiled wryly and glanced across at Gemma, sitting beside her. 'The number of times we've heard that, hey, Sergeant?'

'If I had a pound, guv,' Gemma smiled wearily. 'I could retire by now.'

They kept at him for a while, but he was adamant. On the night Wayne Sutton had died, he'd been working, alone, at the office. In the end, Hillary was inclined — provisionally — to believe him. 'All right, Mr Eaverson, you can go now,' she said eventually. 'But make sure we can find you at that address you gave us. Oh, and by the way, do you know anyone called Annie?'

It was her stock question by now, asked of anyone with anything to do with the inquiry,

193

and she hadn't really expected anything to come of it. But Tommy Eaverson, in the act of rising, suddenly went still. The next instant, he was on his feet. His eyes when they met hers were as innocent as a lamb's.

'Annie? No, it doesn't ring any bells, Inspector,' he said pleasantly.

Hillary, having no other option, had to let him go. When he was gone, Gemma stirred.

'Find out who the Annie is in his life, guv?' she asked quietly, and Hillary smiled. She really was quick on the uptake, never missed a thing, and had an uncanny knack of anticipating her every need and order.

If she didn't have some private agenda of her own, she'd be a godsend.

Hillary nodded. When her DS had gone, she stayed on in the quiet room, thinking. When she finally rose, about ten minutes later, she headed, not back upstairs, but outside to the car park. There she opened all the Volkswagen's doors and windows to let the baking air out, then climbed in and drove north.

She was just pulling up to a set of traffic lights, when she saw them. Keith Barrington's dark chestnut hair was eye-catching enough to attract her attention, and as she braked for the red light, she saw the young man he was with, lean over the table and say something to him.

He was a good-looking youth, early twenties, with a fit, lean body. He looked to be wearing expensive clothes too, and she caught a glimpse of gold on his wrist. Probably a fancy watch. From his salon-style hair cut to his two-hundred pound trainers, he screamed money. His face, however, looked tight and miserable, and was fixed on her DC.

It was his eyes that told her the story.

So, she thought, nodding her head gently. *That* was the way of it.

Barrington didn't look over his shoulder, so didn't see his boss driving away. He did, however, look at his watch, and let out a yelp. 'Shit, I'm so late.'

Gavin threw himself backwards in his chair. 'Oh, of course, we mustn't be late for Detective Inspector Greene, must we?' he snarled.

Keith stood up and looked down at him helplessly. The truth was, he never knew how to handle his lover when he was like this. It only made things worse that, underneath, he could sense Gavin's very real fear and need.

'Look, I'll try to get back early tonight,' he promised gently. 'I'm sure you'll have heard from your dad or Perkins by then. It'll probably all have blown over.'

'Much you care,' Gavin muttered, then

195

shook his head angrily. 'Oh go on, PC Plod, just piss off.'

★   ★   ★

Colin Blake looked surprised to see another police officer, especially since this one was calling at his home, Thursdays were his day off, along with Sundays, and he always spent both days painting.

Hillary sensed he was not too pleased to be interrupted, but he was polite enough not to let it show too obviously.

The butcher, and shining light of the Ale and Arty Club, lived in a fairly large, new-build house on the outskirts of Banbury, with an unexpectedly spectacular view across open countryside. Blake had turned the conservatory into a studio, and in one corner an air-conditioning unit hummed steadily and to good effect. Obviously the side-line in painting paid well. She'd looked around curiously when he'd shown her through the hall and main living-room; all the canvases on the walls had been landscapes, and all had pleased her eye.

'Yours?' she asked now, pausing beside a river scene. There was something about the colour and the rendition of the willow trees that reminded her of something.

'Yes, they're all mine. Ones I couldn't sell, actually,' he said, with a modest smile. Hillary, like Gemma, found him pleasantly good-looking, urbane and likeable. She could understand why Wayne Sutton would have hated him.

Hillary nodded at the landscape. 'It reminds me of something,' she said, and Colin Blake smiled.

'Ah. An art lover. Actually, that's my homage to Constable. No pun intended, officer.'

Hillary smiled. 'Of course. Those Anglian sketches.'

'Thank you for not mentioning *The Hay Wain*.'

They walked on through into the conservatory itself, and a more exotic landscape caught her eye. 'Homage to Gaugin?' she asked, and got a laugh in return.

'Sometimes I do it for fun,' Colin Blake said, lowering his voice as if he was admitting to something scandalous. 'You know, just to see how I measure up to the masters. Of course, copying their style doesn't make you anything more than a good copyist. But at least it does reassure you that you're not wasting good paint.'

Hillary paused beside a painting of a meadow, just before a storm was due to hit, and found herself gazing into the incredibly lovely dark velvet eyes of a cow. 'Oh, you're not wasting paint, Mr Blake,' she said. She would quite happily have hung any of Colin Blake's canvases on her walls — if the *Mollern* had had a wall big enough to accommodate one, that is.

'Thank you, Inspector Greene. Something cold to drink?'

Hillary accepted a glass of real lemonade, mouth-wateringly swimming in ice-cubes, and took a seat. The easel he was working on was standing in the middle of the room, uncovered, and Hillary could see that he was currently painting a cottage scene, one frothing with flowering wisteria. In the foreground, a rusty iron railing fence was awash with a pale pink clematis. A child's bike lay abandoned on a somewhat scruffy lawn.

'Wayne would have called it chocolate box naff,' Colin said, catching the direction of her eye. The painting was almost finished, and Hillary could quite clearly see the peeling white paint on the rotting wooden window frames, the odd missing tile on the roof, the weeds growing through the path. In spite of its loveliness, the sense she got from it was one of acceptable poverty. A novel concept. And, for some reason she couldn't fathom, it aroused a vague, not unpleasant sense of nostalgia in her.

'He was jealous of you,' she said, making it a statement.

Colin Blake looked at her, sighed a little, and shrugged. 'Nothing I could do about it. He just didn't like me.'

'And you didn't like him?'

Colin smiled. 'It's hard to like someone who doesn't like you back, isn't it? Who has no respect for your art or talent, who despises your friends and ridicules your lifestyle and way of living. Unless you're a saint of course. No,' he took a seat in a padded swinging garden chair, and sipped from his own glass of lemonade. 'I didn't like him. But I didn't kill him.'

Hillary nodded. She knew from reading Gemma's notes on their interview, that he was here at the time of the killing, painting this very same canvas, and that his wife, Bernice, could vouch for him.

Not that *that* meant anything. Wives and mothers made notoriously bad character witnesses and alibi-providers.

But why would Colin Blake kill Wayne Sutton anyway? If anything, it should be the other way around. It was Sutton who was jealous and bitter. Now if *Blake* had been found dead, Sutton would have been in the hot seat for sure.

'Do you know anyone called Annie, Mr Blake?'

'Annie Coulson — she lives next door,' he said at once, then smiled, puzzled. 'Why?'

Hillary smiled back. 'Does Mrs Coulson know Wayne Sutton?'

'It's Ms. Our Annie is a feminist. And gay. She'd have a fit if you called her Mrs,' Colin said with a wide grin. 'And no, I don't suppose for a minute she knew Wayne. Why should she?'

'Did Wayne ever mention anyone called Annie to you?'

Colin thought for a moment, then shook his head. 'Wayne and I didn't talk much, though. You should ask his friends. The woman who paints abstracts for instance.'

Hillary nodded glumly, thanked him for the lemonade, gave the unfinished painting a last, regretful look, and took her leave.

On the way out, she passed an exquisite pen and wash drawing of a woman with long, auburn hair. She looked at it and nodded.

'Augustus John. With a hint of Burne-Jones.'

Colin Blake gave an ironic bow.

* * *

When she got back to HQ the desk sergeant beckoned her over.

'Hill, got a live one for you. Man and woman just come in. Wanted to talk to whoever was in charge of the Wayne Sutton inquiry. Husband and wife outfit, wife wears the trousers. Hubby didn't want to be here. I put them in Five.'

Hillary thanked him. 'Call upstairs and send Barrington down will you?'

The desk sergeant cheerfully agreed, and Hillary made her way to Interview Room Five. It looked exactly as Interview Room Two had looked. Inside, a short, dumpy woman sat grimly staring forward. She was wearing a bright, flower-patterned summer dress, tights and sandals, and clutched a handbag as if her life depended on it. Beside her, tall and thin, and casting apprehensive looks at the PC standing in one corner, was a man wearing a pair of creased summer shorts and a faded T-shirt. He had wispy grey hair and long, bony hands. He looked as if a breeze could blow him off his seat.

Hillary smiled at them as she took a seat, and introduced herself. 'And you are?' She looked to the woman first.

'Celia Benson. This is my husband Raymond. Please forgive him, I had to drag him away from the garden.' She sniffed, eyeing her husband's casual apparel with an angry eye. Her husband stiffened, but his mouth firmed into a stubborn line. Hillary suspected a long-running argument, and bit her lip.

Barrington came in, and Hillary introduced him. 'DC Barrington will take notes,' she said softly. 'Now, I understand you have something for us concerning the Wayne Sutton murder inquiry?'

'Yes, we do,' Celia said at once, then nudged her spouse with her elbow. 'Tell her Ray.'

'You tell her,' Ray shot back, his voice surprisingly deep for one who looked so insubstantial. 'You're the one who wanted to come down here.'

'That's because I've got a brain in my head, and a civic bone in my body. But *you're* the one who heard 'em. Now just tell the lady. The sooner you do, the sooner you can get back to that bloody compost heap and your precious tomato plants.'

Her husband heaved a long suffering sigh, and looked, finally, at Hillary. 'It's like this. I was out just before dark — the best time to water tomatoes is after the sun goes down — it can't burn the leaves, then, see?'

His wife rolled her eyes.

Hillary bit her lip again.

'So I don't expect they saw me. They wouldn't have been arguing so loud if they had known I was there. Madge likes to pretend she's such a lady.'

Celia Benson snorted inelegantly.

'Madge? We're talking about Madge Eaverson, yes?' Hillary interrupted, just to make sure.

'That's right. We live next door to where she used to live. Used to be her Mum and Dad's place,' Celia broke in, as if unable to bear being silent any longer. 'Her poor mother would turn in her grave if she knew what she'd been getting up to with that young man.'

'Wayne Sutton?'

'Am I telling this or are you?' Ray Benson asked, turning to look at his wife, and sounding aggrieved. 'Only if you want to tell it, what did you drag me down here for anyway?'

'Oh, get on with it!' Celia huffed.

Ray turned, with ostentatious patience, back to Hillary. 'It's like I said. It was just getting dark, and my tomatoes are against the wall connecting our gardens. Anyways, I heard Madge and that artist chap arguing.'

'You're talking about Wayne Sutton now?' Hillary clarified.

'That's him. Him that rented her place.

Well . . . ' he added, when his wife snorted again. 'Well, whatever. It's none of my business,' he cast his wife a telling look. 'But that night they were going at it hammer and tongs, and I couldn't help but hear. I mean, they must have been right the other side of the wall.'

'When was this, Mr Benson?'

'Ah. Now you got me.'

'He's hopeless with time,' his wife chipped in, smugly. As if it was something to be proud of. 'But I can tell you it must have been a few days before Wayne got killed.'

'Ah, sounds about right,' Ray chipped in. 'They were just beginning to flower. My tomato plants,' he added, when everyone looked at him blankly.

Hillary nodded. 'And what was the argument about, Mr Benson, could you tell?'

'Oh yerse,' Ray said, nodding sagely. 'Couldn't help but hear every word.' Then, when everyone again stared at him patiently, he coloured slightly, and said in a rush, 'she were threatening to throw him out. Said she'd had enough, and this latest floozy of his was the last straw.'

Hillary drew in a quick breath. The latest floozy.

The mysterious Annie maybe?

Hillary took him through it, meticulously

coaxing out every detail he could remember, but there had been no mention of the name Annie, by either Madge or their victim.

By the end of the interview, Ray Benson looked almost to be enjoying himself, and his wife with almost glowing with civic pride. It was obvious that the important policewoman was pleased with them, and when they left, there was not a cross word between them.

Hillary watched them go, then leaned back with a satisfied sigh. 'Right then, let's get Madge in,' Hillary said softly. And smiled. 'This just isn't her day, is it?' First her husband leaves her, now her neighbour drops her in the mire.

Was getting arrested for murdering her lover going to top it all off nicely?

10

Madge Eaverson glanced around the Interview Room and smiled. 'So, the telly has got it right. This room looks just like one I saw on *The Bill* once.'

Hillary smiled. Beside her, Keith Barrington was thinking about Gavin Moreland. Or, to be precise, his father, Sir Reginald. Right now, he'd be sitting in an interview room similar to this one, with the London traffic churning away outside. Of course, he would be surrounded by top-class solicitors, all telling him what to answer and what not to answer, what to admit to, what to fudge, what to deny outright.

But would they be enough? What if he really was going to be charged? What happened then?

'Lots of the television companies have technical consultants and advisors, Mrs Eaverson. Mostly stage-struck retired old coppers.' Hillary said with a short laugh.

'Madge, please call me Madge. I told you before, when you visited last. Whenever I hear 'Mrs Eaverson' I think of Tommy's mother — or even worse, his old granny.' She shuddered, then reached into her bag for a cigarette. Hillary coughed politely and she put it back.

Barrington shifted on his chair again, and Hillary shot him a quick look. He was staring down at his notebook, but she could tell his thoughts were miles away. And she could guess where.

His boyfriend was young and good-looking, and the last time she'd seen him, had been deeply miserable. Were they on the verge of splitting up? Whatever the problem was, it was time to bring her DC back to the here and now.

'Keith, would you like to start?' Hillary asked, and watched him jump.

Barrington, after a startled glance at her, cleared his throat, and looked up at the woman opposite him. This was his first shot at a formal interview with a murder suspect. He knew that it meant Hillary Greene was beginning to trust him, and had decided to stretch him a little. Give him a little responsibility. Damn it, now was not the time to be distracted! He cast around for something to say, something to open the interview and set the right tone. To his dismay, his mind stayed blank. Beside him, he could feel his DI getting restive.

'We understand your husband has left you,

Mrs Eaverson,' he said quickly, and then blinked, wondering if that had been too blunt. Maybe he should have eased into it? What if he'd just alienated the witness and made her clam up? Manfully, he resisted the urge to look across at his superior officer to gauge her reaction, or seek tacit instructions.

Madge Eaverson laughed. She was wearing a pristine pale-lilac trouser suit with an electric blue raw silk shirt. Amethyst and diamond earrings glittered at her lobes, whilst a perfume that had probably come with a fierce price tag wafted around her. But her eyes looked tight, and she was obviously itching for a cigarette.

'Yes, at last!' she said with an exaggerated sigh of relief. 'I've been hoping he'd push off for ages. Well, I've been giving him the hint for some time now, but some men just don't get it do they? I think they wear blinkers half the time.'

Keith nodded. Of course, whatever was happening now in London largely depended on what crime Sir Reginald was suspected of committing. If it was only straight forward avoidance of duty or . . . He cut off the thought and forced himself to listen to what his *own* suspect was saying.

'Do you really expect us to believe that you're not sorry, Mrs Eaverson?' he asked, hoping he'd made his voice sound sceptical enough.

'Of course I do, dear boy.'

Keith smiled briefly. 'But, if that was the case, why not leave him yourself? Just pack your bags and go?'

Madge smiled pityingly. 'Because that's just it. *I* didn't want to pack *my* bags and go. *I* wanted to stay in the house, thus keeping the moral high ground.' Seeing that he still wasn't getting it, she grinned widely. 'I wanted to hold all the cards in the upcoming divorce settlement.' She shot Hillary an amused look. 'He's so young and innocent, isn't he, bless him?'

Keith felt himself flush. Damn, he should have thought of all that himself.

'But with Tommy leaving me, just walking out like he has, I get everything I want,' Madge said smugly. 'I've already got a call in to the locksmith to change the locks, I can tell you.'

Keith nodded. Had Gavin gone back to London? When he returned home tonight, would he find him waiting for him at the bedsit, criticizing the floor space, ordering Chinese and taunting him about a hard day at the office. Or would the place be quiet. Cold. Tidy. As it had been before he came? The thought made a hard knot form in his stomach. No matter how much trouble his relationship with Gavin could cause him, the thought of being left on his own again made him feel cold.

Acknowledging this, he then looked flatly across at Mrs Eaverson. 'I find it hard to believe that you're as relaxed about all this as you seem, Mrs Eaverson,' he said softly.

Madge blinked, and looked away. For a moment, she looked as if she was going to cry. Then she shrugged. 'I'm a tough old bird. When you hit forty you develop a skin like a rhino. You need it.' She glanced across at Hillary. 'Well, you'll know what I'm talking about. Men can skin you alive if you let them.'

Hillary thought briefly of Mike Regis. Mike who hated her boat and wanted her to move in with him. Mike who made her laugh, and worry at the same time. Mike whom she had no idea what to do with.

She glanced across at Keith, silently giving him permission to carry on.

'Did Wayne Sutton get under your skin, Mrs Eaverson?' Keith asked, quite pleased with that. It sounded clever, and it had obviously upset her.

'Wayne?' Madge said sharply, then gave another graphic shrug. 'Oh, well, Wayne was just a bit of fun. A distraction from life's boredom. You simply didn't take Wayne seriously.'

Keith nodded. 'But that's not strictly true, is it? I mean, you took him seriously enough to threaten to evict him because of all his other affairs.'

Madge paled slightly. This time she reached for her bag and lit a cigarette, shooting a defiant glance at Hillary as she did so. 'You can arrest me for smoking in a no smoking area if you like,' she offered with a laugh.

Keith, seeing his witness was distracted, found his thoughts going once again to London. If Sir Reginald was charged, that would mean a trial. And Gavin would have to return home then, right?

'Oh, I don't think I'll arrest you for *that*, Madge,' Hillary said softly, emphasizing the 'that' just enough for the other woman to pale even more.

And if Sir Reginald was found guilty, Keith thought, with a growing sense of desperation, might not Gavin feel forced to take over the chairmanship of his father's company? With no more tennis games, he'd have no more excuses to be away from the capital. No more visits to Oxford. No more . . .

He saw Hillary's head turn sharply in his direction, and he licked his lips. Damn it, *he had to concentrate*!

'We know you argued, fiercely, with the victim shortly before he was murdered, Mrs Eaverson,' he said, trying to sound menacing, whilst at the same time, keeping his voice even and flat, for the benefit of the tape recorder revolving slowly and silently on the table before them. Never let it be said, by any defence barrister, that the police had intimidated a witness.

'How in the hell did you know that?' Madge asked, drawing from the cigarette deeply and trying for nonchalant devil-may-care, but sounding just a shade too surprised. Then, seeing it was no use denying it, she gave another bark of laughter.

'Oh well, might as well come clean, I suppose,' she drawled. 'Yes, Wayne and me did have a bit of a barney. But I quickly cooled off. I'm not one who holds a grudge, or lets things fester inside them. Ask anyone who knows me.'

Keith smiled briefly. 'What, exactly, was this argument about, Mrs Eaverson?'

'Apparently you already know,' Madge said, a shade testily, then sighed, and took another drag of her cigarette. 'It was about his other women, of course. I mean, I didn't mind all those old dears who flattered him and bought his paintings and cooed all over them to their equally daft friends. And that

212

young girl of his — Monica. Well, she was just a lightweight. But he'd got someone else . . . someone he was being very secretive about. And that wasn't like him,' Madge said softly, her voice becoming reflective now. 'It wasn't like him at all.'

Hillary decided it was time to take over. This was beginning to get interesting and it was obvious Barrington's heart wasn't really in it.

'And that sounded the alarm bells, didn't it Madge?' she said softly. 'The others were probably something of a running joke between you, right? The woman who let him have the car, Denise Collier, the Ale and Arty crowd. They weren't anything to worry about, right?'

'Right,' Madge said with a smile, totally oblivious to the fact that that was what all of 'them' thought about 'the others' as well — including Madge Eaverson. 'That Denise was a bit of a pain in the arse though. Too possessive by half,' she mused grimly.

'But Wayne found that funny, I bet.'

'Yeah,' Madge said, relaxing a bit, smiling slightly in remembrance. 'Yeah, he did.'

'But this new girl was different,' Hillary said softly. 'How, exactly?'

Beside her, Keith listened with half an ear. He could ring Gavin's mobile the minute he

213

was out of here, find out where he was. And then what? If he was on his way to London could he really ask him to come back? And come back to what? A lousy bedsit in a backwater city?

'I'm not sure I can describe it, not really,' Madge said, looking at Hillary helplessly. 'He started hiding things from me. Not telling me stuff. He was up to something, and with Wayne that could only mean one thing. I got the feeling she was rich. I mean, seriously rich. I began to get the impression that he thought he was soon going to be able to give all the others the heave-ho. He was beginning to be less cautious around them. Less charming. He'd even allow himself the odd snipe around them. Oh, nothing too bad, nothing to cut off the supply of money. But I noticed it. It was as if he was expecting to be able to do without them soon.'

Hillary nodded. 'It sounds to me as if he was planning on getting married.'

Madge paled even further.

'I mean, how else could he be sure of her?' she pressed on inexorably. 'Unless they had some sort of legal bond, she could have cut off his 'allowance' at any time. But a legal husband — well now, he'd have rights.'

Madge stabbed out her cigarette viciously. 'That's what I was thinking, too. That's why I asked him about her that night. Teased him a bit. Tried to figure out how far things had gone. He got uppity, at first, then downright mad. Told me to leave it alone.'

'Was her name Annie?' Hillary asked abruptly.

'Huh?' Madge looked up from her bag, and the temptingly open packet of cigarettes, and her eyes narrowed. 'No. I don't know. Why? Do *you* know who she is? Has the bitch come forward?'

Hillary hid her disappointment behind a non-committal smile. Still no confirmation that Annie existed. Sutton must have been really keen to keep her in the shadows. But then, if she *was* rich, and he *had* been in with a chance of marrying all that cash, he would have been extra careful to keep his current lifestyle a secret from her. No wonder he didn't want any of his paying fan club to know about her. They might just have paid her a visit and dropped a few home truths in her ear.

Who knows, perhaps one of them already had. Could Annie have found out that her fiancé was nothing more than a gigolo? Had she lured him to that meadow and killed him, leaving behind a taunting red paper heart to show just what she thought of handsome young men who tried to marry her for her money?

'So who's this Annie then?' Madge asked querulously, and Hillary shrugged.

'It's just a name that's come up in our inquiries, that's all,' she said vaguely.

'Well, I don't know if that was the name of his new woman or not,' Madge said slowly. 'But I know she lives in Heyford bloody Sudbury.'

Heyford Sudbury again, Hillary thought. The name of that pretty near-Cotswold village kept right on popping up. 'Oh? How do you know that?' she asked curiously.

And Madge Eaverson flushed. Then she reached for another cigarette and lit up. Hillary, who was slightly allergic to cigarette smoke, bit her lip and leaned back in her chair. The smoke, in the airless room, drifted almost straight up, but she could begin to feel the back of her throat tickle.

'Madge,' Hillary prompted. 'How do you know where she lives?'

Madge Eaverson's eyes drifted around the walls of the room, to the window — which was too high to see out of — ricocheted off the constable standing stolid and silent in the corner and then back to Hillary.

She sighed heavily. 'Look, this is going to sound worse than it is. I mean, it's going to sound bad. But it's not like I'm some sort of loony-tunes or anything. I'm not a stalker. I mean, I'm not that desperate, it's just that . . . ' She took a drag helplessly, and Hillary suddenly twigged.

'You followed him,' she guessed flatly.

Madge shrugged, smiled, then laughed. 'Yeah. I followed him. Pretty pathetic, huh?' She sighed and rubbed her eyes tiredly. 'One afternoon, about two weeks ago, I heard him on the phone as I was coming to collect the rent.' She blushed delicately, and glanced quickly at Keith Barrington, knowing that he must know what she meant by that.

But Keith Barrington looked back at her blankly. She might have been comforted to know that his thoughts were far away from contemplating her afternoon sex sessions with a murder victim.

Hillary wouldn't have been. She'd have given him a lecture that would blister his ears.

'Yes, go on,' Hillary said crisply, not wanting sudden embarrassment on the witness's part to hold up the flow of her evidence.

'Well, I knew he must be talking to her. He was usually so open and loud on the phone. You know, he always had a larger than life personality. But this time he was almost whispering. And when he saw me, he muttered something and hung up at once. He'd never done that before. And all that afternoon he was distracted. I could feel it. Well, a woman can, can't she?'

Madge took another angry puff on her cigarette. 'I wasn't best pleased, I can tell you. Well, when I left, I just drove around the corner and waited. Sure enough, about ten minutes later, he goes out and I followed him.'

Hillary's eyes gleamed. 'To Heyford Sudbury?' she said softly.

Madge nodded. 'Yeah. Well, to the outskirts of it anyway,' she qualified. 'I didn't realize he'd spotted me, but he pulled up on to the side of the road and got out and waved me down.' She laughed. 'I wouldn't be any good as a private investigator, I can tell you. Still, I was daft to try it really, especially in my own car. I managed to keep traffic between us for most of the way, but once we turned off the main roads on to the country lanes, I suppose I stuck out like a sore thumb.'

'What did he say? When he pulled you over I mean?' Hillary asked curiously.

Madge Eaverson flushed an ugly red. 'He was really nasty. I've never heard him so mean. I just drove off. That's when I decided to evict him from the cottage. I was being spiteful I know but . . . well, there's a limit to what I'm prepared to take.'

Hillary sighed. 'So you didn't see where in

Heyford Sudbury he went?'

'No.'

Hillary leaned forward slowly. 'All right, Mrs Eaverson. But please, don't leave Deddington for any length of time without letting us know.'

Madge Eaverson nodded, but she looked relieved. Hillary watched her go, then said flatly, for the tape, 'Mrs Eaverson has left the interview room.' She turned off the recorder and looked over her shoulder at the uniform. She nodded her head, and the man silently left.

If he promised Gavin that they'd get a bigger place, Keith Barrington was thinking, maybe even rent a house somewhere, he could probably persuade Gavin to stay. But it would have to be out in the sticks somewhere. He couldn't risk anyone he knew figuring out he was sharing a house with another man. If . . .

'Constable Barrington.'

The voice, cold and hard, instantly recognizable and yet in an awful way, totally unfamiliar, made his blood suddenly run cold.

His head came up and around in a jerk.

Hillary got up slowly from the chair and walked around to the side of the table to face him. Once there, she leaned forward, resting her weight on her fists and bringing her face close to his. 'If I can't have your undivided attention in an interview room, when questioning a prime suspect on a murder case, exactly when *can* I have it?'

Keith swallowed hard. 'Sorry, guv.'

'Not good enough. I already have one piece of dead weight on this team that I'm obliged to carry — as you've no doubt already guessed, his name is Frank Ross. But I don't have to carry *two*. Do you understand me?'

Keith swallowed again. 'Yes, guv.'

'I gave you a shot at interviewing Madge Eaverson because I've been pleased with your progress so far. I thought you were ready.'

Keith felt himself cringe inside his clothes. Back at Blacklock Green, his old nick, he'd been used to being dressed down by his sergeant. The man had it in for him, and getting a right rollicking was almost a daily event. Keith had despised and loathed him, and felt not a shred of respect for the man.

But so far, since coming to Thames Valley, he'd never been on the carpet. And getting a reprimand from Hillary Greene hurt. It hurt because he knew, this time, he deserved it. And he'd let her down. He'd let himself down.

'I'm sorry, guv,' he said again, miserably.

Hillary straightened up. 'No point apologizing to me,' she said dismissively. 'Think of it as a game of snakes and ladders, Constable. For the last six months you've been steadily climbing ladders. Now you've just slipped down a ruddy great snake. If you want to regain lost territory, I suggest you start climbing again. But it's no skin off my nose, either way. If you don't shape up, I just ship you out.'

Keith blanched.

'Right. Now that's clearly understood, you can start by finding out where Frank Ross is and get him to help you make up a profile for me. Of Heyford Sudbury. I want to know its layout, the name of every person in every house. I want to know if anyone has form, if anyone's been in trouble with the tax man, if there are any old or new scandals associated with the place. I want you to go through the census, check with the council offices, check out any old newspaper reports wherever the village is mentioned — in short I want to know everything about that village. And in particular, I want to know who has the most money. And if anyone who has it is a female by the name of Annie. And make sure Frank Ross pulls his weight. Is all that clear?'

'Yes, guv,' Barrington said crisply.

Hillary nodded and walked out of the room. She left behind her one seriously worried man.

Once outside the interview room, Hillary turned, not left and towards the stairs, but carried on straight across the main lobby to the main doors.

Outside, she walked across the baking car park to her car and undid all the doors and windows again.

She was confident that the fire she'd lit under Barrington would do its job. He'd come to Thames Valley as a last resort to begin with, under a cloud, after thumping his old sergeant. He'd been wary at first, but had quickly settled down, and Hillary knew he'd come to like and respect her. More than that, he'd begun to realize that, on her team, he was not only in an ideal position to learn the job, but would, if he did it right, receive promotion in due course. She didn't play favourites, and she wasn't power-hungry. All her previous team members had left for bigger and better things, and she'd made it clear to him that he was going to be no exception, as far as she was concerned.

Now all that was in jeopardy. Or so he thought.

In truth, Hillary didn't really know how serious the problem was, and would cut him some slack. He was having trouble with his love life — well, who wasn't? The fact that he was gay was more problematical. OK, in this enlightened day and age, it was supposed to be different, and the police force even had a gay rights movement. But in reality, she could understand why he was in the closet.

And she thought he was wise.

If the likes of Frank Ross ever found out about him, for instance, she'd never be able to keep him on her team. Ross would make his life intolerable, and Barrington himself would be back in the same position he'd been in back in London — namely, on his sergeant's shit-list. He'd have to be transferred yet again, with two strikes against him.

Her phone rang and she answered it automatically, not realizing that she'd sighed deeply until Mike Regis's voice said cheerfully, 'You sound about as fed up as I feel. Case not going well?'

Hillary sighed again, then laughed. 'No, just the usual office problems. Nothing I can't handle. What's up?'

'Does there have to be something up for me to call? I just wanted to see if you could make dinner tonight. My place, I'll cook.'

His place meant staying over. Another offer to make room in his wardrobe for her gear. Another conversation about taking their summer holidays together this year — getting away to somewhere hot and exotic. Fiji maybe. She could almost see the entire evening mapped out in her head. Regis was a fair cook — it would be something with red meat in it. Her favourite. He'd have bought a bottle of wine. Maybe flowers. Later, of course, sex in a large, comfortable double bed. No excuses for her to slip out in the middle of the night.

And what was wrong with any of that?

Nothing at all.

So why wasn't she already saying yes?

'I can tell it's a bad time,' Regis said, and Hillary swore softly as she suddenly realized how insulting the long silence must have been.

'It's just that I think the case is about to break,' she said. 'We've got something, a nibble, if not a lead, that's got that feel about it. You know?'

Mike did know. And he knew her well enough to tell she wasn't lying. Nevertheless, as he said something cheerful, and got from her a promise of 'meeting up soon', he hung up feeling morose.

Hillary slipped her phone into her bag feeling guilty. Then she got behind the wheel and shook her head. Hell, here she was, being all wise and superior about Keith Barrington's love life, when she couldn't even handle her own.

Angrily, she thrust the keys into the ignition and gunned the engine.

Puff the Tragic Wagon growled tragically, coughed and died.

Hillary sighed heavily, and tried again, more gently.

★ ★ ★

Nearly three-quarters of an hour later, she stood in front of Heyford Sudbury's church and admired the spire. There was a lot to admire in Heyford Sudbury. The graveyard, for instance, was recently mown, and even the oldest stones were free of ivy. The iron gates had been recently painted black. There was not a scrap of litter to be seen in the immaculately clean streets. Nearly all the mellow Cotswold stone houses sported a plethora of hanging baskets, and front gardens frothed with spring colour. Even the old-fashioned telephone kiosk had been newly painted a dazzling scarlet.

A letter on the village notice board informed all proudly that the village had been short-listed for 'The Best Kept Village award' again that year, which probably explained it all. No doubt the WI had regular marches around the place to make sure no malingerer or backslider was allowed to ruin their chances.

The village was old, dating back to somewhere around the time that William the Conqueror first dipped his toes in the English Channel, and one or two buildings looked Elizabethan. Most cottages were of that pale lemon coloured stone, so beloved of the area, with grey-tiled roofs and porches. Windows were mullioned, oriel, and honeysuckle-festooned.

There was a lot of money here, no doubt about it. She didn't need to see the Jaguars and top-of-the-range four-wheel-drive vehicles parked outside the local pub to know that.

Eyeing the pub thoughtfully, Hillary made her way over. In most English villages, the pub, the church, the vicarage and the manor house, were all cobbled closely together. There was a good reason for that. In the old days, the lord of the manor and the vicar liked to keep an eye on the peasantry to make sure they all went to mass, and the publican liked to keep an eye on them as they all came out. That way, attendances in both establishments could be relied upon.

Heyford Sudbury was no different. As she turned from the church and headed towards the pub, she saw, off to her left, a large set of wrought-iron gates, and an expanse of gravel. Somewhere behind the high walls, she suspected, was the village manor house, and as pretty a piece of prime real estate as you were likely to find.

And the pub was the best place to find out who owned it.

Inside the Three Horseshoes it felt almost chilly, and her eyes blinked in the relative gloom. It was late, nearly closing time, and she made her way over to the bar quickly to order a lemon and lime.

'Like ice with that?' the barman was a youngish, sandy-haired man with a winning smile and very white teeth.

'Swimming in it please,' she replied, hitching herself on to the barstool. 'It's baking out there. Still, brings out the tourists I suppose.'

'You said it. The place would be dead without them.'

Hillary took a long sip and sighed in satisfaction. 'Nice village though.'

The barman smiled. 'Nice if you can afford it. Me, I share a three-bed old council house with two mates in back-of-beyond Burford. We're buying the place together. Only way we can afford a mortgage. Who the hell knows what we'll do if ever one of us wants to get married and have kids.'

Hillary grimaced. 'Know what you mean. Me, I live on a narrowboat. Only thing I can afford,' she lied.

227

The barman nodded thoughtfully. 'The canal, huh?'

'Mind you, even they're getting pricey nowadays,' Hillary warned him.

He sighed. 'I hear you. Still, it's a thought.'

Hillary grinned. 'I wouldn't mind living in that big house next door,' she said. 'I couldn't even see it from the road, but I know I want to live in it.'

The barman laughed. 'Heyford Court. Yeah, it's choice. A bit run-down now though. Could do with renovating, know what I mean? One of those big barns of a place, nearly three hundred-years-old.'

'A young family living there?'

'No, which is a shame. Could have done with some youngsters to cheer it up. No, there's just the one bloke living there. Lucky sod. Still, it's often the way, isn't it? I think his family's been there for donkey's years, but he's the last of his line. Sad in a way. There's no place for the likes of them in this world now. Everyone's waiting for him to get married and have a few kids, but he's in his fifties, so he'd better get a move on, if he's going to.'

'Sounds to me like some woman should have snapped him up by now,' she said craftily.

'Oh, I expect a few have tried,' the barman

smiled, checked that the man sitting down the other end didn't want another drink, and turned back to her. He smiled flirtatiously.

'You might be his type. Care to give it a go?' he asked, flashing that white grin at her.

Hillary gurgled over him lemon and lime. 'Too old for all that.'

'Never!' he said gallantly. 'Mind you, he's not there at the moment anyway. Left suddenly a few days ago. According to the lady who 'does' for him, he went abroad for a holiday. Must be nice for some, huh? To just swan off whenever the fancy takes you.'

'Who knows? Perhaps he'll come back with some dusky young Polynesian bride?' Hillary mused. 'So, what about you? Surely there's some rich matron *you* can marry, who can whisk you away from that three-bed semi of yours?' She blinked her big brown eyes at him and he laughed.

'I wish! But nah, nothing doing. All the birds around here are already married to their sugar daddies and wouldn't give a jobbing bartender a second look.'

'What? No sugar mummies around here at all?'

'Nope. Well, not unless you want to count the countess,' he laughed at the unintended pun. 'She's one of those Germanic types. She's available — lives in the big barn conversion at the bottom end of the village. Trouble is she's eighty if she's a day.'

And somehow, Hillary didn't think her name would be Annie. Damn. She chatted and flirted some more, and discussed various other villagers, but no obvious contenders stuck out.

So just who the hell had their murder victim come here to see? And just how had he expected to make his fortune in this unlikely oasis of carefully-guarded money?

She had the idea that once she knew the answers to those questions, her case would be all but solved.

11

Gemma Fordham woke early the next day. She rolled over in bed, scowled at the electronic 'talking' clock, and saw that it wasn't yet six. She sighed and yawned, and felt the man beside her stir.

She watched him reach out a hand that touched first the table top, then the cord of the clock and, finger-walking along it, reached the clock itself, counted the buttons carefully along and pressed one.

An electronic voice said 'The time is five, fifty-two, a.m.'

Guy Brindley sighed. 'You're awake early.'

'It's this case I'm on. I think it's going to break soon.'

'Got a lead?'

'It's not that so much. But Hillary Greene thinks it is, and I've been watching her. She's good. So, naturally, I think it is too.'

Guy's sightless dark-brown eyes frowned up at the ceiling. 'You sound as if you trust her judgement, and you've only known her a week. It's not like you to make up your mind about someone so quickly.' It also wasn't like her to give someone, especially another woman, so much credit, either. But, of course, he never said so.

He felt her shrug and curl on to her side, her long, lean length pressing against him. 'I researched her before I transferred on to her team. I know DS Donleavy really rates her as a detective, and her conviction rate is impressive. I can just see why, that's all. She's smart, methodical, careful, and well-organized. But she's also good with witnesses, and intuitive. I'd back her instincts any day of the week. And Barrington fairly worships the ground she walks on, she's best friends with the Super, and Paul Danvers, I reckon, fancies her and gives her a wide scope, so she's got plenty of room to play her own game her own way. Why shouldn't she be successful? Given all that, I'd be successful as well.'

Guy smiled. That was more like it. That was the girl he knew and wouldn't let himself love. For his own instincts were fairly good too, and he'd known within one month of becoming Gemma's lover that if he ever let himself fall for her, she'd tear him to pieces. She had ferocious ambition, and a love of the good life, and guarded herself and her emotions as carefully as Fort Knox cared for its gold. As long as he played the game by her rules, things ticked along nicely.

But after nearly three years together, he wondered exactly where a relationship such as theirs could possibly go. But again, he never voiced it. When it came time to leave, he knew, it would be Gemma who did the leaving.

'Well, I'm as good at my job as she is,' Gemma insisted now, and Guy's hand grappled to find hers and squeeze it.

'I know you are, sweetheart. You don't have to keep proving yourself to me.' He was of the opinion that Gemma's family was largely to blame for her emotional make-up. Her father and all four brothers were firemen. Gemma, the youngest, was something of a cuckoo in the nest. The youngest and only girl, her mother had died when she was ten, probably just when she needed her the most. To go through puberty and teenage angst, in an all-male, testosterone environment, probably accounted for a lot of things in her nature. Her hard-headedness and cool heart for one. Her martial arts for another. She'd refused to enter the fire service, choosing the police as being different enough to be rebellious, but tough and challenging enough for her to sneer at any sibling who might take pot shots at her chosen career. It was, he knew, her ambition to be a superintendent by the time she was forty, and commander by fifty. He thought she'd almost certainly make it. In fact, he wouldn't be surprised to see her as chief constable one day.

Now he felt her roll out of bed and get dressed. 'Not going in already, surely?'

'Like I said, the case is breaking. I want to get an early start. I'm still not sure where Greene is heading though. She keeps her thoughts to herself.' She paused in the act of slipping on a pair of dark-blue slacks. 'I don't think she likes me,' Gemma added. She didn't sound worried, or even uneasy, but, nevertheless, it made Guy frown. It was simply not like her to care what *anyone* thought.

When she'd told him she was transferring from Reading to Kidlington, he'd instantly asked her to move in permanently with him, hoping, perhaps, that this was some sort of a sign that she'd decided to settle down with him permanently. And why not? His tenure at the college, plus the money he made on lecture tours and a private income from his father's side of the family, meant that he was always in funds. He lived in a big house, and they took holidays abroad every time her working schedule allowed. He knew she enjoyed the lifestyle he could provide. But now that she was here at last, he was beginning to feel as if there was far more going on than he knew about.

He still wasn't sure why she'd been so set on transferring to Hillary Greene's team, for instance. And the way she seemed to be almost obsessional about her new boss was making him feel distinctly uneasy.

'Does it matter if she doesn't like you?' he asked, cautiously. He knew, from bitter experience, that Gemma would shut down if she thought for one instant he was probing into her life — or, even worse, her psyche.

''Course not,' Gemma said flatly.

'I mean, is she the sort to make life hard for you, just because you don't get on? Is she the spiteful sort?'

'No,' Gemma said, her voice sounding, to his acute ears anyway, almost disappointed.

'Do *you* like *her*?' he asked casually, and from the sharp movement the mattress made, realized that she must have turned to look at him more fully, perhaps sensing just a little too much curiosity on his part for her taste. He kept his face bland. Or at least, he hoped he had.

'Don't know yet,' she said at last, and stood up, slipping a matching blue jacket over her shoulders. She finger-combed her hair, and slipped on her watch. A quick brush of her teeth, wash of her face and hands, and she'd be ready. Gemma despised women who took an hour to prepare themselves for the day. She doubted Hillary Greene, for instance, took much longer than she did herself.

Hillary Greene.

Just how *did* she feel about Hillary Greene now that she'd known her for a few days, and was working a murder case with the woman?

Once, of course, she'd hated her, though they'd never met. Then she'd pretended that she meant nothing. Now, working with her, watching her, always watching her, Gemma wasn't sure any more what she felt.

She shrugged, leaned over the bed and kissed Guy hard, on the lips. 'See you tonight.' It sounded more like a threat than a lover's promise, and Guy smiled wryly.

He listened to her leave, then put his fingers over his tingling lips. He sighed heavily, turned over, and closed his eyes.

But he never slept.

★   ★   ★

Gemma's early start paid dividends almost at once. At her desk, she read through the murder book, then made a check list of all the 'stay outs' still pending. At seven thirty, she was fairly sure of catching most of them having breakfast, and was lucky in two cases. She made an appointment to see one later tonight, after he'd finished work, but the other, a Mrs Sylvia Mulberry, was going to be in all day, and agreed to see her at once.

Gemma left a note on Hillary's desk telling her where she'd gone and her estimated time back at the office. The drive back to Deddington was a fairly easy one at first, since most of the traffic was coming into Oxford, not out. Once nearer Deddington itself, the rush hour traffic for those going into Banbury began to clog the roads around her, and she turned on the radio to listen to the local news.

The more sensational aspects of Wayne Sutton's murder — namely the red paper heart found with the body, and his career as a gigolo — had all been kept under wraps, so the story no longer even rated a mention. But that might all change when an arrest was made. And that an arrest *would* be made, she never for a moment doubted. Failure wasn't part of her make-up, and this was her first murder case as second fiddle, so to speak. Even if Hillary Greene for some reason, fumbled this murder case (and that would be the first time she ever had) she, Gemma, would pick up the reins. After all, she knew everything Hillary knew. Her DI made it a point, with the murder book, to ensure that every member of her team knew all that she knew. A generous act, some would have said. Just asking for trouble, others might have said. But Gemma got the clear impression that Hillary Greene wasn't a glory seeker. She took her training up of younger officers seriously, for a start. Gemma knew that both Janine Tyler and Tommy Lynch, the DS and DC on Hillary's team before her own arrival, had both risen a rank and moved on, and that Greene seemed genuinely pleased about it. And she'd seen for herself how she was handling Barrington, showing him the ropes, giving him gradually more and more responsibility and firmly guiding him in the right direction.

What's more, she knew from her own efforts at getting transferred to Hillary's team, that both Mel Mallow, DS Donleavy, and her own DI back at Reading, were all happy to hand her over to DI Greene for the next level of her education. Without false modesty, Gemma knew that her superiors considered her a high flier. And they wouldn't have transferred her unless they'd all agreed that Hillary Greene would be good for her.

The thought made her feel vaguely uncomfortable. Already Hillary was trusting her with high priority stuff. And she wasn't constantly looking over her shoulder and checking up on her either.

If Gemma Fordham had been anyone other than Gemma Fordham, it might have occurred to her that her uneasy feeling could be put down to a guilty conscience. Instead, she turned off the radio and wondered when she could safely get on to Hillary's boat and search it.

★ ★ ★

Keith Barrington drove into work early too, but even so, saw from the note on Hillary's desk, that Gemma Fordham had been even quicker off the mark.

He sat down at his computer and stared morosely at his desk top. Gavin had returned to London yesterday, but hadn't called him last night, or this morning either, so he had no way of knowing how things had gone at Sir Reginald's questioning.

He suspected that Hillary Greene, who was popular with everyone, and had had twenty years to work up her own network, would be able to find out with a single phone call. If he asked her. But how could he ask her without explaining why?

No. He wasn't ready to trust her with all that yet. Besides, it might all blow over. You never knew your luck.

★ ★ ★

Gemma rang the bell at the cottage opposite the victim's residence, and smiled briefly at the woman who opened the door. She already had her ID card out, and let the other woman scrutinize it.

Sylvia Mulberry was a short brunette with slightly myopic eyes. She looked to be struggling manfully against entering her sixties, but was failing. The fine crepe lines around her eyes and lips told their own story, as did the raised veins on her ageing hands.

'Oh yes, you rang earlier. Please, come on in. I've only just got back from a business trip to Scotland, so I didn't know about Wayne until last night. I suppose it's about him, right?'

Gemma confirmed that it was, and followed the older woman into a small, neat living-room. The art, she noticed, was strictly of the old-fashioned school. So she was probably not one of Wayne's clients.

Sylvia Mulberry sat down on the couch and crossed her legs. She was wearing a long plaid skirt and white blouse, and had a ring on almost every finger. She yawned now, and instantly apologized. 'Sorry. Like I said, I only got back from Scotland late yesterday afternoon. What with unpacking, writing up my report, and then gossiping about Wayne, I didn't get to bed till late. So, what can I tell you?'

'When did you leave for Scotland, Mrs Mulberry?'

'First of May. Travelled up by train, first thing.' She gave a slight laugh. 'I try not to fly if I don't have to.'

Gemma smiled. 'And you knew Wayne Sutton well?'

'No, not well. He moved in over the road some time ago. An artist, I understand. Always seemed very pleasant. I was worried he might be loud — you know, being an artist, that he might throw all sorts of parties and invite around undesirable types, but luckily, that never happened. The only people I saw visiting him were mostly middle-aged women. Very respectable.'

Gemma wondered if she really was ignorant of what Wayne Sutton had done with those respectable middle-aged women, or if she'd guessed and was pretending not to know. Either way, she decided not to push it.

'Did you see anything on the day before you left, Mrs Mulberry? That would be the afternoon and evening of the last day in April. Monday night, in fact?'

Sylvia opened her mouth as if to give an automatic 'no', in response, then promptly closed it again. A near-smile crossed her face, and then she frowned, as if at the inappropriateness of it.

'Well, now that you ask, I *did* notice a bit of fracas over there. About five-thirty, six o'clock time. Mind you, I only noticed because I was upstairs packing for the trip. And it was so hot, I had all the bedroom windows open — as did Wayne I suppose, because I could hear the raised voices quite distinctly.'

Gemma felt her breath quicken, and forced herself to write calmly into her notebook. 'Raised voices? Did you recognize them?'

'Well, his, yes,' Sylvia said. 'But hers — no. Well, why would I?'

Gemma nodded. She had the feeling that Sylvia Mulberry was probably one of those rare women who really didn't care much what their neighbours got up to. Nice for Wayne, probably, but a bit of a blow for the police.

'Could you make out what the argument was about?'

'No, not really,' Sylvia said, instantly confirming her judgement. 'I don't much care for other people's arguments. Besides, I was going back and forth from the drawers and to my wardrobe and back to the suitcase, and then into the bathroom for toiletries, and so on. So I only heard snatches.'

'But those snatches?' Gemma prompted, reluctant to give up.

'Oh, well, I gather the woman was berating

him for something or other. Another woman, I thought.'

'I don't suppose you saw the woman enter Wayne's cottage?'

'No,' Sylvia said, and sighed. 'But I did see her leave.'

Gemma smiled. 'And can you describe her please?'

Sylvia screwed up her eyes in effort, then opened them again and gave a shrug. 'Well she was about my size. Not overly tall, you know. And she had short red hair. She had on a rather bright kaftan thing — it looked expensive. That's about all I can tell you.'

Gemma smiled radiantly.

It was enough.

★ ★ ★

'And the description was a dead ringer for Denise Collier?' Hillary Green said, half an hour later, as she listened to her sergeant's report.

'Right, guv,' Gemma said, having read Barrington's account of the interview with her, which had included a fairly comprehensive physical description of the witness. 'Given what other people have already said about Denise Collier being more possessive and jealous than the rest, it all fits.'

Hillary nodded. Indeed it did. 'And Ms Collier was very careful not to tell us about it when we interviewed her, wasn't she?' she glanced across at Barrington, and smiled. 'OK, you and Keith go and bring her in.'

She glanced across at Frank Ross's empty desk, and sighed. 'Call in at Frank's place on the way. If he's there, roust him out of bed and take him as well. I want you to go in mob handed and rattle her a bit.' Besides, it was the only way of being sure of getting some work out of the lazy sod.

'Right, guv,' Gemma said with a smile. She was rather looking forward to this.

★ ★ ★

At the window of a downstairs kitchenette, George Davies was making himself a mug of tea. The window overlooked the car park, and as he raised his mug to his lips, he saw the striking blonde woman again.

He blew on his piping hot tea thoughtfully.

It wasn't here that he saw her. Not in Kidlington. Of that he was suddenly certain. And it wasn't on a case either. He had a pretty good memory for suspects and witnesses alike — a facility he'd used to good effect on the beat.

So he must have seen her in some sort of a

244

social setting. Or at least, in some kind of situation where he hadn't felt the particular need to memorize her face. But where?

He sighed, and took his mug through to the duty room to check the roster. It'd come back to him sooner or later.

★   ★   ★

Denise Collier was not happy. She wasn't happy to be taken from her home at nine o'clock in the morning, before she'd got her face on. She wasn't happy to be put into the back of a car by three near-strangers, in full view of all her curious, bitchy, gossiping neighbours. And she sure as hell wasn't happy to be taken to a police station, and shown into some dreary little room.

The moment Hillary Greene walked in, she said snappily, 'I want to see a solicitor.'

Hillary Greene smiled, and turned around again. 'All right, Ms Collier. Do you have his phone number? Or would you like me to arrange the duty solicitor to see you?'

'Certainly not! A man from Cummings, Lester and Bolt sees to all my legal needs. Please call them and ask for Mr Milton Lester.'

Hillary smiled again and left, indicating Frank to stay with her. So it was going to be

245

one of those days, was it? Well, she was probably due one. Beside her, Barrington and Fordham glanced at each other uneasily. It was always a complication when a witness asked for a brief.

'OK, Keith, get on it,' Hillary said. 'Gemma, while we're waiting, I want you to take a look at the progress the men have made so far on Heyford Sudbury. See what you can add to it.'

Gemma nodded. 'And, guv, there's no history of stalking or mental illness in Collier's past that I've been able to find.'

Hillary sighed in acceptance.

Outside, the first cloud in days, or so it seemed, passed across the sun and threw the day into welcome shade. The weather forecasters, however, hadn't predicted any break in the heatwave.

★ ★ ★

Milton Lester was a tall, thin, seventy-something, who looked very uneasy to be in a police interview room. No doubt Denise Collier had used him for her divorce and the buying of her house, but he looked the sort who'd run a mile at the mention of the word 'criminal'. Hillary also doubted that he'd seen the inside of a courtroom for years, but she

246

was not about to look a gift horse in the mouth.

She introduced herself to the tape, added that DS Ross, Mr Milton Lester, solicitor, and a PC Davies, were also present. She gave the interview tape number, and then Denise Collier's name.

Then she looked across at Denise and said softly, 'Lying to the police in the course of a murder investigation is most unwise, Ms Collier. If nothing else, it can lead to charges such as wilful obstruction of police officers in the course of their duties, and attempting to pervert the course of justice.'

She saw Milton Lester tug on one cufflink uneasily.

Denise Collier shrugged graphically. 'I have no idea what you're talking about.'

'You told us that on the evening Wayne Sutton was murdered, you stayed at home all the afternoon, evening and night, and never went out.'

'That's right. I did.'

'That wasn't true,' Hillary said flatly.

'Yes, it was!'

Hillary sighed. 'I'm giving you the opportunity to change your testimony, Ms Collier. I strongly advise that you take it.'

'My client has already answered your

question, Inspector Greene,' Milton Lester piped up.

Hillary sighed and stood up. 'Very well.' She terminated the interview for the tape, and a look of vast relief crossed Denise Collier's face.

'I can go?' she asked, making to rise.

'No, Ms Collier, you can't,' Hillary said flatly. 'You will stay here whilst I organize an identity parade.'

Denise stared at her, then looked uncertainly across at her solicitor. 'Can they do that?' she asked faintly.

Milton Lester nodded miserably to indicate that, indeed, they could. For a moment, Hillary thought that Denise was going to give in. Then she got a hard, tight, mean look on her face and shrugged graphically, obviously deciding to take her chances.

Hillary shrugged and left them to it. Frank Ross, arms folded across his chest, continued to stare at her insolently. Milton Lester fiddled with his cufflinks.

Outside, Hillary nodded to Gemma, who was watching from the observation room. 'Go and get Mrs Mulberry.'

Gemma hurried out.

Hillary reached for her mobile and called upstairs. 'DC Barrington,' the familiar male voice answered.

'Keith, we're doing an identity parade. Go out and round up five women for me — shortish, reddish hair. You'll find a few WPC's who fit the description, but make sure they change into civvies. And ask Super O'Gorman's secretary — she fits, oh, and the dinner lady, Vera. It'll give her a laugh. You should have enough with that lot.'

'Right, guv.'

★ ★ ★

Syliva Mulberry didn't look very happy when she walked into the observation room, but she seemed co-operative enough.

After introducing her to DI Greene, Gemma took her through it carefully. 'It's very simple, Mrs Mulberry. In a moment, six women, all carrying a numbered card, will walk in through the door and line up. They can't see you, and will not be told your name. All you have to do is look at them carefully, and tell us if you see the woman you saw leaving Wayne Sutton's cottage on the afternoon of the thirtieth April. If you want a closer look at one of them, just call the number of the one you want, and we'll ask her to step closer to the window,' she added, mindful of the witness's myopia.

'All right. But what if I don't see her there?' Sylvia asked.

'Just say so, Mrs Mulberry,' Hillary said calmly, and the other women nodded, and straightened her shoulders slightly, as if prepared to do an onerous duty. Hillary, satisfied, nodded to Gemma, who pressed a buzzer. A moment later, six women, and a male PC, walked into the room.

Hillary ran her eye over them and nodded. All six women were of a muchness. Nothing there for a defence barrister to cry foul over.

Denise Collier, looking pale and defiant, was number two.

As always, when giving an identity parade, Hillary felt the tension build in her shoulders. It was always the same. There was something intrinsically dramatic about proceedings like this.

'It's number two,' Sylvia Mulberry said firmly.

Gemma smiled triumphantly, and Hillary thanked her.

'Will I have to go to court and say as much again?' Sylvia asked, and Hillary spread her hands in a so-so gesture.

'It's hard to say at this point, Mrs Mulberry. Why? Would it be a problem for you?'

'No,' Sylvia said at last. 'It's her all right.

But I don't want to get tied up in any court case. I'm a busy woman. I'm not sure I can get time off work.'

Hillary nodded, but was largely uninterested in her woes. 'The WPC outside will drive you back, Mrs Mulberry.'

★　★　★

Denise Collier glanced up when Hillary came in to the interview room for the second time. Once again, Hillary went through the routine for the tape.

'Well, Ms Collier, you were picked out of the line-up,' Hillary began briskly, facing her across the table once more. 'The witness who both saw and heard you arguing with Wayne Sutton just hours before he was murdered was quite firm and adamant in her identification. Now, given that, are you prepared to tell us the truth?'

Milton Lester leaned forward and whispered in her ear. Denise Collier scowled. Milton whispered something else, and she sighed heavily.

'Oh all right,' she said petulantly. 'I went to Wayne's cottage that day. It was about four o'clock.'

Hillary coughed gently. 'Our witness puts it closer to half-five, six o'clock.'

Denise scowled. 'Nosy old bat! I suppose it was one of those gossiping old biddies who lived around there? Fine, perhaps it was later. But after we argued, I left, and that's that. I never went back, and I never saw Wayne alive again.'

Suddenly, she burst into tears.

Milton Lester looked appalled.

Hillary sighed and reached for the tissues.

12

Denise Collier dried her eyes, and sniffed hard. She shot Hillary Greene an 'it's-all-your-fault' look and dabbed her eyes again.

'I keep telling you people. *I* was the only one Wayne *truly* loved. *I'm* the only one who's got a right to mourn him.'

Hillary nodded gravely, and asked flatly, 'What did you do when you left his place?'

'I went straight home, of course,' Denise said, sounding surprised. 'I needed a drink and a shower. And before you ask, I stayed home all the rest of the night.'

Hillary nodded, and reached into her case to bring out the red paper heart found on the body. It was now encased in a see-through evidence bag. There had, of course, been no fingerprints found on it. 'Do you recognize this, Ms Collier?' she asked, watching the other woman closely. She didn't think Denise Collier was the sort of woman to have a poker face, and Hillary was fairly confident that if the suspect did in fact recognize it, then it would be evident. But the only emotions she could see on the redhead's face were a faint scowl of belligerence, followed by a touch of puzzlement.

'No. Why should I? What is it?' she leaned forward for a better look as Hillary held it up and turned it around, the better to display it. 'It's just a cut-out, red paper heart,' Denise said, as if wondering what the trick was.

Hillary nodded. 'Yes. Somebody gave it to Wayne Sutton,' she said, with masterly understatement.

Denise Collier laughed spitefully. 'I dare say one of his dozy old women gave it to him,' she said scornfully.

'Are you sure you didn't?' Hillary asked mildly, and again Denise Collier laughed.

'Don't be daft! *I'm* the one who receives valentines, not gives them out. I expect my men to pay court to me — not the other way round. I wouldn't be caught dead doing something so . . . yucky!' And she shuddered. 'Wayne must have laughed himself sick at whichever silly cow gave him that.'

Hillary very much doubted that Wayne Sutton had been alive to do any laughing at the time he was given this particular valentine. She sighed, gave the usual customary warnings about not leaving the area without notifying the police, and let her go.

Milton Lester looked even more relieved than his client.

'You don't like her for it, guv,' Barrington said, as they all trooped back to the office.

'You saw and heard what I did,' Hillary countered. 'What do you think?'

Barrington nodded. 'She might be a very good actress though.'

'Always a thought to keep in the back of your mind, Constable, when interviewing witnesses,' Hillary advised.

Back at their desks, Gemma Fordham picked up the Heyford Sudbury file. 'Guv, I'd like to follow up on some things for this. You need me in the office for a few hours?'

Hillary shook her head. 'No. Keep on it,' she said, and watched as her sergeant collected her gear and left. She was sure, if anybody could find whatever needle in the haystack she was looking for at the Cotswold village, it would probably be Gemma Fordham.

Hillary yawned and reached for the first file in her in-tray, but when the phone rang, she moved the direction of her hand towards that instead.

'Hello, can I speak to DI Hillary Greene please?' The voice was one she vaguely remembered hearing before, and belonged to one of the many white-coated, scientific boffins who inhabited the forensic science laboratories.

'Speaking.'

'Case file . . . ' Hillary rapidly wrote down the digits and letters quoted to her, immediately recognizing it as belonging to her murder case. 'Yes, the Wayne Sutton inquiry,' she acknowledged, thus letting the boffin on the other end know that *she* knew the case number as well.

'Fine. It concerns the victim's car.'

Hillary felt herself being taken by surprise — something she was not particularly used to. Since the victim's car had been parked in the garage throughout the investigation, it had been obvious that Wayne Sutton had walked to his rendezvous with death. Consequently, she hadn't given his car a second thought. Why should she? It couldn't possibly have any bearing on the case.

No doubt its low-priority status was the reason why a forensic report was only now coming in on it.

'Yes?' she asked, curious and wary. Had she missed something? Had she (every cop's nightmare) made a serious, gaping mistake?

'It's basically clean. Plenty of DNA traces, fibres, fingerprints, etc., nearly all the vic's. Evidence of other-people usage, of course, but nothing to ring any alarm bells. But my supervisor thought you might like to know that we've lifted a very recent set of prints from the passenger door. Very recent. They superimpose all others, so were the last fingers to touch the door before we impounded it. They don't fit any member of the deceased's family or, ah, close circle of friends.'

Hillary knew that the uniforms would have arranged for all the vic's nearest and dearest to be printed — including all his 'women'. It was routine.

'Now that's interesting,' she said. A stranger? The mysterious Annie, perhaps? Had they, at last, got some tangible proof of her existence?

'But they do match up with the victim's girlfriend's father. A Mr Victor Freeman.'

Hillary blinked, and immediately focused her mind on the nurseryman. The last time she'd seen him, she'd been interviewing him at his garden centre, shortly after breaking the news of Wayne's death to his girlfriend. And, as she recalled, Victor Freeman had made no real secret of the fact that he'd thought his daughter could do a whole lot better.

In fact, she'd come away with the distinct impression that he wouldn't give Wayne Sutton the time of day. So what were his fresh prints doing on the victim's car?

'Now that *is* interesting,' she said softly, thanked him, and hung up.

★　★　★

Outside, Gemma Fordham walked briskly to her car. She had no intention of going to Heyford Sudbury, or the library. She had only one destination in mind, and it was not five minutes drive down the street.

Also in the car park, George Davies was just starting up his patrol car when he spotted her. 'There she is!' he said, sounding like a twitcher who'd just spotted a Dartford Warbler.

His long-time partner, Ian Gill, jumped. 'What? Who?'

'The leggy blonde, over there. Remember, I told you about her,' George reminded him. 'She keeps ringing a bell in the old brainbox but I just can't place her. I told you about it yesterday.'

Ian, like George, was on the edge of retirement and just as glad of it, and now he stared across the parked cars and gave a slow, appreciative wolf whistle. 'Very nice. Legs right up to her bum. Bit skinny for my taste though.'

'Let your Jenny hear you say that,' George warned with a laugh. 'So she doesn't ring any bells with you?'

'No. Well, I know she's DI Greene's new sergeant. Bit of ballbreaker they say. Does all those kung-fu moves, you know? Half the station's drooling over her, but she looks like one to stay clear of to me.' Thus having given his verdict, Ian turned around to pull on his seat belt, wondering when he'd be clocking off that night.

George Davies, however, still had his mind firmly on the blonde. 'DI Greene. You mean Hillary Greene?' he asked. And the moment he said the DI's full name, in a flash, he remembered where he'd seen the mysterious blonde before.

Of course. Of course! With Ronnie bloody Greene. That wanker.

'Yeah, that's right,' Ian confirmed, oblivious to his partner's revelation. 'Well, she needed someone after her old DS married Mel Mallow. And let's face it, Frank Ross is a waste of space, so she's been coping with only a DC. And he's that Barrington fellah from London. The one who decked his old sergeant.' Ian shook his head. 'You ask me, she could do with all the help she can get.'

George, for once, was disinclined to gossip, or pull the wings off CID butterflies. Like most men in uniform, he had an ambivalent relationship with plain clothes, but now he was too busy thinking of other things.

Shit. Hillary Greene. She couldn't know about her new DS, could she? And then he swore under his breath even more graphically. And neither could the top brass. They sure as hell would never have assigned the leggy blonde to Hillary's team if they knew she'd been Ronnie Greene's one time squeeze.

He felt himself begin to sweat. What the hell should he do? With only a few weeks to go before his retirement, his first instinct was to forget about it. A man in his position didn't need to rock any boats. And that went even more for boats that swam in the same lake as the likes of DCI Paul Danvers, that toady from York, or Mel Mallow. Or Detective Chief Superintendent Donleavy for that matter.

The sweat began to itch between his shoulder blades. No, he should just forget about it and walk away. And yet. Like the rest of the station house, George Davies both liked and admired Hillary Greene. She'd weathered the internal investigation into her bent husband, and herself, with grim dignity. She'd always had a rep for being fair. And lately, she'd handled a few good murder inquiries. Then she'd got that medal for taking a bullet for Mel Mallow. A genuine heroine, no question about it.

Turning his back on her just didn't sit

right. Damn it, if *he* were in her place, *he'd* want to know about it.

It was all coming back to him now. There'd been a bad case over in Reading — a kiddie had been kidnapped. A similar case in the same city, three years ago, had resulted in a child's body being found in a large area of waste-ground and scrub, on the city outskirts. The brass there had asked for, and got, large numbers of uniformed manpower from neighbouring forces to help with the finger-tip search of the area. George and about twenty others from Thames Valley had been roped in.

DI Ronnie Greene had also been around for about a week, since he'd handled a similar missing kiddie case from his own patch, that they thought might match up. As he recalled, neither the kiddie, nor a body, had ever been found.

But Ronnie Greene, billeted away from home, had run true to form, and had quickly found himself a woman — the usual young, blonde crumpet. George could even remember the DI boasting in the pub they'd all used to congregate in of an evening, that this one was a student at the Uni. Which made her a bit more brainy than he usually liked them, but what the hell.

George could see them together now,

drinking at a corner table, heads close together, the girl looking smitten. Yeah, it had been her all right.

And surely Hillary Greene had a right to know her latest DS's history?

But then he thought about just what it was he'd have to do in order to tell her, and the sweat migrated from his armpit and forehead and broke out all over his face. He could almost feel himself heating up.

Embarrassing or what?

What exactly was he supposed to do? Just walk up to her, and say, 'Hey, DI Greene, ma'am. Did you know that blonde sergeant of yours was once a floozy of your late husband?'

'What we doing still sitting here then, George?' Ian asked, sounding amused. And with a start, George realized he'd been sat there like a lemon, staring out of the windscreen for the past few minutes. Gemma Fordham had already started her car and was long gone.

With an amiable swear word, George Davies started the patrol car, and headed out of HQ, still with no idea what he was going to do about his new-found and deeply unwanted knowledge.

★   ★   ★

Keith Barrington drove to Banbury in near silence. He was very much aware of his DI sitting beside him, but Hillary Greene didn't seem in the mood to chat.

Perhaps the memory of the telling-off she'd given him was still too clear in both their minds.

In fact, Hillary Greene was thinking about red paper hearts. There was something about it that just didn't sit right with her but she couldn't, for the life of her, put her finger on what it was.

It hadn't got wet, so the killer must have put it on Wayne's corpse after dragging his head and shoulders from the stream. Too carefully planned? Too pedantic and neat? Would a woman, presumably heart-broken and in a rage, be so precise?

Well, possibly, yes. A woman could have killed in a cold rage. The death was almost certainly premeditated, after all. First with the note luring him there, and the paper heart properly clinched it. Nobody went for a walk in the meadows with a red paper heart already cut out, did they? Not unless they already had a use for it all planned out. No, the killer had meant to kill Wayne, *did* kill Wayne, and left her message. The red heart.

So it wasn't that that was niggling her.

She sighed heavily and shook her head. She

could drive herself crazy trying to figure it out. Perhaps she should just be grateful that no more young men had turned up dead and adorned with the bloody things. A serial killer on the loose was the last thing anyone wanted.

'We bringing Freeman in, guv?' Barrington asked, taking her heavy sigh as an invitation to talk.

'No, I don't think so,' Hillary said. She still couldn't see the car as being all that important. There'd been no signs of it parked near the crime scene, and no one had seen their vic driving it just prior to his death. 'It'll probably turn out to be just something we need to clear up, that's all.'

★   ★   ★

Gemma Fordham turned into the narrow lane that lead to the hamlet of Thrupp. Here, the hedges grew thick and close to the road, shutting out the bright sun and making her feel just slightly claustrophobic. Within seconds, however, she saw the cheerful, khaki glitter of sunlight on the Oxford Canal, and the road opened out, revealing a pub called The Boat. She parked in its car park but didn't go inside for a much-needed long cold drink.

Instead, she got out and walked to the tow-path, glancing both ways down the canal — to her right, leading further into Kidlington itself. Left, and more open countryside. There was a long line of moored craft in either direction, far more than she'd expected.

Guessing that Hillary Greene wouldn't be moored too far from the road, she turned right and began walking, checking the names of the boats as she went.

Further down the canal behind her, she could hear the gentle chug-chugging of an approaching boat. The speed limit on the canal, she knew, was a mind-blowing 4 mph. It would have driven her crazy to be a passenger on anything that went that slow.

She walked on past boats that were mainly painted the bright, primary colours of traditional narrowboats — mostly blues, greens and reds. But it was a narrowboat painted a more sophisticated blue-grey, white, black and gold that bore the name she was looking for.

'*Mollern*.'

With a smile, Gemma hopped on the back and reached inside her bag for her newly-minted key.

★ ★ ★

265

Hillary walked into the small garden centre shop and saw Victor Freeman right away. He was behind a tiny counter, selling a jar of something poisonous to an attentive old man.

'This'll kill elder for sure,' Victor Freeman was saying, 'but you have to be careful. Cut the trunk or side shoots down as low as you can first, and then brush this on. But then you must cover it with something — a polythene bag, an old Tesco bag, something like that. If you've got any pets, or if cats come into your garden, it could kill them, so I'd heap some stones or something over it as well just to be sure. And be careful not to get any of it on any leaves of plants that you want to keep.'

The old man said something very nasty about elder, something almost as nasty about cats, thanked him, paid and left. She noticed that Vic Freeman had noticed her the moment she'd walked into the shop, and had been casting quick, worried looks her way throughout the recital. Now he raised a tight smile as she approached the counter.

'Mr Freeman. You remember me?'

Vic Freeman smiled a bit more. 'Of course, DI Greene. You're unforgettable.' And then the smile fled, and a look of extreme consternation crossed his slightly freckled face. 'Not that I meant . . . I mean, I didn't intend to imply . . . Oh hell.'

Hillary smiled to show that no offence had been taken. 'Your wife not here today?'

'She's out delivering a van load of Leylandii to Cropredy. People *will* still buy them.' He sighed, as if to say, 'what-can-you-do?'

Hillary smiled in sympathy, but got right down to business. 'When did you last ride in Wayne Sutton's car, Mr Freeman?'

Vic Freeman's jaw dropped. 'What? Huh, never. I don't think I've ever been in his car.'

Hillary sighed heavily. So much for just clearing a few things up.

Why did people always have to lie to her?

$\star$ $\star$ $\star$

Gemma Fordham ducked her head carefully to avoid banging it on the roof as she walked awkwardly down the three steep steps that took her into the body of the narrowboat.

And instantly felt uncomfortable.

Stretching before her was a narrow corridor, so narrow in fact, that she almost felt as if she needed to turn sideways and scuttle down it like a crab. Being tall, she also felt as if the roof of the boat was about to crash down on her head at any moment. The windows, although they let in a lot of light, felt stingy, and the relative darkness inside the boat contrasted unpleasantly with the bright sunshine outside. What's more, she felt somehow belittled. It took her a moment to realize that the floor of the boat was far lower than she was used to, and the windows, far higher. Instead of looking out of the windows on a more or less eye-to-eye level, as you did in a house, on a narrowboat the windows were higher, making you look up.

She opened the first door, and found herself looking at a tiny, neat bedroom. The single bed was neatly made. Quickly, she set about a methodical search. She was wearing gloves, of course, and started on the wardrobe first, checking the pockets of jackets and blouses, trousers and coats, careful not to rearrange the order of the clothes.

Nothing.

She ran her clever fingers around the hems, lapels, collars, anywhere a slip of paper might have been sewn in. Nothing rustled, nothing felt unduly stiff. The stitches had that unpicked look. A tiny chest of drawers was next.

Nothing.

Feeling a little like Alice in Wonderland, after drinking from the bottle that made her into a giant in a small world, Gemma moved on to the next door.

Here a minuscule bathroom made her eyes widen. How on earth did a grown woman live in this doll's house? The shower had enough room just about to turn around in, and the loo was obviously one that required some special requirements. It wasn't a chemical one, but neither was it the sturdy kind she was used to that flushed loudly and with copious amounts of water.

She shuddered, and turned away from it, concentrating on a narrow shelf and tiny cabinet. She checked toothpaste and deodorant, even the bars of soap. Nothing.

Gemma, back in her days in uniform, knew a drug dealer who used to keep his stash in bars of soap. He'd cut them in half with a razor, hollow it out, stash the gear, then join the two halves together by wetting them and rubbing his hands over them. No doubt he'd thought that soap was the last place a strung out, filthy junkie would ever think of looking.

Hillary Greene's soap was pristine.

She walked on down the corridor, hearing the sound of the approaching narrowboat getting louder. But just then, the throttle was eased back. Presumably, it was going to moor up nearby. But that didn't worry her much. Why should it? The narrowboat community was, by its very nature, transitory. Even if someone saw her on this boat, how was the newcomer to know that it was not her property?

Gemma found herself approaching the biggest room on the vessel — if anything on this tiny pencil-box of a boat could be called big. The open-plan galley cum living area.

She sighed, and began with the only chair — a padded arm chair. Nothing.

With a sigh, she got down on her knees and started on the first cupboard, opening and checking packets of coffee, looking in cornflake boxes, digging a spoon around the sugar bowl.

A detailed and thorough search took time and patience, and Gemma, suddenly, was glad that the boat was so tiny. After all, there could only be a certain number of places where anybody could hide something in a dwelling like this.

* * *

Hillary Greene walked into the lobby of Headquarters, and nodded at Barrington. 'Take Mr Freeman into Interview Room Four, would you, Constable?' She could tell, by the absence of a light lit up over the door, that it was available. 'I'll only be a moment.'

Keith nodded and ushered through the bemused, and growingly worried, Victor

Freeman. He hadn't wanted to come to the station, but Hillary had been insistent. If he was going to lie to her, he could at least give her the courtesy of doing so on her home patch.

She went up to her desk to check on her messages, and have a cup of coffee. Let the man sweat for half an hour. It would do him good.

★ ★ ★

Nancy Walker hopped off her boat, *Willowsands*, and on to the towpath. She was wearing an old fashioned pair of turquoise hot pants that she'd bought in the seventies, and had worn practically every summer since. Her blouse was white lace — and she was braless underneath. For an old bird nudging fifty-five, she looked, at a distance, like a teenager.

Next, she retrieved a whopping great mallet from the prow of her boat, and proceeded to hammer iron pegs into the towpath, fore and aft, like the seasoned professional she was. She then tied off the ropes either end and stood up, looking around, a wide smile on her sun-kissed face.

She was glad to be back. Stratford-upon-Avon had been good to her, but there was only so much Shakespeare a gal could stand. A long-time divorcee, she liked her men young, and preferably to form a neat and orderly queue. In her time in Warwickshire, she'd been compared to practically every Shakespearean heroine there ever was.

Which was very gratifying. But, after a while, a bit wearing. Time, she'd decided, to return to Oxford, where the student body was far more diverse.

She glanced across at her old friend's boat, glad to see the *Mollern* in such good shape. Hillary must have had her repainted that spring. She was looking forward to catching up with her friend and hearing all her latest exploits.

She hopped back on board *Willowsands* and went to the fridge. She had plenty of ice, still. She'd make up a jug of margaritas, ready for when Hillary finally clocked off work. Then she heard the unmistakable sound of a narrowboat door closing, very close by, and moved curiously to her open door.

Outside, she saw a tall blonde woman hop off Hillary's boat, and she raised an eyebrow. She hadn't thought the dedicated copper would be home at this time of day. It must be one of her rare days off.

Smiling, she quickly made up the jug of booze and, carrying it carefully next door, banged vociferously on the hatch.

'Come on, copper, open up,' she yelled, grinning. The grin slowly faded, a few minutes later, as she realized that nobody was home. And the padlock was neatly re-locked.

She went slowly back to her own boat, casting a curious, just slightly anxious glance over her shoulder as she did so.

She hadn't recognized Hillary's visitor, though she obviously had the run of the place. Nancy felt a sudden pang as she wondered if Hillary had sold the boat, and the striking blonde woman was now her new neighbour.

After all, she'd been gone almost a year. When she'd left, Hillary hadn't had any plans to move off and go land-lubber, but things changed.

With a sigh, Nancy went down below on her own boat and decided to make a solo start on the margaritas.

★   ★   ★

'He just offered me a lift, that's all,' Victor Freeman said, sounding in equal measures exasperated and scared. 'He saw me rush out of the house after Pauline, but miss her, and asked if he could help. I told him I needed to get to the shop, and that Pauline had taken the van. Since my car was in the garage, I said yes, thanks, and that's it. He drove me to the nursery and then went off somewhere. And before you ask, no I don't know where he went, he didn't say and I didn't ask.'

Hillary looked at him thoughtfully. According to the witness, his wife had left their home in Deddington to deliver some plants to a regular customer, just as the phone had rung. Another customer, who could only get into the Banbury nursery that morning, wanted to buy some expensive magnolia trees. Maybe as many as five or six. Although the garden centre was usually closed on a Monday morning, it would have been a good sale for them, so Vic had shot out of the house, hoping to catch his wife. But she'd already pulled away from the end of the road.

'If that's all there was to it, Mr Freeman, why did you say earlier that you'd never been in his car?' Hillary asked, not unreasonably.

Victor Freeman flushed. 'I just panicked, didn't I? It's not every day your daughter's boyfriend gets murdered.' He swallowed hard. 'You threw me, that's all. I wasn't expecting the question.'

'Why did you never mention this lift Wayne gave you when I interviewed you before?'

'I didn't think it was important. I mean, that was Monday morning, hours and hours before . . . well, before he was killed. You only seemed interested in what I did and where I was during the late afternoon and evening. I didn't think it mattered,' he trailed off defensively, shoulders hunched.

Hillary was about to take him through it yet again, when Frank Ross came into the room, leaned over her shoulder and whispered something in her ear. Hillary, ignoring the waft of BO that usually accompanied Frank, nodded, stood up, and told Barrington to stay with the witness.

Outside, Frank nodded his head. 'She's out there. Turned up five minutes ago in a right state demanding to know why you'd arrested her Dad.'

Hillary nodded. 'OK, show her into the next room,' she said, and returned to Victor Freeman. Once again, she took him through his story. Once again he told it the same way. Then she went next door, sat down in front of his daughter, and smiled.

'Now, Miss Freeman. What can I do for you?'

'Mrs Bevis said you arrested Dad. I want to know what for!' the young girl demanded belligerently. She looked badly scared.

'Mrs Bevis?'

'The woman who owns the hairdresser's next door to Dad's shop,' Monica explained impatiently. 'I went to see Mum and Dad to ask them if they wanted to spend the lunch hour with me. Mrs Bevis told me then.'

Hillary glanced at her watch and saw that it was indeed nearly one o'clock. 'I see. But your father hasn't been arrested, Miss Freeman,' she said gently.

Monica Freeman let out a great whoosh of air. 'He hasn't?'

'No. We simply wanted to ask him some questions.' But Hillary found it very interesting to see that Monica had leapt to that conclusion. Why had she? Was she, deep down, convinced that her father had killed her boyfriend? Had she just been waiting, as it were, for the other shoe to drop?

And why should she think that?

13

Hillary Greene decided to eat a sandwich at her desk rather than go up to the canteen, and sent Barrington out for chicken salad bagels from the local bakery. Having her junior officers run such errands wasn't something she'd normally have done, and Barrington knew it, so he was feeling miserable and still very much in the doghouse as he sat back down at his desk, and started to watch the screen of his computer.

He was still compiling data on Heyford Sudbury, and decided to set up a database and run all the reports on the case so far through it. He was rather surprised when two hits came up.

'Guv, two witnesses in the Sutton case mentioned Heyford Sudbury when questioned, both in connection with these highclass friends Colin Blake knew. The ones the vic was so jealous and scathing about.'

Hillary, chewing thoughtfully, raised an eyebrow, indicating that she wanted more information.

'I remember now, Druther, one of them from the Ale and Arty Club telling me about it. Thought the pal lived in Heyford Sudbury, or one of the other Cotswoldy places.' Barrington searched through his files, found the right page, and handed over his interview notes.

Hillary read it through, beginning to frown. She'd had such high hopes for Heyford Sudbury, but now she was beginning to wonder. What if Wayne Sutton had only wanted to put a spoke in Colin Blake's wheels? It sounded the sort of thing their murder victim would do. Knowing Wayne, he'd probably set out to seduce the wife or sister or daughter of the aristo in question, then make it clear that Colin Blake had introduced them. On the other hand maybe he'd found out something about the aristo he wouldn't want bandied about. Had he tried a spot of blackmail? And had the aristocratic blackmailee not liked it and decided to murder his persecutor instead of paying up?

Either way, it had to be a potential lead that was worth chasing up. 'OK Barrington, find out the name of this friend of Blake's — easiest way is to get it straight from the horse's mouth.' Then, when Barrington reached for the phone, presumably to call the butcher, something made her change her mind. 'No. On second thoughts, see if you can find out without Blake's help.'

Sometimes, it paid to keep your witnesses and suspects in the dark.

She leaned back in her chair and finished her sandwich, wondering what Monica Freeman and her father were talking about, right about now. She'd let them go after another hour's questioning, deciding she was just wasting her time. So what if Wayne Sutton had given his girlfriend's father a lift on the morning before he was killed? It was hardly proof of anything. True, they could have used the car journey into Banbury to arrange a meeting later, but why would Wayne agree to meet Victor Freeman in a meadow at eight o'clock at night? It hardly sounded credible.

She sighed and rubbed her tired eyes. Once this case broke, she'd take a few days leave and take the *Mollern* somewhere. Maybe up to Stratford to see if she could meet up with Nancy, and take in a show. Or maybe head towards Gloucester way. All this talk about the Cotswolds was making her yearn for a taste of the real thing.

Either way, it was no good inviting Mike Regis of course — he'd hate it.

She reached for her last sandwich and bit into it with a small frown. She was going to have to do something about Mike. But what, exactly? What was it she wanted?

279

As she considered that, she realized that all she wanted was for things to go on exactly like they were. She didn't want to move in with him, or sell her boat, or worry about maybe, one day, getting married again. She liked things casual and easy. She liked being on her own six nights out of the week. Like most single people, she'd grown selfish, and had got out of the habit of sharing. She liked being able to do whatever she wanted, without consulting anyone else, or wondering if another person would be happy with her choices.

The trouble was, she was becoming more and more convinced that Mike Regis wanted something far different.

Her appetite gone, she put the half-eaten sandwich down, rewrapped it in its grease-proof paper and slipped it into her bag. She'd feed the moorhens with it later. There were a pair nesting more or less opposite her boat, and the fluffy black chicks would be hatching soon.

Suddenly, the thought of ever leaving the canal made her feel abruptly depressed. She muttered something uncomplimentary about a certain vice detective under her breath, and reached for the latest report.

Barrington began to phone members of the Ale and Arty Club. One of them must know the name of Colin Blake's wealthy upper-crust pal.

★ ★ ★

Gemma Fordham drove back to HQ, scowling. She had found nothing on Hillary Greene's boat that remotely aroused her interest. No small slivers of paper with a set of numbers on them, no hidden bank receipts or books, no strange entries on her passport.

The only thing that had been slightly out of place was a Dick Francis book amongst all the highbrow stuff the DI read. It had been enough to make her pull out the tatty paperback for a closer inspection, but then she'd realized that the inscription had been made out by Ronnie, so that was probably why DI Greene had kept it.

If her taste ran to Austen, the Brontës, the metaphysical poets and all classics in between, she couldn't see her boss actually reading the horsy thriller.

Still, searching the boat had always been a long shot, she reminded herself stoutly, pulling into the parking lot and searching for a space. Someone as clever as DI Greene would hardly be likely to leave anything useful where it could be got at so easily. Tomorrow, she'd have to do a little bit of computer hacking, and see if she could find anything more interesting.

Hillary Greene had sold her marital home last winter, for instance, but before that, she must have had some sort of storage lock-up or rental to keep her things in, when Ronnie had still been alive and in residence. Perhaps she'd kept it up. Now a place like *that* was something that Gemma would be very keen to search.

She knew that Hillary's mother was still alive as well, so perhaps she kept something there. But breaking in there would have to be a last resort. And she still had Gary Greene, Ronnie's son, to check out yet.

Patience, Gemma thought grimly, as she locked up her car and walked towards the main building. Sooner or later, she'd find what she was looking for.

She smiled at the desk sergeant as she walked past him and ran lightly up the stairs.

★ ★ ★

Hillary knocked on Paul Danvers's office and gave him an update on the case so far. He agreed that the Freemans seemed, on the face of it, unlikely suspects, and listened, poker-faced, as she ran through all that they had so far.

It wasn't a lot. Apart from the good forensics, which would be useless unless they could find a proper suspect to match them up with, there was nothing that stood out, though he could tell she was industriously following up every strand, as usual. In the end, he knew he could trust her dogged determination to win through, in the absence of luck or inspiration.

'Well, so far, no other dead men have turned up with paper hearts on their chests,' he said dryly, which was probably their only consolation about now. 'What about this Denise Collier woman? She sounds the type we want — a bit unstable, and jealous as a cat. She was heard arguing with the victim. And it seems almost certain that Wayne Sutton was meeting a woman in that field.'

Hillary sighed, and recounted her theory that Collier probably didn't have the necessary height or upper body strength to commit this type of murder.

Danvers nodded reluctant agreement. He was wearing a pale-grey suit, a white shirt with an ultra-thin cerise stripe, and a matching tie that gave a startling splash of colour that contrasted well with his pale-blond hair. He was, as always, impeccably shaved, his nails clean and probably manicured.

Hillary, today dressed in a claret-coloured two-piece suit that was at least five years old, felt dowdy and sweat-stained by comparison. She wished the DCI would get himself another girlfriend, and soon. It made her nervous to have him so obviously available. Especially when he kept looking at her like he was doing now.

'How's Mike Regis?' Danvers asked, right on cue, and as if reading her mind.

Hillary smiled brightly. 'Fine. I was thinking, when this case was over, I might take a few days of my summer holiday, and he and I could take the boat somewhere.'

Danvers smile faded, his blue eyes darkening somewhat. 'Splendid. Mind you, it doesn't look as if the case is about to crack anytime soon. You seem to have plenty of theories and suspects, but no solid leads. This Annie character still being elusive?'

'Very,' Hillary agreed grimly. In fact, she was beginning to have severe doubts about Annie.

Her boss sighed and put both hands down flat on the table in a 'well-let's-get-on-with-it' gesture. 'Keep me informed if anything interesting turns up,' he said by way of dismissal, already reaching for a file from his tray. When he sensed her turn around to walk to the door, however, his eyes quickly rose to follow her progress. He watched her leave, and gave a mental shrug.

Patience, he told himself grimly. Patience.

★ ★ ★

Gemma Fordham glanced up as a stranger approached their desks and took the chair in front of Hillary Greene.

Her DI looked up and grinned widely. 'Sam! What's up?'

Sergeant Sam Waterstone, a big man with dark hair and instantly forgettable features smiled back. 'Got something you might be interested in. A nasty little weasel by the name of Coles. Ever come across him? He's been around for a while.'

Hillary's eyes narrowed. The name rang a bell. 'Malkie Coles? A smash-and-grab merchant? Responsible for a whole outbreak of ram-raiding a few years back?'

'That's the little scrote,' Sam agreed, nodding. 'Done for aggravated burglary, GBH, and his last stretch was for a jewel heist up Birmingham way.'

'What's he been up to now? I thought he only got out a while ago.'

Sam shrugged graphically. 'So he did. But you know Malkie. Not the sharpest knife in the box. Whilst he was doing time in

Birmingham, he hooked up with this bloke who worked a gang who specialize in raiding security vans.'

Hillary groaned. 'Don't tell me.'

'Right. We got a tip-off last week about this van getting heisted this morning. Set up a sting and voilà. A nice little haul of scumbags.'

'Congratulations,' Hillary said, and meant it. She knew how taking down blaggers could give a whole station house a lift. 'Kept that quiet, didn't you?' she asked with a grin. 'I never even heard a whisper about it.'

Sam shrugged. He was fast getting a reputation as a master thieftaker, and she could see him making DI on the back of this latest success. 'You know how it is,' he said grimly. 'The less people know . . . '

'The less they can hurt you,' Hillary agreed flatly. Although neither of them liked it, they knew leaks were a fact of life in any station house. Mostly it was down to some gormless uniform with a pet reporter who fed him a couple of hundred here and there. But sometimes the leaks were far less harmless.

'Anyway, it seems Malkie has got himself a woman,' Sam took up the story again, and Hillary blinked in surprise. Unless she'd got it wrong, Malkie Coles was a weasel-faced, bucktoothed, scrawny little runt with practically no hair, and killer halitosis.

'Yeah, I know,' Sam laughed, reading her expression. 'It made my mind boggle, too. Apparently she's one of these women who hang around hair salons as a private contractor doing nails (fingers *and* toes, apparently) and beauty treatments and what not, while the women sit under the dryers waiting for the perm to set. According to Malkie, this angel of mercy has turned his life around.'

Hillary grunted. 'Not enough to stop him trying to turn over security vans, apparently,' she said sceptically.

'No,' Sam said with a grin. 'Well, according to Malkie he more or less had to do the job because he'd promised his old cell mate back in Birmingham, and he didn't feel he could let the gang down. But after that one job he was going to go straight.' Sam held one hand over his heart, and the other up, as if petitioning God, and rolled his eyes.

Hillary grinned. 'Such cynicism, Sam,' she shook her head sorrowfully.

'Yeah. Well, the upshot is, Malkie had been seeing wedding bells in his future, a little house without too much graffiti damage in Blackbird Leys and maybe one or two little nipper Coles running around, snatching purses off unwary pensioners.'

Hillary shuddered. 'Don't.'

'Thing is, our Malkie has suddenly twigged to the fact that this time he could be looking at twenty years inside, max. And not even the little angelic manicurist is going to wait *that* long for him. So he's anxious to do a deal and try and cut down on his time.'

Hillary raised a brow. 'All very interesting, but why bend my ear? Doesn't your guv'nor want to go for it?'

'Oh, he's fine with it. But Malkie's dropping everyone he can think of in the mire. We've got people from burglary in with him now, and the sex crimes unit want a word as well, 'cause he reckons one of his other cell mates from ten years ago bragged of several rapes he got away with, back in the late eighties. He also claims that someone you may be interested in, recently hired him to beat someone up.'

Hillary tensed as Sam checked his notebook. 'A Mr Thomas Eaverson. Malkie claimed he was approached by Mr Eaverson to beat up Wayne Sutton. That's your murder vic, ain't it?'

Hillary smiled grimly. Behind Sam, Gemma, who'd been listening to every word, caught her eye.

Hillary nodded. 'Yeah, bring him in,' she

said to her DS, making Sam turn around to look at her. 'Sam, this is Gemma Fordham, my new sergeant. Gemma, Sam Waterstone. And Gemma, find Frank and take him with you.'

The two sergeants nodded at each other, a shade warily perhaps, and Sam watched her go. 'Good idea getting her to take Ross. He's not much use, but he's a vicious little bastard and a good one to have in your corner if a suspect cuts up rough.'

Hillary gurgled with abrupt laughter. 'Oh it's not that! Gemma's one of those kung-fu experts. She'd probably tie Eaverson in a knot if he even so much as laid a finger on her. No, I just wanted her to take Ross so I'd know where the lazy bugger was.'

Sam Waterstone laughed, but with real sympathy.

★   ★   ★

Ten minutes later, Hillary looked across the scratched table at Malkie Coles, and offered him a polo mint. It wasn't to put him at ease, so much, as to fend off the bad breath that wafted across the space between them.

'Ta, DI Green,' Malkie Coles said, and took two of the mints. It was a curious fact that Malkie Coles was always very polite. He always said please and thank you, and after swearing at police officers arresting him, very often apologized. His mother, it seems, had raised her son to have manners. No moral conscience mind you, or even a rudimentary grip of right and wrong. But manners — definitely.

'My pleasure,' Hillary said politely back, and beside her, saw Sam Waterstone raise a hand to his lips to hide his smile. 'So, tell me about Mr Eaverson,' she said casually.

'Who?'

'The man who wanted Wayne Sutton beat up,' Sam said sharply. Having put Hillary Greene on to him, he didn't want the little weasel showing him up.

'Oh, him. Right. Comes up to me in my local, and introduced himself as Mr Robinson. I ask you!' Malkie appealed to them both, and both obligingly smiled. 'Still, I suppose it was better than Mr Smith,' Malkie said. 'At least he made a bit of an effort to be original like.'

'And I'm sure you appreciated it, Malkie,' Sam said, a shade impatiently.

'Course, I soon found out who he really was,' Malkie said complacently.

'Very wise of you, Malkie,' Sam said flatly.

'Nice of you to say so, Mr Waterstone.'

Sam sighed heavily. It was, he knew from

bitter experience, pointless trying to hurry Malkie Coles along. The villain could only go at one speed — his own.

'Why don't you just tell us all about it,' Hillary said, having learned the same thing. 'This man just walks up to you one night in the pub. When was this?'

'Dunno. About three weeks ago maybe? He asked me if I was Malkie Coles, and I said yeah, and he said, 'Somebody told me you did odd jobs like. With your fist', and I looks at him funny like. I mean he was talking quiet, but we were in the *boozer* for crying out loud! So I says 'Why don't we talk about this outside', and he looks a bit sick like, as if I'm going to take him round the dustbins and duff him up. Well, I shrugs. I mean, no skin off my nose is it? But then he grows a bit of a backbone like, so he says 'all right', and we go outside.'

Malkie paused to give his polo mints a vigorous sucking and take a much needed breath. Hillary sighed and reached inside her pocket for the rest of the roll of mints, and handed the whole lot over. Whoever inter-viewed him next had better appreciate it.

Malkie beamed and thanked her nicely.

'So anyway, we goes outside and I sits on this wall,' the armed robber carried on blithely, 'still drinking my pint like, and this bloke asks me how much it is to beat up some punk. As if there was a price list or sommat!' He snorted a laugh, and Hillary shook her head.

'Some people, hey Malkie?' she said softly.

'Yeah, some people,' Malkie echoed sadly. 'So, anyway, I say 'How much you got on you, then', and he looks all sort of surprised. Then he takes out his bloody wallet then and there and draws out a wad of tenners. I mean, well, I nearly cried. Is this pigeon asking to be taken down or what?'

'Practically crying out for it, Malkie,' Sam Waterstone said drily.

Malkie nodded, glad to have two such knowledgeable cops talking to him at last. Those last morons from burglary didn't seem to know nothing. Both in their twenties and still wet behind their ears. No, give him proper coppers, like these two, any day of the week.

'So anyway, he goes 'I've only got a hundred and seventy' and I says, 'that'll do', and he hands the stuff over. Then he brings out this picture of this bloke. Looks like it was taken at a party or something. And he says, 'His name is Wayne Sutton. His address is written on the back.' And so I turns it over, and sure enough, there was this address written on the back. Funny kind of place name. Deddington. I mean, who'd want to live in a place called that?'

And Malkie, who'd lived for part of his life in Newport Pagnell, shuddered.

Hillary shook her head. 'The things some folk do,' she agreed sadly.

Malkie nodded, ripped into the polo mints and popped a few more into his mouth. 'You can say that again. So, anyways, I tells him the job's as good as done, and does he want any bones broken, or any organs ruptured, or what.'

Malkie chewed vigorously for a while, then smiled, revealing nicotine-stained teeth. 'That made the geezer turn a bit pale, I can tell you. So then he says, 'Oh no, nothing too violent. Nothing life-threatening.' Honest, that's how he put it. Very lah-di-dah. 'Nothing life threatening.' I nearly laughed in his face,' Malkie said bitterly.

Then he shrugged philosophically. 'Still. Then he said he wanted me to make sure his pretty face got properly rearranged. Seemed most insistent about that. So I said, sure, I knew what he wanted. Pop a few of his teeth out for him, smash his nose up good and proper, that sort of thing. I could tell from his photo that he was a good-looking sort of lad. I figured he'd been bonking 'Mr Robinson's' missus, that's why he wanted his face rearranged.'

'Good guess,' Hillary said drolly.

Malkie nodded in satisfaction. It was nice to be right. 'So I tell him not to worry, job's good as done, then went into the pub and stood everybody a round.'

'And when were you going to rearrange Wayne's face for him?' Hillary asked, and Malkie's small, watery eyes rounded slightly.

'Hey? Never. Don't be daft. I just took his money, didn't I? I wasn't actually going to go traipsing off to bloody Deddington to give someone a pasting. Why bother? It's not as if 'Mr Robinson',' Malkie quoted the name again with a sneer, 'was going to complain, is it? I mean, what's he going to do?' Malkie laughed. 'Silly sod. 'Sides he paid me up front, didn't he? Why do the work if you've already been paid, that's what I say? I mean, what muffin pays up front?' Malkie asked, scandalized.

Hillary sighed. 'So there really is no honour among thieves, huh? All my illusions are shattered.'

'Eh?' Malkie said, looking puzzled. 'He weren't no thief, just some silly sod who wanted someone duffed up.'

Hillary nodded. 'Right. Sorry, Malkie, don't know what I was thinking. So, if I bring

Mr Eaverson in, you'll formally identify him and testify that he hired you to give Wayne Sutton a beating?'

'Sure,' Malkie said magnanimously. 'So, you think he done him in then? That good-looking kid who was boffing his wife? When I read in the papers he'd ended up dead, I wondered if our 'Mr Robinson' had got tired of waiting for me to biff him and decided to take him out himself.'

'I don't know,' Hillary said, amused. 'What do you think?'

Malkie chewed his mints and thought judiciously. He thought for so long and so hard, that both police officers were almost prepared to swear they could hear the clogs clanking around in what passed for Malkie's mind. Then the old lag shook his head.

'Nah, can't see it myself. If he hadn't the bottle to duff up the kid himself, but needed to hire out for it, I can't see him having the bottle to actually off the kid. Can you?'

Hillary thanked Malkie politely for his help, nodded a thanks at Sam, and left. Outside, she nodded at two officers from the sex crimes unit. 'Thanks for waiting. He's all yours.'

★ ★ ★

Gemma Fordham looked up as DI Greene walked into the interview room. It was getting on for late in the afternoon, and she and Ross had been baby-sitting Tommy Eaverson for what felt like years now.

Frank heaved an ostentatious sigh as Hillary took her seat. If the tape hadn't already been running, she might have made some caustic comment along the lines of being sorry for making him do his damned job. But she merely glared at him instead.

Taking the hint, Ross slumped down in his seat and stared at the wall behind the suspect. He looked so heavy-lidded, Hillary suspected he'd probably fall asleep at some point, if he wasn't careful.

Gemma introduced DI Greene for the tape and Hillary smiled across the table. 'Mr Eaverson, I'm sure DS Fordham has told you that you're entitled to have a solicitor present?'

'Sure she told me,' Tommy Eaverson said, with a scowl. 'But I can't see why I need to bring Jim Watson into this.'

Hillary's eyebrow lifted. James Wilberforce Watson wasn't a solicitor but a QC. And if he was Tommy's personal friend and legal adviser, he obviously had friends in some very high places.

'Very well,' she said blandly. 'I have, next

door, a man by the name of Malkie Coles. He tells me . . . '

'I want a solicitor,' Tommy Eaverson said flatly.

⋆   ⋆   ⋆

Four hours later, Hillary drove home feeling exhausted. James Watson, on receiving Mr Eaverson's one allotted phone call, had promptly sent down to HQ a legal eagle by the name of Geoffrey Whiting, who was so sharp he could cut diamonds. And eager to impress the great James Watson.

Consequently, it had been a struggle to get Tommy Eaverson even to admit to knowing Malkie, despite the fact that Malkie picked him out at a line-up. Whiting had then pointed out that an old lag such as Coles was hardly a credible witness, and that if no other witnesses from the 'alleged' pub could be found, his client was leaving now.

Hillary had promptly dealt with that nonsense, but it had been an uphill battle all the way.

She'd then proceeded to tackle Eaverson from all angles — from leaving his wife, to having a vendetta against the murder victim, to hiring a hit man and even playing on his inability to keep a wife sexually satisfied. The last had had the fancy brief almost incoherent with outrage.

Towards the end of the interview, she'd even been goaded into an enormous bluff, and told Eaverson that they knew all about 'Annie', although Gemma hadn't yet had time to track her down.

This had proved interesting, in that Eaverson had immediately said that his mistress, and the soon to be second Mrs Eaverson, was nothing to do with her. Whiting had managed to shut him up fast, but not before the damage had been done. It had been a brief and only partial victory, but after that gruelling battle with Whiting, it had been sweet indeed.

Eventually, of course, she'd had to let him go. Coles's word wasn't enough to charge him with conspiracy to cause actual bodily harm, but she'd put Barrington up to casing out the pub in question tonight. If anyone *had* overheard any of the conversation between Coles and Eaverson, she wanted to know about it.

But since Eaverson had paid Coles with money straight from his wallet, she knew there would be no bank withdrawal evidence to confirm his having paid Coles any set amount, and she knew in her bones that she could kiss any chance of charging

Eaverson goodbye.

Nevertheless, as her final order of the day, she'd told Gemma Fordham to make finding out all about Eaverson's Annie a top priority. Who she was, how long they'd been having an affair, and, most important of all, if she could possibly have known, or have any connection with, their murder victim.

But again, in her bones, she knew that wouldn't pan out either. Eaverson's Annie would probably turn out to be a respectable PA or secretary-type, on the look out for a rich husband to make her middle-age nice and comfortable. And she almost certainly wouldn't have known Wayne Sutton if he'd prodded her with a big stick.

★   ★   ★

That evening, Hillary turned into Thrupp, never more happy to see home. A long cold shower, a glass of wine, and a doze on top of the boat in the last of the rays, that was what she needed now.

She parked in her usual place in The Boat car park and walked tiredly along the canal. The May blossom was out, casting a heady, slightly sickly scent on the air. As expected, the moorhen chicks had hatched, and already the parent birds eyed her hopefully. She tossed them the sandwich she'd kept back, then gave a small cry of delight as she recognized the boat moored up behind hers.

Willowsands was back.

She hurried her pace, and ignoring her own boat, knocked sharply on the roof. 'Ageing reprobates beware,' she yelled. 'This is a police raid.'

'It's a fair cop, guv,' a voice yelled back cheerfully from the depths of the boat. 'I've got two nineteen-year-old divinity students, one Polish foreign exchange student and a stoned wood carver down here. Give us a break, guv. The Pole doesn't even speak a word of English.'

The door opened, and Nancy Walker's head popped up. She'd recently dyed her head a dark brunette, and she was looking fabulous. Hillary, who wouldn't put it past the predatory divorcee to have just who she said she had already stashed on board, grinned.

'You decent?'

'Hardly!' Nancy snorted. 'I'm already half-plastered. Come on down, I made some margaritas. You can help me finish them off.'

Hillary almost groaned out loud. 'After the afternoon from hell I've just had, I could kiss you.'

'Sorry,' Nancy called back, over her

shoulder. 'I don't swing both ways.'

Once inside, Hillary kicked off her shoes and accepted a drink, guzzling it down in three swallows. Nancy watched, impressed, and took the glass for an instant refill. This one Hillary sipped more slowly.

The two old friends spent the last of the daylight hours reminiscing and catching up.

'You know, it's funny you should come back now,' Hillary said, at last, as Nancy went around turning on the 40-watt bulbs. Like most boat-dwellers, she had a constant battle not to use too much electricity, thus running down the generators. 'I was actually thinking of taking the *Mollern* up to Stratford some time soon, to see if I could catch up with you.'

Nancy smiled. 'Well, you still can — go to Stratford I mean.' She hiccoughed and smiled, a trifle foolishly. She'd always been a very amiable drunk. 'Actually, *I'm* relieved to see *you*.' She poured the very last drop of margarita into her glass and sighed. 'I thought you might have sold up and moved on.'

Hillary frowned. 'Oh? Why?' And then listened with a growing sense of grim anger as Nancy described what had happened that afternoon.

'So, who was she then?' Nancy asked, when

she'd finished. 'By the look on your face, you recognize my description of her.'

Hillary forced herself to smile. 'Oh yes. Sorry, I forgot for a moment, I asked her to drop by. That's my new Sergeant, Gemma Fordham. I gave her my key and asked her to pick something up for me,' she lied, without a tremor.

'Oh, that's all right then,' Nancy said. It was a good job she was a bit tipsy, Hillary knew, otherwise the older woman might have picked up on her angst. Not much was missed by the sharp-eyed divorcee.

'Well, now that I've drunk you dry of margaritas, I'll say goodnight,' Hillary said, struggling a little bit herself to get up. She walked up Nancy's steep stairs with extra care, and jumped off on to the towpath with more caution than usual.

Nancy waved her a vague goodbye through her porthole, and Hillary waved back.

Once on her own boat, Hillary washed her face in cold water and looked around with a cold, gimlet eye.

Nothing looked out of place, and nothing was missing. If Nancy hadn't spotted her DS leaving the *Mollern*, she might never have known she'd been there.

Hillary made herself a large mug of coffee, forced herself to drink it, and then sat down in her chair for a good long think.

Well, this explained what Gemma had been doing rifling through her bag. She'd obviously had a key cut. Hillary made a mental note to change the padlock tomorrow, which smacked somewhat of shutting the stable door after the horse had bolted, but still. At least it would prevent the nosy DS from coming back for a second search.

But the question was of course — just what the hell had she been doing here?

What did Gemma Fordham *want*?

14

Hillary Greene awoke that Saturday morning with a hangover and vague sense of foreboding. She lay in her narrow bed, the *Mollern* rocking slightly beneath her as a passing narrowboat went by too fast, and listened to a skylark, trilling high above.

She closed her eyes against a throbbing headache and let everything wash over her.

Gemma Fordham.

The murder of Wayne Sutton.

Mike Regis.

Life, the universe and everything.

What, exactly, was she supposed to do about it all?

Well, first things first. She swung her legs out of bed and reached into her handbag; taking out a bottle of aspirin, she dry-swallowed two and coughed. Dragging herself to the bathroom, she took a quick two-minute shower, then dressed in a clean pair of black slacks and a cream T-shirt. Over it she slipped a beige cardigan and thrust her feet into beige pumps. Once in the galley, with a cup of coffee in her hand, and the sound of the morning papers landing on her roof, she felt, if not happier, than at least not so grumpy.

OK — Gemma Fordham. There were several possibilities there, she reasoned, and none of them was good. She could be simply a bent cop, or one who was so ambitious that she was trying to find something on Hillary that she could hold over her, thus gaining promotion or easy assignments. That fitted in fairly well with what she knew of Gemma so far. According to Mel, she was something of a high flyer with an impressive record behind her. But then, if she was used to prying out secrets about her immediate superior officer, then she probably *would* have just that rep. What's more, her DI in Reading would have been ecstatic to transfer her out of his hair, and endorsing her to Thames Valley would accomplish just that.

But for all that, Hillary hadn't got that vibe from the tall blonde woman. Gemma was too competent, too able, too sure of herself and her abilities to go down that route.

OK, so what else? She took a sip of hot coffee and wished her head would stop thumping. Well, Gemma could simply be carrying out orders. If Hillary herself was under investigation, then Gemma Fordham's assignment to her team made sense. She'd been short a viable sergeant for some time, so she'd have no reason to be suspicious of a new appointee. The only problem with that was — what could the brass possibly think she'd been doing that needed investigation? The most obvious answer, of course, was the old trouble with her late husband, Ronnie Greene. But he'd been dead nearly five years now. There was still the question of the money he'd stashed, but Marcus Donleavy knew exactly what had happened to that, and although he wouldn't be in any hurry to blab about it, he would surely have been able to put a discreet stop on any further investigation into trying to find it. Besides, that was old, old news. And it just didn't feel right. If she was still under suspicion, she thought she'd have felt it by now.

She had a good nose for trouble.

And if Gemma *was* working undercover, either Donleavy, Mel, or maybe Danvers would know about it. And whilst she could see Danvers keeping quiet, and maybe, at a pinch, Donleavy, she knew her old friend Mel would have found a way to tip her the wink.

So what did that leave? Did Gemma Fordham have some sort of personal vendetta against her? Hillary blinked her tired, gritty eyes and sipped her coffee morosely. She was sure she hadn't met Gemma before, so if there was something personal going on, it couldn't be a direct link between them.

Of all the possibilities, though, this one seemed to be the most likely. But what did she do about it? Confront her? Hillary sighed and shook her head. Gemma was tough — she'd almost certainly flat out deny it, and then where would she be? No proof, and Gemma on the alert that she'd been sussed. No, she had no other option but just to wait and see. Do a little discreet digging, find out more about her, see if she could find out what the problem was before it escalated even further. It was deeply unsatisfactory having something like that hanging over her head, but she didn't see what else she could do about it.

What else.

Mike Regis.

Well, there were only two things she could do there — either call it all off, or sit him down and tell him straight how she felt about things. Neither appealed. But as soon as the case was over, she'd have to bite the bullet and choose one.

That left Wayne Sutton, and the only thing she could do about her murder victim was drag her sorry, hungover backside to HQ and knuckle down to it.

She drained her coffee mug, wisely deciding to leave life, the universe and everything for another day, and headed aft.

After she'd walked up the stairs, the act of shutting the padlock reminded her of another chore she had to do. Change the lock.

She stashed the weekend papers under one arm, and glanced wryly at *Willowsands* as she passed. Nancy Walker's curtains were still firmly drawn against the cheerful skylarks and bright sunshine.

It was all right for some.

★   ★   ★

When she got to the office, Barrington was there ahead of her. She nodded at him as she took a seat, then went straight to the coffee pot for another mug. Her headache was receding a bit, but she still felt like something no self-respecting cat would ever dream of dragging in.

She sat down stiffly, and glowered at her in-tray. She'd cleared it last night before going home, but it had magically started to overflow again. She spent some much-needed time dealing with her other cases, signed off some reports, read and passed on inter-office memos and generally cleared the decks. By the time she'd finished, Gemma Fordham was at her desk, and so, incredibly, was Frank Ross. It was nearly ten o'clock, and she had no idea then, that in less than forty minutes, she'd have solved her seventh murder case.

★　★　★

Keith Barrington glanced across at his boss as she dealt with the last file in her in-tray and looked towards the coffee pot again. It was his opinion that she drank far too much caffeine, but he was not idiot enough to tell her so.

'Guv, I've got the name of the chap in Heyford Sudbury that Colin Blake is friendly with. Man by the name of Jasper Fielding. He owns a place called Heyford Court. Family used to be big in biscuits or something. You know, back in the Victorian era, owned a huge factory and made a mint. Course, the factory closed down during the wars and never got up and running again. I reckon the family's been dwindling along with the fortune ever since. Now it's down to a last remaining son — Jasper. I've been ringing him on and off all morning but no reply.'

'He's away at the moment,' Hillary said vaguely, making Barrington give her a double take. *How the hell did she know that?*

'I don't suppose there's anybody called Annie in his life?' she asked, but Barrington shook his head.

''Fraid not, guv. And he's got no record.'

Hillary got up and refilled her mug, then sat back down, staring at the morass of paperwork strewn across her desk. She'd reread every ongoing file on the Wayne Sutton murder at least three times by now, and she just couldn't face doing it again.

She reached instead for the morning papers (well, technically, it was supposed to be her day off) and, as was her habit, turned first to the Weekend/Arts section of the *Oxford Times*.

And found the answer to her murder case staring her in the face.

But it didn't hit her at once.

Firstly, she found herself staring at two portraits, placed side by side. Both were of the same woman, a rather plain-looking brunette, in a blue-and-white lace dress with a lace cap in one, and wearing a rather more formal, dark-brown gown in another. The caption read 'JANE AUSTEN — Another Portrait Found!'

Hillary began to read the write-up.

Dr Matthew Brownlow, an art expert on several painters, including Fletcher Crispin-Jones, is expected today to give his verdict on the so-called 'found' portrait of Jane Austen, discovered earlier this month in the attic of an Oxfordshire manor house.

The portrait is signed by Fletcher Crispin-Jones, a little known, but documented artist (b 1770, d 1848) and was discovered by the owner of the house when he was forced to do an attic clearance so that more modern insulation could be installed.

According to our sources, the owner of the house, who so far wishes to remain anonymous, was said to be 'astounded' by the find. He went on to tell this reporter, that, at first, he'd assumed the painted lady to be one of his own ancestors, but after getting the painting cleaned and restored by a local specialist, intriguing 'clues' came to light as to the identity of the sitter. On the back, presumably in the artist's own writing, was a small, badly faded and worn note, giving the date of the sitting, and the startling information that 'Miss Austen' had kindly given him permission to use sketches of her previously done in Bath to paint a full portrait.

'Well, naturally, we were intrigued,' the owner of the portrait told us. 'I know my family once lived in Bath, and were famous for giving soirées for the beau monde, so in theory it was perfectly possible that Jane Austen, who also lived in Bath for some time, would almost certainly have been a guest of my ancestor at some point.

'I immediately contacted a friend of mine from the Ruskin, who told me that Dr

Brownlow knew more about the artist than anyone, and I subsequently got in touch with him. Dr Brownlow, naturally, was most anxious to see the portrait, and has been studying it and running tests on it for me ever since. I must say, I can't wait to see what he has to say on the matter.'

This newspaper has tried to contact Dr Brownlow, but his personal assistant would only confirm that he has indeed been consulted about a portrait of a woman, purported to be by Fletcher Crispin-Jones.

The piece went on to give a brief biography of the little-known artist. A spokesman for the National Portrait Gallery also said his piece, insisting, not unnaturally, that they still had the only known, authenticated portrait of Jane Austen in existence, and added, somewhat stiffly, that the Gallery would, of course, be interested in Mr Brownlow's findings, but pointed out that, even if the portrait was genuine, there was still no proof that the sitter was the famous authoress herself.

But by then, Hillary had stopped reading.

Instead, she let the paper fall to her lap and stared blankly in front of her, as it all became clear.

It explained everything. Annie, and the

reason for the paper heart. Wayne Sutton finding his fortune in Heyford Sudbury, and no longer needing his coterie of ladies. Everything.

'Well for crying out bloody loud,' Hillary said, and, walking past the startled Barrington and Fordham, took her newspaper into Paul Danver's office.

★   ★   ★

Danvers looked up as the door to his office opened without a preliminary knock, but one look at Hillary's face had his heart leaping. Not only did she look radiant and fierce, enough in itself to get his loins tingling, he also knew from old what that gleam in her eyes actually meant.

'Sir, I think you should read that,' she said, dropping the newspaper article in front of him.

And as he read, Hillary filled him in.

★   ★   ★

At his desk, Barrington's phone rang and he reached across for it absently. He'd seen Hillary Greene before when she'd suddenly had a brainwave, and knew that it meant that things would be happening — fast.

313

'Hello, DC Barrington,' he muttered into the phone, his own eyes, like those of Frank and Gemma, fastened on the DCI's door. What could she have read in the papers that had . . .

'Keith?' Gavin Moreland's tense voice broke across his thoughts and made him jump.

'Hey!' Keith said, casting a quick, nervous glance at Frank Ross who was fiddling with a pen and trying to look busy. 'I was hoping you'd call,' Keith said, wishing he could talk properly. 'How are you? Are you all right?' he asked anxiously.

Gemma Fordham glanced across at him curiously, realizing it was a personal call, but she went back to her computer terminal almost at once, obviously uninterested. Ross, however, was beginning to catch on too, and gave Keith a leering grin that was probably meant to be supportive. Barrington felt his guts clench. He mustn't mention Gavin's first name.

'They've only arrested him, haven't they?' Gavin said in his ear, his voice hoarse and thickened, and Keith realized, with dismay, that his lover was drunk.

'What for?' Keith asked blankly, unable to think of anything else to say.

Gavin laughed bitterly over the phone.

'Does it matter? He's been charged, and his team are arranging bail so he can come home. At last. You bastards have kept him in for nearly three days.'

They must have asked for, and been granted an extension, Keith thought automatically, then registered the personal pronoun in the accusation.

'Hey, hold on,' he said softly. 'It's nothing to do with me . . . darling.'

There was a startled silence on the other end of the line, and then a harsh bark of laughter. Barrington winced and held his hand over the phone, in case Ross picked up on the masculinity of it.

'Oh, I get it. Can't even call me by my name, huh?' Gavin slurred hysterically. 'Afraid someone will hear you and twig that you're as bent as a corkscrew, eh? Just like me? Well, you know what? That won't be a problem for you anymore. You think you coppers can do this to my Dad? Well, *darling*, screw you!' Gavin screamed and crashed down the phone.

Shaken, Keith lowered his own receiver.

'Woman trouble, huh, Red?' Frank Ross laughed. 'They're all the same, mate, and plenty more of them in the sea.'

Keith, hating himself, smiled grimly back at the older man and shrugged. Could he get time off and drive down to London? Damn, if the case was breaking, now was the worse time ever to ask for leave. He glanced up as the door to Danvers's office opened, and his heart fell as he saw the tight, hard look on Hillary's face, and the avid, eager look on the DCI's.

'I'll take the brief to Mel, and we'll get the warrants as fast as we can,' Danvers was saying, and since it was a Saturday morning, and slow, his words carried clearly across to Hillary's team. 'You going to bring him in now?'

'Yes, I think we should. I don't like the fact that Fielding is in the wind,' Hillary said sharply.

'Right,' Danvers agreed, and strode off towards the door.

Gemma got to her feet as Hillary approached, and the curvaceous brunette shot the tall blonde a quick, thoughtful look, and said, 'Gemma, come with me. Barrington, Ross, I want you to find out where Jasper Fielding is. Check with airports, ports, hell, even his local travel agents. Go through Interpol if you have to. I want him found and brought in.'

Barrington nodded. 'Yes, guv.' There would be no trips to London for some considerable time, he could tell.

Frank sighed heavily. The case was breaking, and as he expected, it was the new girl who was going to be in on the kill. It didn't matter that he had seniority. Oh no. It was all girls together now.

'Bloody women,' Ross muttered, as he watched the two of them leave at a brisk walk. 'Mark my words, Red, those two are as thick as thieves.'

You could always trust Frank to get it wrong.

★   ★   ★

They took Gemma's car, with Gemma driving. Hillary watched the scenery flash by as they headed towards Banbury, glad that her hangover was all but gone. She was going to need her wits about her for the next few hours.

'We're bringing in Blake, guv?' Gemma asked quietly, speeding up just a bit as the traffic lights in front of her went from green to amber.

'Yes,' Hillary said tersely.

'For the murder of Sutton?'

'Yes.'

Something about the crisp, monosyllabic answers warned Gemma not to push it further, and they drove the rest of the way in silence. They parked illegally on double yellow lines not far from Blake's butcher shop, and walked quickly through the narrow alleyways.

Colin Blake looked surprised to hear the caution, and his assistant, watching open-mouthed, felt as if he was watching an episode of *The Bill*. When Hillary had finished, Blake merely said flatly, 'Take over Baz. And call William for me. Tell him what's happened.'

'OK, Col, I will. You want me to call your wife?'

'No!' Blake said sharply. 'I don't want to worry her.' He walked around the counter, taking off his apron as he went, and looked more surprised than ever when Gemma Fordham expertly cuffed him.

They walked through the crowded streets, attracting a little attention as they did so, but nothing major. At the car, Hillary removed the parking ticket from Gemma's windshield and slipped into the back seat with her prisoner.

The drive back to HQ was completed in absolute silence.

★　★　★

An hour later, the atmosphere in Interview Room Four was tense, but calm.

Sitting on one side of the table was Colin Blake and his solicitor, Mrs Judith Coulson, who'd arrived at the station shortly after they did. Opposite them sat Hillary Greene and Gemma Fordham. A po-faced constable stood beside the door. In the observation room, Barrington, Danvers, Mel and Frank stood watching and listening carefully.

Inside, the tape ran smoothly and quietly as Hillary began the interview.

'Mr Blake, you've been charged with the murder of Wayne Sutton on the last day of April this year. Do you understand the rights that were read out to you?'

'Yes.'

'We can waive the usual preliminaries, Inspector Greene,' Judith Coulson said blandly.

She was a large, grey-haired woman somewhere in her middle fifties, and wore a dark-blue suit that screamed bespoke tailoring. Hillary instantly put her down as an ex-Oxford Reader of Jurisprudence.

So she'd have to be careful.

'Mr Blake, I'd like to take a sample of your DNA. Do you have any ob — '

'Have you got a warrant for that, Inspector?' Coulson interrupted.

'It's being drawn up as we speak.'

'Well, when you can actually produce it,

we'll deal with it then. Not before, if you please.'

Hillary shrugged. It was no skin off her nose. 'We also have a warrant to search Mr Blake's premises. That is being carried out, also as we speak.'

Colin Blake shifted on his seat. 'I don't want my wife upset.'

'I'm sure the officers will be as discreet as possible, Mr Blake,' she said, looking at him curiously.

He didn't look particularly nervous, or angry, or even worried. She wondered if his blankness was down to shock, and hoped so. Shock wore off, leaving you vulnerable. But if he was just plain stubborn, or hunkering down for the duration, she knew she'd never get a confession out of him.

'On the evening of the thirtieth of April, you arranged to meet Mr Wayne Sutton in the meadow outside of the village where he lived, didn't you Mr Blake?'

'No.'

'You went there with the express purpose of killing him.'

'No.'

'You took with you a note you'd already written, supposedly from a woman called Annie, which you placed on his person after you'd killed him, and also a heart, cut out of red paper, which you also placed on his body.'

'No.'

'Do you have anything to substantiate these allegations, Inspector?' Judith Coulson asked quietly.

'We will have, once we have Mr Blake's DNA for comparison Miss Coulson,' Hillary said, equally quietly.

'You see, Colin,' she turned back to Blake, who stared back at her blankly, 'you left one of your hairs on the body. It's amazing how much hair is shed during a single day. The human body is constantly growing and replacing shed material. Take the skin cells off your hand for example.'

Colin Blake glanced compulsively at his hands, then quickly away again. 'When you hit Wayne on the head with the stone, you realized, quite rightly, that stone wouldn't take fingerprints. But dried skin cells, like hairs, are constantly being shed. Millions of them apparently. And the forensic labs were able to take traces of the killer's skin cells from the stone. And with that, and the hair sample you left behind, we'll be able to prove you were there when Wayne Sutton was drowned.'

'So far this all sounds like speculation, Inspector,' Judith Coulson said, but her voice was a bit tighter now, a bit less sanguine.

321

Colin Blake glanced at her quickly, then away again. His lips tightened.

'The note from Annie and the red paper heart were carefully thought out red herrings, weren't they Colin?' Hillary carried on smoothly. 'You knew Wayne was a gigolo, and you knew it would be one of the first things we found out about him. So we'd already be predisposed to look to that area of his life to try and find his killer. After all, when a good-looking young man, who makes his living off gullible middle-aged ladies is found dead, it's the first thing you think of, isn't it? Either that one of his women became jealous and murderously angry, or that one of his women's husbands, fathers or lovers, took exception to him sponging off their loved one and took the opportunity to get rid of him. The red paper heart was just to make sure that we concentrated our efforts on that aspect of his life, wasn't it?'

Judith Coulson sighed heavily but said nothing.

'But Annie was a bit of a mistake, Colin,' Hillary said softly, leaning forward a little in her chair. 'You see, there *was* no Annie in his life. And we looked for her, as you intended we should, wasting our time and efforts on a hiding to nothing. But you see, the more we couldn't find her, the more we smelt a rat,' she continued, not quite truthfully. 'You'd have done better just to leave it at the paper heart.'

Colin Blake blinked, but said nothing. If she was making any dents in his self-confidence, she couldn't see it. She felt her anger grow, and quickly held it back. Now was not the time to lose it.

'Wayne Sutton didn't like you did he, Colin?' she said flatly, deciding to change tack. 'He didn't like the way you painted, or managed to sell your canvases regularly.'

Colin shrugged. 'That's no secret,' he admitted.

'What did *you* think of *his* style?' Hillary asked, partly to get him talking, partly because she was genuinely interested.

'He tried too hard,' Colin Blake said, after a moment's thought. 'He wanted to be original, but in trying to do something different, he squashed his talent, rather than fostered it. But try telling him that!'

Hillary nodded. 'He must have hated listening to advice from you,' she mused. 'Wayne didn't just resent you, or dislike you, he positively loathed and hated you, didn't he?'

Blake swallowed hard, but otherwise looked unimpressed.

'Everything about you offended him,' Hillary pressed on relentlessly. 'That you could paint better than he could, that you sold your canvases strictly on their own merits, even that you earned an honest living, whereas he, as he must have known deep down, was something of a local joke. And then, there was your greatest sin of all.'

Blake shifted on his seat again and Coulson looked at Hillary, fascinated in spite of her professionalism.

'You were actually achieving the lifestyle that he wanted for himself,' Hillary murmured knowingly. 'You were getting in with the 'right' set. I'm talking, of course, about your friend, Jasper Fielding.'

Colin Blake licked his lips and glanced across at Coulson. 'Do I have to listen to this?'

'I'm afraid so,' Judith Coulson said wryly.

'Let's consider Mr Fielding for a moment, shall we?' Hillary went on brightly. 'How did you meet him?'

Blake stared at her.

Hillary glanced at the solicitor, then back to Blake. 'Is there some reason you don't want to answer that, Mr Blake? It seems a simple and straightforward question to me.'

Colin Blake sighed elaborately. 'OK. Fine. I met him about five years ago. I had an exhibition at a local gallery, and Jasper bought one of my canvases. After that, he recommended me to some more of his friends, and I regularly sold to them.'

'A fact that your fellow Ale and Arty members knew about. So when Wayne joined, he learned about it too. It must have driven him mad,' Hillary mused. 'There he was, a working-class lad, just like you, who wanted to make a name for himself as a serious, professional artist; what he needed were rich friends in high places, too, who could hook him up to the posh galleries and introduce him to the movers and the shakers. He probably saw himself as the next Andy Warhol right?'

Colin smiled. 'I imagine so. But in reality he was only a second-rate artist, and probably a second-rate gigolo, come to that.'

'Right. You mutually loathed each other. So when Wayne tumbled to your little scam with your friend Jasper Fielding, you had no other option but to kill him, did you?' Hillary pounced.

Judith Coulson coughed loudly. Hillary ignored her.

'How did it start, hmm? Did he ask you for money? Or did he threaten to go direct to Jasper and blackmail him for a share in the cut? Either way, you knew it would come down to killing him, didn't you, Colin? Because it wasn't really about the money, was it? Not for Wayne. If it had been, you'd have probably cut him in on the deal, and that would have been the end of it. Am I right?'

Blake folded his arms across his chest and stared over her head.

'Oh, it would have rankled, but you could have lived with it,' Hillary soldiered on. 'But you knew Wayne better than to trust him. You knew, ultimately, that he wouldn't be able to resist bringing you down. In the end he could always have a cosy life living off his women. But the chance to see you disgraced, to see you behind bars, to see you taken down a peg or two . . . *that* would just have been too good for the likes of Wayne to resist, wouldn't it?'

Colin blinked, and she could see in his eyes she'd hit the nail right on the head. But just then the door opened, and Barrington came in with a message. She took the slip of paper from him and read it, careful to keep her face blank. Barrington silently left, not expecting a reply.

The note was from the head of the search team:

'*Blake's house clean, but neighbour told us suspect rents an old barn from a nearby farmer as studio-cum-storage shed. Have applied for extension of warrant, and will search there ASAP.*'

326

Hillary folded the note, hoping they'd strike lucky at the barn, because she was becoming more and more certain that Blake simply wasn't going to crack.

'You know Jasper will spill his guts, don't you, Colin?' Hillary asked casually, changing tack yet again. 'His sort always do, believe me.' She smiled at him and nodded. 'Oh yes, we know all about Jasper. His family had money, didn't it, back in the old days, living in Bath, entertaining the beau monde. And later, with their biscuit factories. A rather vulgar way to earn money for the likes of the Fieldings, of course — trade. But very profitable.' Hillary shrugged, leaning back in her chair. 'And then came the slow decline. The gradual selling-off of the property. The sale of the fancy Bath residence, and the move to the country, where the lack of ostentatious wealth wouldn't be so obvious. The discreet sale of the odd suite of jewellery, the parcels of land, probably, ironically, the odd portrait or two.'

Colin Blake, apparently, didn't see the funny side of that, because it was only Hillary who smiled.

'Who was it who first came up with the idea of the scam?' she asked softly. 'I can't, somehow, see Fielding having the nous for it. It had to be you. And picking Jane Austen for your subject was a stroke of absolute genius.'

She saw Judith Coulson look at her client curiously, before bending her head back over her notes.

'All the ingredients were right, weren't they?' Hillary said, letting her voice become almost dreamy now. 'It really was very clever,' she flattered softly. 'Fielding's family lived in Bath, and were known to entertain the leading lights of the day. And Jane Austen could easily have attended a soirée there. So the provenance is, if not rock-solid, at least reasonable. And the choice of a little-known artist was inspired. I imagine, when the art fraud squad begin to check it all out, that they'll find that Fletcher Crispin-Jones really *did* spend some of his time in Bath, painting the celebrities of the day?' She nodded, for all the world as if he'd confirmed her hypothesis. 'So who's to say that he didn't attend one of the Fielding family's famous dos? That he didn't sketch the shy and retiring Miss Jane Austen? And, if he *did* paint her portrait, why shouldn't it end up in the Fielding family attic? Stranger things have happened.'

Hillary leaned forward on the table and smiled at Colin slowly. 'Jasper must have jumped at the chance when you put it to him. He was badly in need of a boost of money, wasn't he? And you had all the materials there right to hand. I daresay there were several canvases of the right age and period just hanging on the walls of Heyford Court going spare — the worthless daubs of long-forgotten, second-rate artists. I'm no expert, but I know that a lot of artists reused old canvases. So when the art experts came to check the phoney Austen portrait, they wouldn't be surprised, or even suspicious, to find signs of another painting underneath. In fact, it would only help to confirm that it was the genuine thing. And you, of course, are an expert copyist, aren't you, Colin?' Hillary smiled. 'A man who can combine Augustus John and Burne-Jones, a man who can paint like Constable — well, a man like that wouldn't have any trouble copying the style of a little nobody like Crispin-Jones, would he?'

Blake swallowed hard but again said nothing. Hillary noticed that, beside him, Judith Coulson had become very thoughtful. No doubt she was thinking of her fee, and all the kudos a long, complicated case would bring.

'You know, I have to hand it to you,' Hillary said admiringly. 'Between the two of you, you had the perfect scam. Fielding, with his genuine family history and background to back-up an 'accidental find' in his attic. And you, with all the skills to forge the portrait. And you were so clever. That's what really impresses me. You see, most people when they forge a painting, do so because of the *painter*. People want to believe they've got a genuine Monet, or Rembrandt, or who-the-hell-ever, because of the fame of the *artist*. What they actually painted is almost beside the point. But you went one better. You deliberately picked an obscure painter, because it was the fame of the *sitter*, that was going to net you the money. Who'd bother to forge a Crispin-Jones? Apart from a handful of artistic academics, nobody would know or care about a painting of his. But a genuine portrait of Jane Austen! Well now, the Yanks alone would go mad for that. Especially since there's supposedly only one painting of her in existence — that little daub by her sister that hangs in the National Portrait Gallery.'

She reached for the glass of water and took a long, deep swallow. She'd been talking for what felt like hours, and she wasn't getting anywhere. But at least she could rattle him a bit with the scope of what they *did* know.

'There have to be plenty of rich Jane Austen fans who'd pay a fortune to have a genuine painting of her, or even only what *might* be a genuine painting of her. That's what made your scam so clever. Even the

330

possibility of owning such a rare object would be enough to start a bidding war.' She shook her head in admiration and took another sip of water. 'So, there you were, with everything ready. You'd forged the painting, Jasper had 'found it' in his attic, and the experts had been contacted and the ball was rolling. All you had to do was sit back and wait for it to sell to the highest bidder. Then disaster struck. Wayne figured out what you were up to.'

Hillary leaned forward, frowning. 'Just how did he figure it out, Colin?'

Blake stared at her blankly.

'Do you even know?' she asked. 'No? Well, no matter,' she shrugged. 'Juries don't need to have all the ins and outs to bring back a guilty verdict. And we'll soon have DNA evidence linking you to Wayne's killing, and Jasper will sell you out in a nano-second once he realizes he could be charged as an accessory to murder.'

She paused as Barrington came back in, smiling. Hillary read the message and glanced up at Blake.

'This is from the team searching the barn-studio you've been renting. They're confiscating everything. Presumably, forging a painting from the early eighteen hundreds isn't all that easy. You'll have had to mix the paints to the specifications of the day for a start, and stuff like that?'

She saw him shift hard on the chair, and smiled. 'I thought so. The art squad have experts in that sort of thing, you know. How hard will it be for them to prove that you had everything you needed to fake the portrait? Soon the whole world will be in no doubt that the Fielding/Austen portrait is worthless. So Wayne will have won after all.'

Blake stared at the wall behind her head and said nothing.

It was her final shot, Hillary shrugged, gathered up her papers, and left.

You couldn't win them all.

Gemma Fordham signed off on the tape and also went, leaving Blake and Coulson to discuss his defence. No doubt, it would be a long talk.

★   ★   ★

'Too bad you couldn't crack him,' Mel Mallow said, a few hours later, as they all gathered in his office for a celebratory drink. The warrant had come through for a DNA sample to be taken from Blake, and nobody doubted that it would prove a match with the samples taken from the crime scene. Even better, Barrington had been informed by Interpol just twenty minutes ago that Jasper

Fielding had been arrested in Biarritz, and would be accompanied back on the next flight to Heathrow. Apparently, he was already singing about what he knew, and was claiming to have fled the country in panic and fear when he'd read about Wayne Sutton being murdered, fearing that he himself might be next.

A very chuffed art fraud squad was all over the 'Austen' portrait and the Crown Prosecution Service were happy with the case against Blake and all ready to sign off on it.

'A confession would have been nice,' Hillary agreed drily, 'but I could have gone at him all day and not got anywhere. When that sort close down, they're like limpets. There's just no moving them.'

Mel laughed. 'Well, here's to another successful case.' He'd already opened the wine, and now poured the last of it into their glasses.

Frank Ross drank his quickly, and left. He preferred beer or whisky. Barrington too, seemed fidgety, and Hillary watched him with a jaundiced eye. He wanted to be somewhere else, badly. Perhaps she'd give him the rest of the weekend off to try and get it sorted — whatever the crisis was. There were still a lot of loose ends to be tied up, but she could tell he'd probably be useless to her in this state.

Gemma Fordham was the only one drinking orange juice. She looked very satisfied to be associated with a successful and high-profile murder case, for already the media, scenting something glamorous and a touch out of the ordinary, was sniffing around.

Yes, she'd let Gemma handle the bulk of the cleaning up, Hillary mused. It would keep her busy, and that patrician nose of hers out of Hillary's business for a little while.

'Well, if nobody objects, I think I'll call it a day,' Hillary said, getting up. 'Gemma, I'd like you and Ross to stay for a while. The art squad will probably have questions and the media need to be seen to.' She glanced at Mel, who nodded that he'd see to it from here on in.

Outside, Hillary walked across the car park, and once level with Puff the Tragic Wagon, stretched luxuriously. It felt good to be out in the fresh air, after the tense afternoon inside. She was just opening her car door, when she heard someone cough apologetically behind her. She turned around, and found herself facing a chubby man in uniform.

'George Davies, ma'am.' His smile looked distinctly uneasy. Hillary, puzzled and eager to get home to relax, wondered what was up.

'Something I can help you with, Constable?' she asked, firmly but pleasantly.

George Davies nodded miserably and glanced around, but they had the parking lot to themselves.

'Thing is, ma'am, I was wondering if you knew about your new DS,' he began, and flushed uneasily.

'DS Fordham, you mean?' Hillary asked sharply, turning away from the open door of her car to face him more squarely head on.

'Yes, ma'am,' Davies confirmed, staring down at his boots. 'Thing is, ma'am, I recognize her from a brief stint I did down in Reading. Oh, she weren't in the force then, not when I saw her. She was a youngster, like, still at Uni.'

Hillary blinked. 'Yes?' she asked, wondering why the constable was looking so furtive. Surely the fastidious Gemma hadn't been up to something naughty? Like paying for her student fees by doing a bit of prostitution on the side?

'Yes. Thing is ma'am . . . she, er . . . that is . . . ' When it came to it, George faltered. This was a DI, after all, a woman who'd earned a medal for valour.

'Just spit it out, constable,' Hillary advised quietly. 'I won't shoot the messenger, and it's obviously something important, or you

335

wouldn't have come to me. If it's nothing official, I shan't repeat what you say, or mention your name.'

'Oh no, ma'am, it's nothing to do with the job, like. It's just . . . I thought you should know. You're held in high regard round here, ma'am, and I think you should know . . . well . . . '

He met her calm, dark-brown eyes, and blurted out, 'That sergeant of yours was with your husband, ma'am.' And then he promptly stared at his feet again.

Hillary felt herself go cold then hot. Damn! Did the humiliations never end? Even five years dead, that bastard of a husband of hers was still making her life a misery.

She drew in a long, hard breath. 'I see,' she said calmly. 'Thank you for telling me, Constable Davies. I take it nobody else knows about this?'

'Oh no, ma'am,' George looked appalled. 'I ain't told no one and never will. I just thought that you should know, ma'am. Seeing as how it might be awkward like.'

Hillary nodded and forced a smile. 'Thank you, George, I appreciate it,' she said, sincerely. 'If I see you in the canteen sometime, I'll stand you to dinner.'

George Davies nodded, relieved she was taking it so well. 'Right-oh, ma'am. I'll be off then,' he said, and with that, turned and scarpered.

Hillary didn't blame him.

She felt like scarpering herself.

Instead, she got in her car and drove numbly home. On her boat, she opened another bottle of wine and poured a glass. She drank it slowly, with her mind whirling.

So Gemma had been one of Ronnie's old girlfriends. Blonde and young, she'd been just his type. But Ronnie must have dumped her long before he died in the car crash, and Gemma herself had gone on to join the force and rise to the rank of sergeant. She couldn't still be holding a candle for Ronnie, or, by association, a grudge against herself.

So why had she transferred to Hillary's team? What was she after? What had prompted her to search the boat?

The answer came in a flash, and Hillary abruptly sat up in her chair, sloshing wine over her slacks.

Of course!

Gemma Fordham was searching for the money. She was trying to track down Ronnie's dirty millions.

Hillary Greene leaned back in her chair and began to laugh.

We do hope that you have enjoyed reading this large print book.

Did you know that all of our titles are available for purchase?

We publish a wide range of high quality large print books including:
Romances, Mysteries, Classics
General Fiction
Non Fiction and Westerns

Special interest titles available in large print are:
The Little Oxford Dictionary
Music Book
Song Book
Hymn Book
Service Book

Also available from us courtesy of Oxford University Press:
Young Readers' Dictionary
(large print edition)
Young Readers' Thesaurus
(large print edition)

For further information or a free brochure, please contact us at:
Ulverscroft Large Print Books Ltd.,
The Green, Bradgate Road, Anstey,
Leicester, LE7 7FU, England.
Tel: (00 44) **0116 236 4325**
Fax: (00 44) **0116 234 0205**